CHASING SHADOWS

DETECTIVE INSPECTOR ANGELIS CRIME THRILLER
BOOK 1

MATTHEW J. EVANS

Chasing Shadows © Copyright Matthew J. Evans 2021

All rights reserved. No portion of this book may be reproduced, copied, distributed or adapted in any way, with the exception of certain activities permitted by applicable copyright laws, such as brief quotations in the context of a review or academic work. For permission to publish, distribute or otherwise reproduce this work, please contact the author at matt@matthewjevans.co.uk.

Disclaimer

Chasing Shadows is a work of fiction. Names, characters, businesses, police operations, criminal cases, police warrant numbers and telephone numbers are a product of the author's imagination or used in a fictitious manner. Any resemblance to actual persons alive or dead, or actual events are purely coincidental.

ACKNOWLEDGMENTS

I would like to thank my wife, Valerie, for her love, patience, and encouragement as I wrote this novel. I also would like to thank my daughters, Beth and Caity, for their invaluable suggestions and proofreading skills. Thank you also, to Bob Lock and Terence Gregory, for kindly agreeing to read through my manuscript and offering your words of wisdom. I am very grateful.

Finally, a big shout out to the real police and especially 'E' Section Response in Chichester. Thank you for being so supportive of Special Constables like me.

ABOUT THE AUTHOR

Matthew Evans lives in Chichester, West Sussex, UK. He is married to Valerie and has three grown-up children: Beth, Caitlin and Zac. His daughters have flown the nest, and now Matthew is a carer for his son, Zac, who has Down's Syndrome.

Matthew has been a police officer for 16 years and is now a serving Special Constable with Sussex Police. He's also practising Christian, a folk musician and proud owner of 'Betty', his 1962 Morris Minor.

Chasing Shadows is his debut novel.

Email: matt@matthewjevans.co.uk
Website: https://www.matthewjevans.co.uk

DEDICATION

Dedicated to my mother, Sybil Evans (1932 - 2021)

And my wife, Valerie,

My better half.

PROLOGUE

22nd June 2020

'So, tell me, David, what happened that night in Brighton?'

'I nearly died.'

Professor Allen's student tries to engage me, but I don't want to go through this again. How many more times? I look out through the blinds to a bright, warm day outside, where a few lucky nobodies are walking in the sunshine around the hospital grounds. But I'm stuck in here. This office is in shadow, with grey walls, a brown desk and a beige, stained carpet. There's nothing to look at in here, apart from bookcases full of stuffy books written by Professor Allen.

The student adjusts his position and tries again. 'Can you be more specific, David?' He glances to Professor Allen, who is watching him, making notes with a scratchy fountain pen.

Be more specific? He wants me to scrape the nerves of an open wound so he can write his dissertation. I sigh, my heart beats faster, I'm sweating.

'What do you mean?'

'Go back to the beginning. Think back to why you were there.'

I put my head in my hands. I can feel them tremble.

'Think back? It was only six months ago. It was a Friday evening...'

December 2019

I'm outside Brighton Police Station, and as I get near the car, I see a fresh-faced probationer waiting for me, perched on the bonnet, engrossed in his mobile phone. He looks up and quickly puts his phone away.

'DS Angelis? Are you ready to go, Sarge?' he asks.

'What's your name?'

'Tom Hobbs.'

'Let's go, Tom.'

We get in the car, and Hobbs is driving. We head out of the station into the evening, down John Street, right into Edward Street and right again at the lights into Grand Parade. The city is buzzing with revellers heading for the bars, and I see a Christmas theme is already creeping over the city. We slow down as we pass a crowd in the middle of the road. It's a gaggle of girls on a hen night.

'Are you married, Tom?' I say.

Hobbs laughs. 'No, Sarge.'

'Stay well clear of it.'

We're driving towards the north of the city, cutting through the side streets, away from the garish Christmas lights, and finally, we stop outside the address.

'Let Control know we're here and ready to make the arrest.'

'ABH, Sarge?'

'Yes, a domestic caught on CCTV. He's got warning markers for violence against police. So be careful.'

I knock on the door, and a short woman in her forties answers, her face bruised and swollen. I show her my warrant card.

'Harriet, I'm DS Angelis. This is PC Hobbs. We need to talk to Henry.'

'You're not coming in,' says Henry's wife.

'Come on, Harriet. You know we need to talk to him,' I say. 'You can't go on like this, and he shouldn't even be here.' She shakes her head and curses me under her breath. 'We won't go away. We need to get this done and dusted.'

Harriet steps away from the door, and we move into the hall. It's dark and damp inside, and a single low-energy bulb emits a ghostly glow up the stairs. The air is thick with cigarette smoke. I know I'm going to reek of it all night now.

We move into the lounge, and Henry is sitting in front of the TV. The place is a mess, with dirty plates and empty beer cans on the chairs, clutter everywhere. It looks like they're having a party amongst themselves. There's a kid here—he's about 17. He doesn't look happy we're here, and he backs away to a table.

As Henry stands, I nod to Hobbs to let him know I'm going in. He puts his hand on top of his cuffs and unclips them—I have my own ready. Hobbs looks anxious, and Henry is sneering at him.

I turn my face away as Henry belches stale beer breath over me. 'Henry, I'm Detective Sergeant Angelis, from John Street Police Station. After reviewing the CCTV from last night and the photographs of injuries from that altercation, I'm arresting you on suspicion of assault, occasioning actual bodily harm on Harriet, your wife. You do not have to say anything—'

'You can't!' shouts Harriet. 'He didn't mean it. I love you, Henry. I won't let them take you!'

Hobbs pushes in between Harriet and her husband. He's remembered he has to separate them. I just wish he'd done it sooner.

'Get your hands off my wife!' Henry says to Hobbs.

'But it may harm your defence if you...' I take Henry by the arm, and I have my handcuffs out. Henry tenses up, so I strike his forearm and bend his hand behind his back. '...do not mention when questioned something which you later rely on—'

'Leave my dad alone! Get off him!' the kid bawls from behind me.

There's the double-tone sound of the emergency red-button press on the radio. Shit!

'One-zero-three—we need more officers here! Urgent! Male with a knife!' shouts Hobbs.

I don't see it coming. I hear the rip of cloth and feel the air rushing from my lungs—excruciating pain. A baton racks open, but it's too late. The blade strikes again. My back is hot with blood, and I fall. The room grows dark. Another strike and again to my front, and it's all over when he stamps on my head. The last thing I remember is the horror on Henry's face...

22nd June 2020

The student has caught up with his notes and looks at Allen, who just raises his bushy eyebrows at him.

'Thank you, David. That must have been hard for you.'

'Hard?'

'Can you remember what you felt before you entered the house?'

'What's your name again?'

'Marcus.'

'I felt like shit, Marcus. I didn't want to be there. My ex-wife was stopping me from seeing my son. I was depressed, lonely, and most annoyingly, I was hungry.'

'Ah, okay... Please carry on.' Allen shifts in his seat, and Marcus sees it. He scribbles furiously on his pad.

'There isn't anything else. It's all I remember.'

It's then that Allen coughs twice into his hand—it's his signal to me. He wants a demonstration of what I can do. Marcus writes another note and looks at Allen, who nods at him to continue.

'Since your sight returned, has the frequency of the disturbing images you've been seeing decreased?'

I'm reading Allen—I need something personal, something only he will know. Now, I focus on Marcus. There's a way in. Everyone has a way in.

'If anything, they've increased—more vivid too.'

'And what do you see, typically?'

'People, creatures, changes in light around people. I see this room as it was weeks ago, years ago, the patients sitting here, Professor Allen sleeping in his chair.'

Marcus is making lots of notes now. He looks back at me, and I'm sitting back, relaxed, looking straight back at him. He doesn't see what he's doing, what I'm making him do. Professor Allen has put down his pen and is shaking his head.

'Can you describe what you see now?'

'Yes, Marcus. I see you've written all over your shirt. I'm not sure that will come out very easily.'

Professor Allen coughs.

Marcus looks down. He's written Allen's bank card PIN all

over his hands and shirt sleeves. He stands, staring wide-eyed at me. He's completely confused.

Allen looks at me, tilts his head, and purses his lips for a moment.

I slowly stand. My legs are still out of sync with my brain.

'Is that enough of a show for you, Professor Allen?' I say.

'Thank you, David,' says Allen. 'I'll see you next week.'

ONE

25th February 2022

Ancient yews surround me, and it's silent here, like the hushed reverence of a cathedral. I see the ghosts of a thousand journeys made through these trees, criss-crossing the ancient pathways, their impressions etched into this other-worldly forest.

I walk further along a narrow pathway that leads me to the oldest yew of them all. He's a wrinkled man, with a hollowed trunk as his gaping mouth and his red, flaking beard of snaking roots. A little beyond, behind the furthest extent of his beard, a robin alights on a bramble cane. She pauses a moment so I can see her, then she flits to an oak sapling further away. As I follow her, a shaft of sunlight highlights a track hidden beneath a layer of tangled brambles. I continue until I come to another space tucked away, with only the robin for company and the sound of my heartbeat.

I crouch and run my fingers through the moss. A shadow falls over me, and I shudder. I glance up to the looming branches of another yew, where a pendulous silhouette appears suspended high above me.

The crack of a twig and a sudden voice brings me back.

'There you are, David! Are you hiding from me?' It's Kate, my neighbour. 'Come on—it's getting late! I don't want to be stuck in the woods with you after dark.' She looks around where we're standing. 'Besides, this place gives me the creeps.'

I laugh and dig my hands into my jacket. 'But I'm waiting for *you*. Where's Max?' He is her orange-roan cocker spaniel.

He finds me, wags his tail, and darts off into brambles.

Kate looks at me—she likes my eyes. They're bright blue, unusual for someone with brown skin. As I return her gaze, the setting sun catches her red hair and sets it on fire. She looks amazing.

'What's up?' she says. 'I thought I'd lost you. How long have you been standing here?'

'Not long. I just wandered in here. It's peaceful, isn't it?' I look up again and only see the branches this time.

'Come on.' Kate takes my arm to lead me back to her car. 'Am I too noisy for you?'

'Maybe.'

She thinks that's funny. I have only known her for a few months, but she's growing on me.

We walk the short distance back to the car park, and Kate drives us back. I watch the last drops of sunlight strobe past the trees along the winding lanes, and I see her from the corner of my eye, snatching glances at me. I catch her out, and she looks away and laughs.

We pull up into her driveway, and I walk her to her door.

'I could do with a cuppa now,' she says, looking into her house. 'It looks like Vee's out. Do you fancy coming in for a quick one?' I decline. 'Another time, then?' She's pulling a funny, sad face at me.

'I'm sorry. I've got a lot on my mind. My new job starts tomorrow—a big day.'

'Of course, that's fine. That's come around quickly! I hope it goes well.'

'We'll go out for a drink soon, I promise.'

'That'll be good.' Kate slowly closes the door with a smile and a wave.

I'm getting my clothes ready for the morning and responding to a few emails. Tomorrow is my first day back on the frontline. It's a big deal. I've been working in a backroom office at HQ for the last few months, keeping my head down and achieving the rank of inspector.

My mobile rings. It's Giles Walsh, Detective Superintendent, my boss.

'David Angelis,' I sound in control, business-like.

'Hello, David. Can you spare a moment?' he asks.

'Yes, sir. Fire away.'

'I just wanted to check you're still fit for tomorrow?'

'I'm all good, sir.'

'Are you ready for this, David? It's been two years, and now you're a DI. A huge well done to you. You should be proud of yourself.'

'Thank you. I'm more than ready.'

'I won't be in the office, but a great team is waiting for you—they're good people.'

'I've met some of them, sir. I'm looking forward to working with them.'

'That's good, David. Anyway, keep in touch. And...' I'm waiting for it—here it comes. 'I'm just checking through my notes... Occupational Health has signed you off as fit, but they want you to continue with the psychiatric assessments. I'm sure that will be all fine, don't you think?' Why is there doubt in his voice?

'I can do this. They thought I'd never make it—I proved them wrong.'

'What did they call it again? The syndrome, where you see people?'

'They thought it was Charles Bonnet Syndrome, but it's not that at all. The hallucinations interact with me. They still continued after my sight returned.'

'That must be frightening.'

'It was, but not now. To paraphrase the words of Professor Allen, it's my brain constructing images from my subconscious observations. It's okay. It's something I can control.'

But I can't, not in the slightest. I've just made them believe I can.

'Great, you'll probably not want to tell too many people about this.' Walsh sighs. 'Well, if you need anything, David, call me. Good luck for tomorrow. Keep in touch.' He ends the call.

I'm showered, dressed for bed, and I'm jittery. Paranoia wasn't in the package I left the hospital with, but I feel someone is watching me. I've had dreams of faces at my window and eyes on the ceiling. It's probably nerves about the job.

I see myself in the bedroom mirror, standing there in my boxer shorts. There are the scars on my side, just under the ribcage. Running my fingers along my forehead, I feel the indentation in my skull. I get a flashback of Brighton, the stale beer breath in my face, and I'm unsteady for a moment, breathing through it until the panic subsides. That was over two years ago. The physical injuries have healed, but my emotions are still raw and infecting my thoughts daily. But I'm getting through it one day, one hour, one minute at a time.

My normal is not the same as everyone else's. I have this gift that opens a door into the souls of others. It gives me sight of their memories, their hopes, and fears. I see the ghosts that haunt them, the skeletons in their locked closets, and I smell their lies like rancid meat. There are times I can see through the layers of time and turn them like the pages of a book. Look at me! I've become a freak with superpowers.

So, yes, I'm okay. I *can* do this. Here goes for tomorrow. 'Good luck,' I say to myself. I glance at my unopened bedside drawer and think about the face on the photo inside. 'Wish me luck, Josh.'

Hudson Biotech lies within a clearing of mixed conifers, at the end of a grandiose, winding driveway, an unsubtle nod to their Canadian headquarters. The Hudson building is a striking architectural design, a wave of curved glass framed in steel. To the front, a water fountain washes over a sculpture of hands holding a child, the logo of The Hudson Corporation.

Doctor Dean Dettori is walking along a woodland footpath that weaves around the perimeter of the site. He finds a bench facing the fountain. It's out of sight from anyone and basks in the golden light of the late afternoon. He closes his eyes and takes a deep breath, listening to the bubbling water. He's thinking of home, his childhood in Venice, his very first love. So far away from him now, that innocence. How did he get to be here?

'You took your time,' says a voice behind him, breaking his thoughts.

'Sit down, Nathan,' says Dettori. 'No one can see us here.'

A man in a black leather jacket sits beside Dettori. He's tall and muscular. His blue eyes are bright. Dean watches Nathan as he observes everything around him. It's something Nathan does now, constantly scanning the smallest of movements, the slightest of sounds, the droplets of anxious perspiration. Dettori finds it unnerving.

'You're nervous, Dean,' Nathan says. 'What's wrong?'

'My wife wants a new house. She's seen one in Poole, Dorset, right by the water. Fourteen million. That makes me nervous. But you're not interested in my problems. I can guess why you want to see me. You want your fix, I assume?'

'I don't have a lot of fucking choice, do I.'

Dettori hands him a plastic package. 'Use it within six hours. You're wishing you never started this, aren't you.'

'It was great to start with, but now look what you've done to me.'

'Don't give me that bullshit. You love it, Nathan. The women, the power. One little fix from me, and you're stronger than an ox.'

'And without your little fix, I'm one dead ox.'

'As long as you keep your end of the bargain when I need you to, you can have as much of it as you want.'

'And you keep the control.'

'Always.'

Nathan Wheelhouse walks away with his package, leaving Dettori to dream of Venice again.

Helen McCall is drinking alone. She's just removed the man she met two hours ago from her flat. She can't even remember his name, but his cheap aftershave still lingers. What was she thinking?

She pulls at the wisps of blonde hair that have fallen loose from behind her ears. At least her nails are still perfect, and she spills a little wine on her red dress as she inspects them.

'You're not twenty anymore,' she says to herself. It's gone 11.30 p.m., the time when she used to get ready to go out for the night, not get ready for bed. She's alone, single again, and pissed. Perfect.

Her eyes are itching, so she takes out her contacts and tries to find her glasses. She's always doing that in the wrong order, but she remembers where she left them in the bathroom. As Helen looks at herself in the mirror, she can see she still looks good, considering how rough she feels. Then she sees in the reflection the answerphone is flashing—one message.

'Hello Helen, it's Mum.'

Helen rolls her eyes. Who else?

'Just checking you're okay, as we haven't heard from you this week. Dad's been in the garden today, doing his own thing. At least it keeps him busy. I've been baking, although I'm a bit bored, to be honest. I need to get out more, while I still can, with Dad still able and all that. Anyway, hope we can chat soon. Love you, dear. Speak soon.'

'I'm a terrible daughter,' she says to the answerphone. She will call after work tomorrow. It's an early shift, and her new boss is starting.

Helen stumbles into her bedroom and checks her wardrobe. There's nothing in there to wear for the morning, and the laundry bin is full. Helen carries a bundle of dirty clothes to the washing machine, dropping knickers and socks as she goes. She fumbles to get the machine to work, and it starts before she's noticed the trail of clothes she's left on the floor.

'Bollocks, bollocks, bollocks!'

Helen resigns herself to downing the unfinished half glass of red and curls up on the sofa to drift off to sleep.

Martina Hayes can see Nathan through the spyhole of her front door. She lives in a flat on the second floor, one of the new developments in Chichester. She can see he's buzzing, fresh from a hit. Martina's sleepy and ready for bed. She has to be in early for work at Hudson tomorrow—she doesn't need this. She reluctantly opens the door.

'You're looking lovely as ever,' he says to her.

'It's late. What do you want?'

He pushes his way into her flat and checks her bedroom before heading to the lounge.

'No guests then?' He's sneering.

'I do what I have to do. You know that. What are you doing here?'

'I'm just looking out for you. And I need a drink.'

Martina goes to the kitchen cupboard and pulls out a bottle of single malt and two glasses. She knows he's watching her—he's in one of those moods. She pours herself a drink and hands the bottle to Nathan.

'Help yourself, you normally do.'

Martina pushes back her hair and attempts to cover her modesty with her nightdress. Nathan half fills a glass with whisky and downs it in one. His hands are trembling, his legs twitching constantly.

'What do you think of it?' Nathan asks her, refilling his glass.

'Of what?'

'You know what. It makes you feel alive, doesn't it—fight the fucking world!'

'Keep your voice down, you dick!' Martina pauses for a while, and a smile builds on her face. 'Yeah! It does.' She laughs.

'Just keep him happy. We need to work out a way to get our hands on his supplies.'

'They account for everything at Hudson, moron. That stuff costs a fortune. I should know! Not even I can get my hands on it. Believe me, I'd take the lot if I could.'

'He's got a shit-load of it stashed away somewhere. He said so himself. We've got to find where he keeps it, Martina. I don't want anyone else having this. We're fucking superheroes because of this. I want it all!'

'Easy, Nathan! The trials have stalled. He can't carry on without authorisation.'

'He doesn't give a fuck about that!'

Nathan drains his glass and pours another. Martina knows what's coming. She can't stop him—she never could.

'Come on, Nate,' she says. 'I have work in the morning. You've got a whorehouse to check on.'

Martina can see the drink is kicking in.

'I never wanted to be like this, Martina. You know me better than anyone... Anyone! I wanted what everyone else wanted. Life just got in the way. If I could go back and change everything, I would. You know that, don't you? Don't you, Martina? I'd be looking after you—keeping you safe. Fuck Dettori! We could've done so much better than this. So, so much...'

'That's the drink talking now,' she says.

'Rich tossers like Dettori and bloody Dalton. They think they can rule it over us. Dalton ain't that clever, Martina. He just got lucky. Just lucky. That whore of a wife of his—nice tits but no brain.'

'Just bide your time, Nate. He'll get what's coming to him.'

'Too fucking right he will! We will be in control of our own... destinies...'

Martina rolls her eyes. She picks up the bottle and puts it back in the kitchen.

'Come on, Nate. You can sleep on the sofa.'

She can see the tears welling up in his eyes. She knows what she has to do, what she always does. She sits beside him and pulls his head onto her shoulder, stroking his hair. Within a few moments, she is on her back, with Nathan on top of her.

Kate hears the latch on the front door close. The dog looks up at her, and she reaches down to stroke him. She gets out of bed, walks to the window, and looks down at the street below. The streetlights have switched off now, but she can see Vanessa's shadow as she turns the corner.

Kate isn't sure where Vee's going, but she has an idea. It's okay; she has to leave her to it. She must feel the world is against her right now.

Kate picks up her mobile and logs onto an app. She brings up a live camera image. It's in night mode, so everything appears in greens and greys. The battery levels are down to 40 per cent, but that's not her problem. She just needs to report that in, and someone else will handle it.

She studies the image closely and records what she sees. There's nothing out of the ordinary tonight, unlike last night—that gave her the shivers. How much longer does she need to do this? She's getting paid for it, but it just feels wrong. The psychiatrist is lapping up the footage. Kate thinks he's probably going to make millions from writing a book about him. Everyone is screwing him over somehow. She doesn't want to be a part of it anymore.

She closes the app and looks at her photos on Pinterest: the Scottish Highlands, the mountains and lochs, the heather, the morning dew. There's another of her dream cottage, a total fantasy, she knows. But it's something, at least, she can aim for. She and Vanessa, with Max, walking alongside. Pure bliss.

She just has to trust that Vee will be okay. There's still more to do, but they will make that bastard pay for their dream. Dettori has used so many people. Why not give him a taste of his own medicine? She laughs at the pun.

Kate lays her head on the pillow, and Max is licking her fingers.

'Go to sleep, Max,' she says. 'Or you won't be coming to Scotland with us... I don't mean it, boy. Of course, you will.'

It's gone one o'clock in the morning. The streetlights are off here, and Vanessa likes the solitude the darkness brings. It's a 30-minute walk to the house from where she lives. As she gets closer, the familiar roads draw a sense of sadness and regret. The reason she left him wasn't so she could be with Kate. That came almost by accident, an unexpected crash of people in need of solace against a common enemy. She left to protect him from the trouble she would bring, but he would never believe that, not now. She isn't even in love with Kate. She realises now it's purely for comfort.

Vanessa follows the pathway through the underpass, and she turns on her torch as the footpath is uncertain. There's someone up ahead. Vanessa can hear footsteps scuffing on the pavement, a man's voice humming to himself. It's one of the street drinkers, looking for a place to put his head on this chilly night. Vanessa steps onto the road and lets him pass by. She's not afraid. With her training, why should she be?

A light in the distance catches her eye. It's the cathedral spire, illuminated from below. She used to go to church as a young girl. She had little choice, with her father being a vicar. But her father's drinking and gambling poisoned any trust in her family, leaving Vanessa broken and without faith.

She stops again, looking skyward. The stars are peeking out of the breaking cloud. She wonders if God can see her in the dark and remembers the verse, *'But the night shineth as the day: the darkness and the light are both alike to thee.'* God doesn't need a torch as she does.

She crosses the road opposite the green and walks up Norwich Street. After a few hundred more yards, she comes to the house. All the lights are off, and his car is in the driveway. She takes out the notepaper and pen. Vanessa realises she should have written the note before she left, especially as she has nothing to lean against and has to hold the torch in her mouth.

She writes the note and places it inside the envelope. *'To Peter,'* she writes on the front and carefully posts it through the letterbox, making sure she doesn't let the flap make a sound.

Vanessa stands there for a moment and wipes away her tears. Regret is so painful and utterly pointless. So many memories sleep behind this door. What has she done with their journey together? She's thrown it all away.

4th February 2022

. . .

The murmur of conversation fills the church hall, dispersed by a little laughter and the sound of cups on saucers. It's hot and stuffy in here and a cold, dark day outside. The windows run with condensation from the bubbling urns, making gallons of tea and sympathy on demand. The cloying fruit punch is being avoided, and the ample supplies of rich fruitcake still wait to be consumed on their paper plates and folded napkins.

Terry Galloway is in the corner, out of the way. He's people watching. There's a mix of dress formality going on, and a few people are still wearing face masks, unsure how safe things are after the multiple lockdowns of the last two years. Some people are wearing black, expecting a wake. Terry concludes they are distant family who didn't know Alison so well. Her friends and close family are in bright colours, pinks, and blues. One fella, the one who said the grace, is in a Hawaiian shirt and shorts in early February. Terry can see he's regretting it, but it's a great effort.

Terry is an old school friend of Alison. He remembers her as funny and kind, and seeing all her church friends here, the photos of her stuck around the walls, is a warming tribute to her. But as warming as it is, Terry can't help but question why any god would want to take her so young? It doesn't seem fair to him.

Terry recognises a few faces from school. Some have aged well, like he has, but others not so well. A lot of the men have spread sideways and are even going grey.

'Another fruit punch, Terry?' says Robbo, holding out a plastic cup.

'Lovely!' says Terry, grimacing. 'I'd rather have the tea.'

'Nice send-off,' says Robbo.

'Absolutely. How about we stay another 15 minutes and then find a pub?'

'Music to my ears, Terry. Where's Davey? Didn't he get the invite?'

'God, I didn't think of that!' Terry pulls a face.

'Didn't he go out with Alison for a bit?'

'He did. He even got religion for her.'

They both laugh. Terry is watching a woman he recognises. She's tall and slim, with short blonde hair and looks slightly older than him. Robbo is watching Terry.

'Laura's still got the looks,' says Robbo.

'A fine woman, Robbo. I may have to introduce myself shortly.'

'Good luck with that one!' Robbo gives a wheezy laugh—too many cigarettes. 'She didn't like our Davey, by all accounts.'

'I can't remember, to be honest.'

'Talking of Davey,' Robbo leans in as he speaks. 'How is he now, after… you know?'

'He's mostly there now. He recovered from his injuries quickly, considering. It's his head that isn't there yet—that and the family problems. He said he's hoping to go back to work in a few weeks. I just think it's too soon.'

'Shit! He's a brave fella, considering what happened.'

'He's one of the bravest people I know, Robbo, and I wish I could be more like him. I'm the only one who's got his back. I can't see anyone else looking out for him.'

Terry turns away and clears his throat. He suffers the last drop of stewed tea and looks over to the slim blonde woman.

'Go on, then Terry,' says Robbo. 'You know you want to. She can only say no.'

'I'll engage her with my charm, shall I?' says Terry.

Terry makes his way to where she's standing and waits for his moment.

TWO

Doctor Katherine Jacobs to camera:

It's 2.30 p.m. on Monday, 7th February 2022... My name is Doctor Katherine Jacobs, and I used to be a Lead Researcher for Hudson Biotech. This video is my account of everything that's happened just in case I don't get the opportunity to tell it in person.

Firstly, about Hudson Biotech. You may have heard that Hudson was one of the first companies to develop a Covid-19 vaccine. But the main thrust of Hudson's research has always been developing medicines based on altered virus proteins, enhanced by nanotechnology. Proteins are biomolecules composed of amino acid chains. They are essential for biological functions such as DNA replication in cell division, muscle growth, and so on. We use these enhanced proteins to build machines in the nanoscale. We can build complex structures using these proteins, such as meshes, tubes and valves.

26th February 2022

The letter arrived three months after Vanessa walked away from eight years of marriage. So, Peter Grant thinks it's strange to see her cursive, handwritten script again on the envelope that was pushed through the door—delivered by hand. The writing is scruffy for her, even rushed. He always thought that she had beautiful handwriting for such a thug. She has addressed the letter: *To Peter*—full of melodrama, like some mournful ode. But he can't bring himself to read it yet, expecting a prelude to divorce proceedings.

Peter hasn't dressed, and he's taking things easy today with his breakfast of tea and toast. The envelope remains unopened on the table as he looks over the lawn, enjoying the cool air through the open French doors. The white muslin curtains *she* had chosen are billowing in the breeze; an idyllic day, haunted by Vanessa.

Through an acquaintance, Peter heard Vanessa had moved in with someone. When he asked this so-called friend, they couldn't say who he was. *Get on with your life*, they told him—*she's happy now*. How could they know? How was he supposed to get on with his life when she was the biggest part of it?

Vanessa was good at her job, and covering her tracks is her forte. He didn't see it coming. The other man was a complete surprise. *It's something I must do*, she said to him in tears that day, and then finally, there was, *I need to find myself*, and *I need to have fun again*. Who knew that all she needed was an existentialist comedian all this time? But none of it rang true—she was still hiding something.

Peter sniffs the envelope as if it would smell of her—it doesn't. Her old clothes are still in her wardrobe, along with her matted hairbrush. He could sniff those if he were that desperate. Why won't he let it go? The letter is the first time she's made contact since she walked out, and he can't deal with it right now.

His mobile rings, and he clears his throat. It's Dean Dettori, his boss.

'Hi, Peter. Sorry to bother you on your day off, but there's a problem.'

'Can't it wait until Monday?'

'No, and we can't talk over the phone. Something's gone wrong, big time. Important material is missing. We need your input on finding it.'

'What information?'

'Not over the phone! Come into the office. We'll meet you in an hour.'

'We? Who's we?'

'One hour—don't be late.' The line goes dead.

So much for a day off. He folds the envelope and stuffs it into his wallet for later.

After a quieter drive than usual, it surprises Peter when he passes straight through Hudson Biotech's main gates without the standard inspection by security. The car park has more spaces than he's ever seen before; perhaps he should work every Saturday if it is going to be this quiet.

Peter walks into the reception and then takes the lift three floors into the Hudson Research Centre. There's the dramatic video-wall demonstration playing on a loop—people in lab coats, physios with injured soldiers, doctors with a child in a wheelchair—all to impress the clients. They've dimmed the lights for the weekend, giving it the air of a classy hotel lobby. He sees Dettori with Martina Hayes waiting for him. He feels in his jacket for his passkey, but Martina has opened the glass security door for him.

'No need,' she says. 'I've booked you in.' Martina is the new Head of Security, replacing Vanessa after she left. She's dressed for the weekend, and he's never seen Martina in tight jeans. She catches him smiling to himself.

'Thanks, Peter,' says Dettori, walking at pace in his Armani Chinos and shirt. 'Sorry to drag you out, but I'm missing my golf as well!'

Peter rolls his eyes. He glances back at Martina, who stays fixed straight ahead of her. 'This must be some serious shit!'

'It is,' says Dettori, 'and you're right in the middle of it.'

They're in a meeting room, and Dettori waves at Peter to take a seat at the end of a large table, with a spotlight above him.

'Peter, thanks for joining us,' says Dettori.

'How can I help?'

'Your wife is causing us significant problems.'

'I haven't seen the woman for months. She left me to torture some other poor bugger. She has nothing to do with me anymore.'

'Vanessa stole a laptop computer containing confidential files. Has she spoken to you about it or asked you to look after anything for her?'

'You're not listening to me! I know nothing about it. I'd tell you if I did. Vanessa's not returned to the house, not even to pick up the rest of her stuff.'

'Martina has kindly been monitoring your home, just in case. Even going through your rubbish, poor girl.'

Peter glares at her.

'What right do you have to pry into my private affairs! What you're alleging Vanessa has done has nothing to do with me. I don't know where she is or who she is with now.'

Peter's mouth is dry.

'I get it,' says Dettori. 'She left you—terribly sad and all that—but that's rather suspicious considering the timing. Can you at least suggest who she is seeing? Has she contacted relatives?'

'Look, I don't know who she is seeing! Frankly, I don't care. It's not my problem. And her parents don't even talk to each other, let alone to her or me! There is no one else. Nobody! Have you thought about calling the police? Isn't that what they do? Catch criminals?'

'We would prefer to keep this internal for now,' says Martina. 'In the same way, we wouldn't want to bring their attention to the PPE you've been pilfering from us over the last two years, either. How much have you been making on the auction sites? A handsome profit, I imagine.'

Peter shakes his head, and beads of sweat are forming on his top lip. 'What do you want me to do?'

'If you hear from her, then let me know immediately,' says Dettori. 'I have people looking for her, but it would be better for her if she came of her own volition.'

'That sounds like a threat, Dean?'

'A threat? Take it how you like. I just hope for your sake that you're not hiding something from me.'

The new Chichester Investigations Centre, fronted with tinted glass and blue cladding, sits alongside the Custody building. The original red-brick police station still stands nearby and is the hub for police response and neighbourhood teams in the district.

It's a Saturday morning, so the car park has plenty of spaces free. I walk into the office, adjusting my eyes to the bright lights and white walls. Someone needs to turn it down in here—it will give us all a headache. This place is as shiny as a probationer's florescent jacket. It needs dirtying—more mess. It's started already, with the reassuring smell of burnt toast coming from the kitchen, and the first of the coffee stains has christened the blue carpet. We're not immune from the grime of life we deal with every day, and neither should this place be.

Like any other open-plan office, there are boards for everything, from whiteboards to message boards. Back-to-back desks have the latest terminals. It's all modern and must have been expensive. There are offices along the far wall. One of them is mine, another is empty, and the big one in the corner is for Detective Superintendent Walsh.

'Good morning, sir,' says a detective. She's been watching me taking in the new environment. 'I'm DS Helen McCall—we met a while ago. Sorry I couldn't get here sooner. I got caught up in Custody.' She takes a moment to tie back her hair that's fallen over her face. She has that hard-cop face gained from years of experience, but it softens when she smiles. I met her several weeks ago at HQ for a meet and greet. I remember she struck me as having a sharp mind and flawless eyebrows. I'm not in the habit of judging people by their eyebrows, but I'm drawn to hers and her brown eyes.

'I've only just got here myself,' I say. 'I remember you from HQ.' There's an awkward pause. 'I've been briefing myself on our current cases. I'm looking forward to catching up with you.'

'Great. DS James Harris is on late shifts, but he said he'd come in and see you.'

'You're looking at the intel from the house in Broyle Way. Any concerns?'

McCall drops her bag on the desk next to a mug with a photo of two young, grinning girls printed on it. 'Sorry, I'm clumsy today. Someone reported seeing several men coming in and out of the house at night and possibly dealing from there. I've been watching it with DC Lang, but we've seen nothing yet. I've got a meeting set up this morning with the informant who lives over the road. I don't know if you want to come along? It might be useful to get your opinion on it.'

'That would be good.' I sound so stuffy. 'Where are we meeting this informant?' I can't stop myself. She's going through her iPad to remind herself.

'Inside the coffee shop on the canal at 11. We're paying.'

There are several jobs I need to review today. There's a GBH, a rape, a cold case murder review, a spate of shed burglaries. James Harris and Helen McCall are dividing the load between them.

'Great.' Another pause. Why am I so awkward? 'See you then... then.'

Peter is sitting in his car after driving to the waterfront at Bosham Harbour. He's staring towards the horizon, hoping for inspiration from the silver-bottomed clouds. The tide is out, boats are sleeping on their muddy bellies, and wading birds are scouring the shallow pools for food. The tourists are idling away their time between the artisan craft shops and the church, searching for the stone marking the grave of King Canute's drowned daughter.

Peter's phone rings. He sees it's that unknown number again, so he cancels it.

Vanessa has dragged him into a mess of her making, and now he's expected to find her. What a bloody awful weekend this has turned out to be. His heart jumps as he remembers: 'Shit, the note!'

Peter scrambles into his pocket and pulls out the crumpled letter from his wallet. He pauses for a moment and feels his stomach tightening.

> *Dear Peter,*
>
> *I'm sorry to have put you through this, and I owe you an explanation. I've done something stupid, but it means I can pay you what I owe. Come to 24 Alcott Gardens, Chichester. I'm staying there with Katherine Jacobs. You'll remember her. Please come tonight at 9 p.m. I will explain everything, and I hope you'll forgive me.*
>
> *V x*

He's reread it at least six times now, and it's too late for her apologies. But he can still hear her voice, smell her perfume. No—he's not having any of it. She can answer to Dettori first.

He unlocks his mobile and finds Martina's number. She only takes a few seconds to answer—she sounds breathless.

Martina is still on top of him, but he's finished—his timing was impeccable. She notes the address Peter gives her on a scrap of paper and puts it on her bedside table. She heads to the bathroom for a few minutes while Dettori pulls up the covers and looks at the address.

'Vanessa has found Katherine?' he shouts out to Martina. 'Both together! How perfectly squalid.'

Martina returns, and she's still naked. She sits on the bed next to him and turns Dettori's head.

'I need it now, Dean. You promised,' she says. Her voice has a hint of desperation.

'Ah, yes, I did, didn't I. You should stop soon, my dear. The more you have, the harder it gets. Just look at young Nathan. If he stops now, it will kill him. I don't want that for you.'

'Look at me! I've never felt so alive, so strong. How much of it do you have?'

'Enough for several hundred lifetimes, and I can make more. But that's still my secret.'

'Where are you storing it? How do I know it's safe?'

'I'm never going to tell you or Nathan that. I'd be dead by the end of the day. I know it's safe. As long as I'm alive, there will be a supply.'

'Nathan is getting worse, Dean. He's so angry. Is that going to happen to me?'

Dettori leans over and strokes Martina's back, running his fingers down her spine. Her skin is sensitive, and goosebumps appear under his fingertips.

'That's not the drug, Martina. That's just the way he is.'

'I guess I'm the lucky one.' Martina kisses his hand. 'I need it now, Dean.'

Dettori gets out of the bed, walks over to his briefcase, and removes a clear bag with a syringe. He hands it to Martina, and she goes back to the bathroom.

I'm walking with McCall along the canal basin, a hundred yards from the police station. As we walk beside the railings, McCall is glancing at me.

'Glad to be back, sir?' she says.

'You know what, Helen,' I say, 'I actually am. It's been a long time, so if I'm rusty and awkward, then you'll have to forgive me.' I stop, so she has to look at me. 'I wanted to let you know before we start, you may find some of my methods somewhat unorthodox—not what you're used to.' I don't know how else to tell her.

'Sounds intriguing. I'm looking forward to it.' She's looking me over. 'You're looking better since the last time I saw you. You've got more meat on you, with respect.'

I laugh. 'Thank you, I think.'

'You can relax now, sir. We've done the introductions, and I'm easy to work with.'

She's sussed me out quickly.

We go into the coffee shop, and McCall greets a pale-faced young woman wearing a grey tracksuit. She has tied back her greasy hair into a tight ponytail, pulling up her eyebrows. She must like it like that, but I think it looks ridiculous. She's sitting at a table overlooking the canal. This isn't the type of place she typically goes, so no one knows her here, at least.

When she sees me, she stares at my eyes.

'Megan,' says McCall, trying to get her attention. 'Thanks for coming over here today.' Megan is still staring. 'This is my colleague, Detective Inspector Angelis.'

'You've got amazing eyes,' she says to me. 'They're really weird.'

'Thanks,' I say. I can see McCall looking away, trying not to laugh. 'Nice to meet you, too.'

'You've got a hole in your head. Shit, that must have hurt.'

'Shall we get drinks?' McCall changes the subject.

'Are you new?' Megan asks me. 'I wasn't expecting anyone else.'

'Nothing to worry about,' I say. 'I work with DS McCall.'

'He's my boss,' says McCall.

'That's okay,' she says, smiling. 'He's checking up on you, is he? It doesn't bother me.'

Our coffees arrive, and we're relaxed, watching the volunteers scrub the sightseeing boats that carry the tourists along the old canal. But only I can see the ghost ships from two centuries ago moored along the basin. And the gangs of hefty men unloading carts of coal.

'Megan,' says McCall, 'you told me you'd be happy to continue our arrangement. Is that still the case?'

'I'm here, aren't I?' says Megan.

'I need to know who's coming in and out of number 17, Broyle Way. Are you happy to talk about that here?'

'Yeah, no worries,' Megan says with a sideways smile at me. I must be irresistible today.

'So,' says McCall, 'what's new? What have you seen?'

'Much the same as before. Gary still comes every morning and every evening. He's in there for about half an hour and then locks up. I think he's picking up his post, that's all. It's all quiet, apart from the odd visitor at night.'

Something is happening. I'm seeing someone standing with Megan. First, there's a man. He's a tall, rough, but handsome type with a distinctive jawline. He must be Gary—it's how Megan remembers him. Then I see a girl: she looks Thai, around fifteen years old, as a guess. She's frightened; her black hair is lank, clinging to her face. She's looking at me and then listens to Megan. She must be the memory of someone that Megan's seen.

'Have you seen anyone else visit the house?' says McCall. 'Anyone at the window, coming to the front door?'

'No, no one.'

How do I do this? She's not telling us everything. She could be scared, so I need to press her.

'Megan,' I say, 'we've had some intelligence to say there are young girls living in the house. What do you know about that?'

McCall is looking at me. I can read the surprise in her eyes, but she calmly goes along with it.

Megan is fidgeting, drumming her fingers on the table. She's looking around now for anyone who may be listening.

'I know nothing about any girls,' she says.

I'm watching a black snake squeezing its way out of her mouth. Snakes appear when people lie to me. It slithers out down her chin and vanishes under the skin of her neck.

'You're scared,' I say, 'but I also know you're lying. It's okay, Megan. No one will know it's come from you.'

'Shit! What do you know? Look, I can't say nothing.' The tone of her voice has changed. I can feel her heart is racing—her breathing is rapid. 'They'll know it was me!'

McCall makes a note on her iPad. She's looking puzzled. I expect she's wondering why I hadn't shared this information with her.

'No one else will know anything,' I say. 'We can protect you.'

'How are you going to do that? You don't have a clue what he's like. He's a nasty piece of shit.'

'Has he threatened you before?' asks McCall.

'Not me. But I've heard what he does to anyone who's a grass. Believe me. And I've got my little girl.'

'Who does he work for?' says McCall.

'How do I know?' Megan shrugs. She's restless, shaking her knees against the table.

'Tell me about the girls at the house,' I say.

'Gary keeps them locked up there, poor cows. They're his

little bitches—young ones. The older fellas must love them, especially the men in suits. I see them most evenings, going in and out. Sometimes I've seen four of them go in at once.'

'I don't know who this Gary is,' says McCall. 'Do you know his full name?'

'No. Just Gary. He'll kill me if he finds out I said anything. Look, you're still paying me, right?'

'How old is this Gary?'

'About 25.'

'Helen,' I say. 'May I have a word?'

'Here we go,' says Megan. 'Look, I need the money. I've got no food in the house!' She folds her arms like a petulant teenager.

'Give us a moment, Megan,' I say. 'I just need a quick word.'

McCall and I get up from the table and walk a short distance away.

'That was news to me, sir,' says McCall. 'Have I missed something?'

'I can't explain it to you right now. It was a hunch, that's all.'

'A lucky one, sir!' She doesn't sound convinced.

'I told you, I'm a little unorthodox. We need to move quickly on this and get those girls out of there. We can't wait to see who this Gary character leads us to. They're in real danger of further harm.'

'Okay, boss. I'll get the ball rolling.'

'We'll need to get Megan and her daughter into protection if she'll agree to it. We don't want any repercussions later.'

'Megan,' says McCall. 'How do you fancy going on a holiday for a while?'

What to do for lunch had slipped my mind. I'm sitting in my office, and I'm hungry. There's an exodus of detectives heading to a sandwich van, which has just pulled up, leaving McCall on her own, staring unhappily into her lunch box.

'Helen, do you have a minute?' I say as I approach her desk. I can see what she's turning her nose up at now. It's some sort of brown bean salad. It looks bleak.

'Yes, boss?'

'Nothing in for lunch, then?'

'Nothing I like the look of.'

'Great! Let me treat you. We need to talk, so it's a working lunch on me.'

She's got her jacket on within seconds. We head down to my car, and there are a few interesting looks as they see us getting into my Mercedes.

'Everything okay, sir?' she says as I'm driving. I notice she's rubbing her neck with her lanyard, leaving a red mark.

'Nothing to worry about. I'm taking you somewhere where they do a great coffee and baguette—it's my favourite.'

I've taken her to *Hogs*, an all-day restaurant a few miles west of Chichester. It's one of my favourite places to eat, and it's seldom busy unless the races are on at Goodwood. We take a table by the window, which comes with a delicate floral arrangement and folded napkins. It's probably not McCall's usual choice of a place to grab lunch. We're overlooking the rear garden, but it's not warm enough to sit out there yet. We both order, and she surprises me by going for the meat feast baguette.

'You don't want a veggie option then?' I say.

She laughs. 'I've been trying to eat more healthily recently, but I'm losing the will to live.' She looks around and absent-mindedly twists the ends of her ponytail around her finger. 'This is different. It's a nice place, thank you. But what was it you needed to talk about?'

I'm trying to read her and have sensed nothing about her that concerns me. It's all easy. She's a what-you-see-is-what-you-get type of person—quite reassuring. I don't think she would take any bullshit, either. What I don't know is how freaked out she's going to be. I can tell her, but she may not want to work with me again. I wouldn't blame her. I once thought I could use this gift to help people, but I soon realised people don't like it when you know their secrets and lies. It's going to be a step of faith with her. So, just a hint of the weird shit, not too much.

'Helen, you need to know something about me.'

'Okay?' Then she suddenly blushes in horror. 'Oh shit! You don't think I've been coming on to you! Look, I'm not—'

'No!' I can't help but laugh. 'Nothing like that.'

'Thank God! Not that you're not... It's a work thing... I'll stop digging. You were saying, sir.' I can see that she's kicking herself.

'So, roughly two years ago, pre-pandemic, I was attacked in Brighton. I was following up on a domestic ABH. A husband arguing with his wife, him beating her head against the floor. Another officer and I turned up later to arrest him, but their son objected and stabbed me four times out of nowhere. They put him in a secure mental health facility. I'm carted off to the hospital.'

'That's awful, sir. I knew you were injured on duty, but none of us knew the details.'

'I was in a coma for a while, not that I remember.'

She's too engrossed to see the bulging baguette and latte that's landed in front of her.

'Yet, you recovered?' She rolls her eyes at her own comment. 'Obviously, you did.'

'I woke up in a hospital and ended up there for six months. I was blind at first. They weren't sure if I'd see again, but my sight returned, as did my mobility. I had to learn to walk again—the whole works. But I'm fitter than I've ever been now.'

'I'm not sure I could have come back after that,' she says and then looks down wide-eyed at her baguette.

'It took a long time, and I got a lot of help. I eventually returned to light duties, and that's when I made inspector.

'Look, I'm not telling you all this because I need a pat on the back. The experience has changed me, Helen. I think differently now. Let's just say it's given me a different level of perception and intuition, and you may find that difficult to work with. There's a lot more to it, but that's all you need to know for now.'

I'm trying to read her as she chews her mustard and ketchup-dripping baguette. She's thinking about it, tilting her head slightly and frowning.

'It's all fine by me, sir. It's spooky how you knew about the girls in the house, but you seem pretty normal, if you don't mind me saying so.'

'I'm glad you think I'm normal.'

'I didn't mean that how it sounded.'

'I'll be working with DS Harris too, of course, but I'm limiting my confessions on directions from the Superintendent. I don't want everyone thinking I'm a nut job.'

'Okay. As long as you don't see dead people and shit.'

'What, like your great aunt sitting on your shoulder?' I feign horror.

'That's okay, sir. I'm a newly divorced woman living on my own. Nothing frightens me anymore.'

'Are they your kids printed on the cup?'

She stares at me blankly for a moment and realises. 'Ah, on my desk? No, we never had kids. They're my sister's kids, Beth and Caity; they live in the US, Oregon. I love them to bits.' She sips her coffee for a moment. 'Are you married?'

'No.' I wonder if she's seen me twitch.

'You haven't missed much. Mine wasn't the best example of a normal marriage. I scare men off now.'

'I'm sure you get scared along with the rest of us.'

'I scare myself sometimes. I met this fella last night, and I must have invited him back for a coffee. I don't even remember doing it. Now that scares me!'

I laugh and get a momentary image of the man she met from her memory. He's standing in front of her with his hands behind his back. He looks vaguely familiar, but I must cast him out of my head. He may be someone we work with, and it's none of my business.

'Anyway,' I say, picking up my cheese and tuna panini. 'That's what I wanted you to know. This has to stay between ourselves, okay?'

'Of course, sir. Just like what I told you, that stays between us.'

'Agreed.'

I went for a run after work, took a shower, and I've just got off a video call with my mum. She wanted to know how my first day back went. Dad was there in the background, half-listening. He was busy fiddling with some engine part of Gracie's, his beloved Morris Minor.

Now I'm standing outside Kate's front door, waiting for her to answer. She opens the door in her pyjamas, and she looks embarrassed.

'David! Are you okay? How was your first day back?'

'Fine, thank you,' I say. 'I'm hitting the ground running.'

I pull out a plastic box from behind my back, and there's a tweak on the curtains of Kate's other neighbour.

'I made you flapjack.' Kate bounces a little with delight on the doorstep and takes the box.

'Thank you! Are they safe?' She laughs, and I pretend to be offended.

'Do you fancy a drink tomorrow night? The Wheatsheaf is back to normal now, no restrictions.'

I can hear someone moving around in her front room.

'Hi, Vanessa!' I shout through the hall.

Vanessa pops her head around the corner with a phone against her ear. She's a tall woman, with shoulders like an Olympic swimmer. She smiles and waves to me before disappearing again.

'Sure, I'd love to go out for a drink!' Kate says. 'I'm not doing anything. Just let me know the time.' She's grinning, but there's a shadow at her feet that lingers for a few seconds. I can't make it out.

'Only if you're sure? Sometime around 7.30?'

'Yep. No worries.'

I'm thinking about that shadow as I go back into my house when there's a video call request from my friend Terry.

'Davey boy!' he says. The picture quality is rubbish, but I can see he's standing in a dark field somewhere. He knows I hate being called Davey. 'Terry, where are you? On the moon? I can barely see you.'

'Dartmoor, filming, with permission, of course.'

'I haven't spoken to you for weeks!'

'I know, that's why I'm calling.' He's showing me the view. I imagine it would be beautiful if I could see in the dark.

'Very nice. You haven't broken your drone again, have you?'

'No. I nearly lost it in a stream, but it's all okay. I'm driving back tomorrow. I was just wondering if you were free for a pie and a pint tomorrow night?'

'Ah, no! I'm seeing my neighbour tomorrow—I've just arranged it. You should have called ten minutes ago.'

'Davey, what are you doing to me?' There is genuine disappointment hiding behind the bravado. 'Who is she and does she have a sister?'

'Ha! I don't know, but I can ask her for you. You know Kate —she's just a friend. She has a housemate, though. Kate's attractive, but you know where I'm at with all that crap at the moment.'

'You will have to get yourself out there soon, my friend,' he says, 'before you go all old and crinkly and your dick falls off.'

'You can talk! I'll call you after the weekend. We'll get a romantic date in, just you and me.'

'You're not my type. Your hair's too curly.'

'Not being racist, I hope.'

'You know me. No worries. Hope the job's going okay?'

'Slow but sure,' I say. 'There's a good-looking DS I could fix you up with. Her name's Helen.'

'As in of Troy? Sounds like a heap of trouble. Look, I must go. Call me, you bastard, or I'll break your door down.'

'Will do.' He's gone. I feel lighter now.

I've known Terry since I was five years old, and he's the best friend I have. We grew close when he found out about the attack. I wasn't always a good friend, though, and I pushed him out of the picture when I met Karen, my now ex-wife. Terry's the only one who knows everything about me, about what happened and how it changed me. It's not a big deal to him, even though he's not into paranormal or *weird shit*, as he calls it. I appreciate him more than he knows.

I'm hungry now, even after stealing a few pieces of the flapjack for myself. I microwave a lasagne ready-meal for one, and as sad as that sounds, I'm happy with that. As I watch the oven timer counting down, I'm thinking about Helen telling me she's divorced and why I didn't say *me too* at the right moment. Then I'm wondering about Josh and what he's doing right now. I have to stop because that thought hurts too much. The same reason his photograph hides in my bedside drawer.

I feel the hair rise on the back of my neck, and there's that feeling I'm being watched. It keeps happening. I look around, but there's nothing here to haunt me tonight, no visions nor phantoms. So, what is it I'm feeling?

THREE

Doctor Katherine Jacobs to camera:

Apart from the Covid-19 vaccine, Project Oberon is Hudson's most important development in recent years. Oberon is a research programme developing a powerful drug developed using nano-enhanced viruses and an altered amphetamine. This drug is code named Y9-Alphapase or Y9 for short. It preserves and enhances muscle and brain tissue, and could potentially be useful in the treatment of stroke, brain injury, and various diseases that cause dementia. Initial tests, yet to be published, showed very positive results in animal testing, but that was to change. We also observed vast improvements in response times to nerve stimuli and even increased longevity in mice.

27th February 2022

. . .

I've spent the day in my office reviewing cases and completing a ton of admin. It's as tedious as it gets, but necessary. Police work is nothing like the TV, where they never seem to do any paperwork.

I'm taking a break, searching online for a video doorbell for my house, when a giant of a man walks into CID wearing jeans and a tight t-shirt. He's ripped, and he knows it. He looks like a wrestler: bald with no eyebrows. I really shouldn't judge people by their eyebrows. He has a little banter with a few female DCs before he seeks me out and finds me.

'Afternoon, sir,' he says. I look up casually, making like I'm busy. 'I'm James Harris, DS.' James is on a different shift pattern to me.

'Ah, James,' I say, closing my browser. 'Good to meet you at last. I wanted to catch you this week. How are things for you?'

'Cheers, boss. All is well, just really, really swamped.' He leans against my door and shakes his head.

'I'm trying to find more resources from the district. It's not like we're short of room in here. I was just reviewing the Colin Decker cold case. You said there was some partial DNA found on his clothing. Are you doing door-to-door enquiries again?'

'"That and delivering leaflets to the locals. We're considering taking voluntary DNA samples too.'

McCall comes in, back from the raid on Broyle Way.

'Hey, Helen!' says Harris as she walks into my office. 'You've taken out that Broyle Way address.'

'News travels fast,' she says. 'We found two girls on the premises, sir,' she's updating me. 'Can't be certain of their ages—both look under sixteen. No passports, no ID at all. We're suggesting Thai initially, just trying to sort out translators now. They were left in squalid conditions. All the doors and windows were locked, and they had little food. Even I'm shocked. There was no Gary there, unfortunately. Anti-trafficking is taking the case off us, so if you would both excuse me, I have lots of writing to do and property to book in.'

'Thanks, Helen,' I say. 'Great work.'

When McCall leaves the office, I signal to Harris to close the door.

Harris is sitting in front of me, and I'm reading someone who is ambitious, confident, and trustworthy. I can see he's trying to read me too, and he's another one intrigued by the colour of my eyes. He and McCall have led this team successfully for a while now. I need him to trust that I won't undermine that.

'Thanks for coming in, James,' I say. 'I really can see you have a lot on your plate, especially with the Colin Decker case review. Is there anything I should know about?'

'Yes, sir. Several documents are missing, and some of the work is substandard, in my opinion.'

'For example?'

'Well, I can't see we ever spoke to Decker's employer, for one thing. He was drinking in a pub the night he was killed, and the witness statements taken were poor. We know he was with a woman that night, but no one knew who she was or could give a description of her. I've got the statements out of storage, and I'm going through them with the team.'

'This shouldn't just fall on you. I'm doing what I can to find help.'

'Thank you, sir.'

'And how about you? Any issues you need me to be aware of?'

There's a slight change in the temperature of his skin, an opening of pores. He's hesitating to tell me something.

'No, all fine, sir. Just snowed under.'

'I'll try to find some more resources for you.'

'Thank you. That will take a load off.'

'Are you local, James?'

'Not too far, Tangmere.'

'Family?'

'I live with Paul, my husband. He's a paramedic, so our shifts mean we don't see each other as much as we'd like.'

'This job can be hard on relationships.'

'True. I'm looking forward to working with you, sir. We've heard a bit about how you came to us.' He's looking at the hole in my skull.

'Thanks. It's good to be frontline again.' I pause. 'Look, just to let you know, and I've said this to Helen, I do have some unusual working methods. Nothing to worry about, but intuition plays a big part. Don't let it disturb you. I get results.'

'Ha! No worries, sir. Whatever it takes. You call it intuition, my old man used to call it a copper's nose.'

'It probably is. Let me know if there's anything else. I have a PC on secondment for you starting this week.'

'Thanks, sir. I'm grateful.'

I'm watching him go and realise that Walsh has been kind to me by giving me this team to start with. James's talking with Helen now, and he's telling her what I said. Hopefully, they don't think I'm a complete dick in my first week.

Swampy lives alone with his dog since his dad passed away. He doesn't want to be alone, but it seems to him it's a life fate is trying to force upon him. There's one girl, though, he can't get out of his head.

Swampy wonders how many times she's pushed him away now? Three at least, he reckons, but the knock-backs won't put him off. Furzzle is watching him from his bed, and he knows his master's moods better than anyone. Swampy puts his head in his hands and groans.

'I just can't get her out of my head, mate!' he says to Furzzle. The lurcher wags his tail in sympathy.

Swampy remembers it was in November that Kate first came into the pub. She came in alone then; this was before her friend came on the scene. She wore that short denim skirt and long boots. God, she looked sweet! She came straight over to him, no one else, just him. She ordered a rum and coke and asked for his name. Swampy's mates, Del, Mick and Chester were there, all eyeing her up. She's way too good for them.

'She's only a frigging doctor!' Swampy told them after she'd left.

'I reckon she's taken one look at you, Swampy,' said Kevin, 'and has got herself all unnecessary.' Kevin is his boss, the landlord. He was elbowing Mick and laughing.

'I reckon she's talking to you for a bet,' said Chester.

'Tossers, you're just jealous,' said Swampy.

'Are you going to ask her out to do a bit of lamping with you, Swampy?' said Del.

'You know what? I think she's the sort of girl who'd be up for that,' said Swampy. 'Can you imagine it, her in my van in the dead of night!' There was a cheer around the bar.

She came in twice more that week, and she told him the name of the road where she lived. So, she must have been interested. Swampy has thought this through many times over the last month. She asked him for help that first time. She'd had too much to drink, kept going on about how lonely she was, how people let her down. Swampy told her he wouldn't let her down, never. She asked him for a lift home. It was obvious what she wanted. So, when the time was right, he went in there. She just pushed him off. He didn't mean to put his hand up her skirt; he was helping her out of her seatbelt. She said nothing about it afterwards, though, so it must have been okay.

Next time, she came in with a friend. Vee, she called her. Swampy's dad would have called her a handsome woman; it's how he described Swampy's mum. Chester came over to try his luck with Vee. She would have had him for breakfast. Chester went off with his tail between his legs and called her a dyke. He got himself barred because of that.

With her friend there, Swampy asked Kate out for a midnight walk and to shoot some rabbits with him. There're too many rabbits on the Downs, he told her when she objected. Kate would have loved it, but she just laughed at him. That was unkind. She can't keep coming in dressed like that and not want him. She's just a prick-teaser.

Swampy has followed her home a few times now, but not bothering her, respectfully keeping his distance. He just likes the way she walks, with her head held high, confident, full of life. He thinks she knows he follows her. She must like it because she doesn't complain.

Then there was last week. Kate threw her drink over him. He wasn't trying to touch her, not there. His hand was just resting on the stool. He thinks she thought he was someone else. She wasn't half-embarrassed afterwards—she had to walk out.

Swampy has some secret photographs of Kate, taken at the pub when she was sitting on the stool. He likes to relieve himself when he looks at them. She wouldn't want him having them, but she doesn't know. She never saw the camera, so it's okay.

'What am I going to do, Furzzle?' he says. 'I just want to be near her. She'll change her mind—I know it. If she doesn't, then you and me will change it for her.'

The Wheatsheaf is my favourite pub. It's only a ten-minute drive from home, yet far enough out of the city to enjoy the quiet of the countryside. It has farmland to one side and a steep hillside forest on the other, sloping away into the darkness towards the ancient yew forest of Kingley Vale.

I open the door of the Merc for Kate and help her out. The air is chilled, and frost is expected.

'I haven't been here for ages,' she says to me. I can see that she's a little nervous.

'Are you hungry?' I ask.

'Not particularly. I didn't know this was a dinner date.'

'It's not, don't worry, but they do great food here if you were.'

The pub is cosy and warm, scented sweetly with wood smoke and beer, and alive with locals laughing between themselves. We find a small table by the open fire, and I order our drinks at the bar. While I'm waiting, I turn to watch Kate for a while. She's in a short denim skirt and a long, green chunky jumper. Comfort clothes, I imagine, but she looks great in them. Then I see a shadow, whispering something in Kate's ear. She looks up and smiles at me, but there's something on her mind—she's waiting for an opportunity.

'So,' says Kate, as I hand her a large glass of Sauvignon Blanc. She's sitting forward and looking into my eyes. 'How's work? Is it everything you hoped it would be, coming back after all this time?'

'Well, I know where the kitchen and the toilets are now. I've convinced everyone that I'm an inspector—so far so good.'

'I bet you're a great detective inspector.'

'How about your research work?' I sip my shandy—there's

something coming. 'I'm not really sure what you're researching, but you always seem busy.'

'Oh, it's fine. Researching away as normal, thanks.'

She definitely wants to say something. She keeps fiddling with the stem of her wine glass, running her fingers up and down.

'Is there's something you want to tell me? You seem a bit on edge this evening.'

'Me? Why do you think that?'

'I'm a great detective inspector, remember?'

She swallows and studies her glass for a moment. 'Well, there is something. I don't really know where to start.'

'Okay, try the beginning.'

The room fades out, and Kate is talking to me, but I can't hear her. There's someone else here, standing over me. He's the man I saw in McCall's memory, and now I can see he's the same man Megan remembered, Gary from Broyle Way. He shows me a knife he's been hiding behind his back. And there is McCall—what is he doing? He's gone back for McCall.

I pretend I've got a message on my phone.

'Oh shit! I have to go!'

Helen McCall parks outside her Victorian-style converted flat in Bognor Regis and sees the man she met last night waiting on the doorstep for her. He's sitting there in the shadows with a hood up against the cold night air. She can see his face lit up by the mobile phone he's engrossed in. Helen holds her mobile and walks to her door. He looks up and smiles.

'Hi, Helen,' he says. 'Remember me? You're back late.'

It's either Steve or Simon. She knows so many Simons. He's

looking rough now. She must have been more drunk than she thought last night.

'What are you doing?' says McCall.

'I just wanted a little chat.' He stands on the concrete steps above her.

She feels uneasy and steps back into the street. In her handbag is an attack alarm, and she pretends to look for door keys.

'The keys are in your hand,' he says. He smiles like it's funny.

Helen finds the alarm fob and keeps her finger on the button. 'Look, Steve, Simon, whatever your name is. I'm tired. I've had a hard day, and I want to go in and have a bath. I thought I told you last night—it's not happening.'

'I can help you with your bath.' She's creeped out now. A car pulls over further down the road. He's checking it out.

'No, you're alright, thanks. Go now, please.'

'Come on, Helen! We have a lot to talk about.'

'Wait, David! Please let me explain,' says Kate. She's trying to tell me something, but Helen's in trouble. She takes my hand, and I pull away.

'Look, there's an emergency. I'm so sorry, Kate! Someone's in serious trouble.' I pull three notes out of my wallet. 'Get yourself a taxi home. I must go now. I'll try to come by later, honest.'

She looks miffed but nods her head. 'Okay, don't worry. Drop by when you can.'

I pick up my jacket and run out the door, calling DS Harris on the way back to my car.

'James, it's Angelis. Look up Helen's home address for me.

She's in danger. Get a response car over there straight away—there's someone with a knife. I'll head over there, too.'

'Bognor Response units are tied up with a fight on the seafront. I'll see if anyone can break away.'

'Do what you can.'

'Talk about what?' says McCall.

'About your day, for example.' He's put his hands in his pockets. 'And it's Gary, by the way, Gary Parkes.'

'Look, I'm a police officer. If you don't want to get nicked for stalking, fuck off. Is that clear enough?'

'I already knew you're the filth, Helen. And you had to stick your nose in where it didn't belong, didn't you.'

McCall tries to make a call, but he knocks her mobile out of her hand. The phone clatters to the floor.

'What the fuck are you going on about!'

'We paid good money for those girls. You stole them! What have you done with them?'

'Gary Parkes, Broyle Way. How do you know where I live?'

'You've been snooping about for a while. It wasn't hard to follow you home one night. You lot are so stupid.'

He's going to make a move. She's pressing the panic alarm, but nothing is happening. Then it comes, and he's strong, and his arms are crushing her against him, her back is hard against his chest. She's struggling to kick him. She catches sight of something glinting in his hand. A serrated edge, and it's under her throat. She lands an elbow, making the knife snag.

'Now, you bitch, you're going to make a terrible mess.'

Someone runs towards them from the shadows. It's Angelis.

'Let her go!' Angelis shouts. He's catching his breath, facing

Parkes square on. Parkes drags Helen backwards with him, and she grunts in pain.

'Who the fuck are you!' he says.

'I'm a police officer. Let her go!'

'Fuck you!'

Angelis looks down and closes his eyes. Parkes drops the knife, and it falls into the gutter. Helen breaks away. Parkes wets himself, and his eyes roll back. He grips his head, digging his fingernails into his temples.

'Make it stop!' says Parkes.

He falls to the ground, and Angelis pins him down. There's a siren and strobing blue lights. Parkes is still. It's over.

'What just happened!' says Helen.

Angelis checks the nick on her throat. 'Are you hurt?'

'No.' McCall is shaking.

'You're going to be okay. Breathe slowly.'

'Is he dead?'

Angelis places the back of his hand against Parkes's mouth. Parkes is grunting. 'No, just pissed off.'

Inside McCall's flat, the response officers have finished taking the first accounts from McCall and Angelis.

'God, Sarge!' the female officer says. 'Are you okay? You've got a little cut on your throat there.'

'It's just a scratch. I'm fine,' says McCall. 'How's Parkes?'

'Delightful.' The officer shakes her head. 'He left screaming like a child, but he's okay. He's being booked into Custody now. We'll get the nurse to check him over.'

'Great, thank you.' McCall is watching Angelis, who is casually walking around her living room, looking at her family photographs. She turns to the officer. 'Honestly, I'll be fine. I'm really grateful.'

The officers leave, and there's silence for a while between McCall and Angelis. He's drinking the last few mouthfuls of tea while she pours herself a glass of wine.

'What did you do to him?' says McCall.

Angelis swallows his tea and gently puts down his mug.

'I did nothing,' he says. 'He must have had a seizure. Was he waiting for you?'

'Sitting on my doorstep. He told me he'd followed me home. Apparently, he didn't like me snooping around Broyle Way.'

There's another silence, and McCall downs her wine quickly.

'How did you know to come, sir?' she says.

He takes his time to answer. 'I was having a drink with a friend, and I realised I'd missed something. It could have been Parkes you met the other night.'

'That's really some wild intuition! Almost too—'

'But you're okay now?'

'Yes, sir, thank you.' She can tell he doesn't want to talk about it. 'I'm just glad you're on our side.'

McCall sits down on her sofa, examining her wrecked mobile phone. She's feeling the wine now, and it helps. She can feel hot tears running down her cheeks, and she hides her face from Angelis.

Angelis sits beside her and puts his arm around her shoulders. 'Did I scare you more than he did?' She's shaking as she's crying. 'I didn't want him to hurt you.'

Angelis spots a box of tissues and hands them to her. She

walks out to the bathroom and washes her face. Parkes's scent is still on her.

'Were you on a date?' McCall calls out from the bathroom. She doesn't know why she's asking and regrets it.

'Not really, just a friendly something or other.'

'A something or other?'

McCall comes back in, and the colour is back in her cheeks.

'I'd better go,' says Angelis. 'If you need time-out tomorrow, just let me know.'

'I'll be fine, sir.'

She looks at Angelis in front of her and has to push the inappropriate thoughts out of her head. She's not used to strong, caring guys, not good-looking ones. She must stay professional, especially now.

Kate is sitting on her sofa with Max, stroking his ears as she's surfing the Internet on her phone. Max wags his tail and buries his head against her chest.

'So, David just left you there?' says Vanessa.

'He gave me money for a taxi,' says Kate. 'He said it was some sort of emergency. He had to go right away.'

'Do you think he knows?'

Kate shrugs and puts down her mobile. 'You've seen what he can do, Vee.'

'So, what now? He'll find them soon—you know he will.'

'We tell him everything,' says Kate. 'Get it over and done with. He said he'd try to drop by when he's finished.'

'Your boss wouldn't be too pleased. Haven't you signed something?'

'Yes, but we'll be gone before she can do anything. We'll have the money, and it'll be just you and me.

Vanessa hesitates and looks into Kate's eyes. 'Kate, I asked Peter to come over tonight. I owe him an explanation. It's not fair.'

'Coming here? Is that safe! What did he say?'

'I wrote him a note, and I've tried phoning, but he's not answering. I expect Martina's watching the house, his house. Dettori would have sent her looking for me. I didn't want to stop by in case.'

'After everything you've done to him, do you think he'll come?'

'I hope so. If he doesn't, then... It's understandable. I'm not sure I would. It won't take long. I just want him to know and move on.'

'That's fine. I sort of guessed you'd contact him, eventually. But we're doing this, okay? This is it. If Dettori doesn't pay, then his proverbial fan is going to get covered in it. I'm serious, Vee! I'll expose everything. I want to get out of here, and I want you to come with me.'

Vanessa is showing doubt on her face. Is this what she wants, too?

They hear a vehicle pulling up outside, and the engine stops. The dog is barking.

'That's Peter now,' says Vanessa. 'Get the dog in the garden for a minute. Max will only jump all over him.'

Kate takes Max's bowl to the garden and fills it up with food. The dog attacks his extra treat as the backdoor closes.

The doorbell rings, and Vanessa goes to the front door.

It's late, nearly 10.45, and I'm home. The lights are off in Kate's house. I guess I'll have to talk to her tomorrow. I'm shattered now, anyway—I hope she understands.

I've taken myself off to bed, and I can hear a dog barking somewhere. I'm hoping it will stop soon. Something in my head is bothering me—I don't know what it is. Was it to do with Gary Parkes? No, it's something else—why won't that dog just shut up! There's just so much information struggling for my attention. I'm trying to sleep, but now there's a high-pitched squeal coming from outside. It's not stopping and turns into a mournful howl. Kate must have left Max in the garden. I check my watch, 11.30 p.m. Can't they hear the dog? I'm going to have to wake her up if I'm going to get any sleep.

I put on some jogging bottoms, and I'm outside Kate's front door. I ring the doorbell—there's no reply, but Kate's car is in the drive. Why leave the dog outside? The dog continues to bark, and a light goes on outside Kate's other neighbour's house.

'What's that awful noise?' comes a voice. A woman is peeping out of her front door.

'I'm just trying to find out,' I say.

'Those girls have left that dog outside, poor thing,' says the neighbour.

I can see a yellow light inside the house, but I know it's only visible to me. It moves closer and pauses behind the front door. Then the light comes through the door and towards me as if it's seen me. I reach out a hand to touch it. There's a hand inside the light, reaching back, outstretched fingers, but as I'm about to take hold of them, the light ascends over the rooftops and escapes into the night. I know who that was!

'Shit! Kate!' I'm hammering at the door. 'Kate! Open the door!'

'What's wrong with you?' The neighbour has come outside.

'Call the police! Tell them someone is dying. I need to break the door down. Quickly!'

I'm kicking at the door for what seems like ages, but it won't budge. I look through the window into Kate's front room, and I see a coffee table turned on its side. I need something to break the double-glazed glass. I'm thinking of grabbing my tools from the shed when I see strobing blue lights fill the road. Four police officers pile out of their cars.

'I'm police—Inspector Angelis,' I say. 'Get that door open! Someone's dying in there.'

An officer grabs a metal ram from the back of his car. He smacks it against the door three times. There's a loud crack, and shards of PVC fly everywhere. The door breaks apart, and I push my way through it, followed by another officer—his torch is lit.

We freeze as his light hits the kitchen.

'Holy shit!'

Kate is half hanging off the kitchen table. Her eyes are staring at me, and congealing blood covers everything. It's sprayed all over the walls and ceiling. She's tied by ropes to the table legs. The gaping neck wound is the last I see of her as I turn away. There's a confusion of shadows, too many to see, and my adrenaline isn't helping. Where's Vanessa? Is she hiding? I run upstairs.

'Police! Vanessa!' There is no one here.

A crowd of neighbours has gathered outside, and their phones are out taking photos, videos, tweeting, and messaging. There's a reporter and photographer here, too. Voyeurs, all of them, craving the likes, the wows, the loves, the attention. The shits are filming the SOCO team kitting up beside their van, trying to get a shot through the smashed front door to see the body, the blood, and the shock of the macabre, just before a large blue screen blocks their view. They're getting off on someone's demise. What if she was your wife, your child, your friend?

I'm standing next to James Harris and Superintendent Walsh, just outside the outer police cordon. Walsh is wearing a rain mac with an upturned collar. He looks like a classic, silver-haired private eye. Someone has put the dog in my back garden, where we can hear him whimpering again.

Walsh is here to make clear my involvement in this. I knew her, and I met with her tonight. He's now on the phone, swearing at someone. DS Harris is organising a rota of scene guards with the neighbourhood sergeants.

'Good grief!' says Walsh as he comes off the phone. 'It's all over Twitter already! And now the reporters are here.' He shakes his head in disbelief. 'I heard what happened to McCall. Is it a full moon or something? Okay, David. Talk to me about you and the victim.' He's only in the mood for facts, not feelings.

'Sir, Kate is my neighbour. She is Katherine Jacobs. She shares the house with her friend Vanessa. I don't know her last name. Kate and I are... were friends. Nothing serious. We went out for a drink at 7.30 tonight, to a local pub. I left her there at about 8.15 to help Helen. I called James about that time. Before I left, I gave Kate money for a taxi. I got home from McCall's about 10.45 and went to bed. I heard the dog howling outside about 11.30 and grew suspicious that something was wrong.'

'So, the dog alerted you. What was it that made you suspect something was seriously wrong?'

'Excuse me, sir,' says Harris. 'I'll get the door-to-door enquiries going.'

'Yes, thank you, James,' says Walsh.

'I looked through the window and saw a table in the front room was on its side,' I say. 'It didn't look right. Possibly a burglary in progress.'

'So, just from that, you concluded that there was a serious threat to life?'

'Yes, sir. It was my honest held belief.'

'A little tenuous,' says Walsh. He sighs. 'I'm taking charge of this inquiry initially, just until we can check out your part in all this.'

'Yes, sir.'

Walsh leans closer to me. 'We need to keep your friendship with Kate at a low profile, especially with the media jumping in so early. I'll ask you this once, so be honest with me. Were you in a physical relationship with Katherine Jacobs? Were you sleeping with her?'

'No, sir.' It sticks in my throat. 'We were just friends.'

'Okay, good. Where is this Vanessa? Has there been any friction between her and Kate, do you know?'

'Nothing that I know of. Kate told me Vanessa had men trouble, but no more detail than that.' Walsh can see that I'm flagging.

'Go and write your statement, then get some rest. You've got one of your catch-up appointments with the doc tomorrow morning, haven't you?'

'Yes, sir. So, unless you need anything?'

'No, off you go.'

The *victim*. That turns my stomach tonight. We use these terms all the time: the victim, the aggrieved, the witness, the suspect. It's real people with real futures ahead of them, and so hard to get my head around. I'm looking up to the heavens and wonder where Kate's light has gone.

My pathway is just on the edge of the outer cordon. I go inside my house and close my front door to all the madness out there. I jump when I see a small dog running towards me, wagging its tail. I must have left the back door open—the house is cold. Poor Max, I wonder if he knew what happened?

. . .

I've uploaded my statement and crashed out on my sofa, lying in the dim light. Kate's corpse appears on the floor in front of me. She's wearing her chunky green jumper and her short denim skirt. Her head is partly removed, and her mouth hanging open. Her glassy eyes are watching me; they blink as she waits for me to figure this out. I can't—I have nothing. God, Kate, what happened to you? Where's Vanessa?

After two large whiskies, her spectre fades away. It's one way I can switch it off, and now I'm drowsy.

The SOCO inspection lights intrude through the curtains, the officers casting unwelcome shadows on my wall. I can hear their voices, and they are moving things next door. Max is with me now, and he whines at me as he lies on top of my feet for comfort. What am I going to do with him? I can't think anymore, and I close my eyes.

January 2020

I'm not sure where I've come from, but I know I don't want to be here. Am I awake in this darkness? Is this all that's left of me? I hear the repeating tones of diagnostic machines and the hiss of air near my face. Then there's the passing squeak of soles on Lino, the brush of cloth on my skin, and the whisper of words whirling around me.

'Hello, David. It's Friday. It's so cold out there, but at least the sun is out at last. It's the weekend! Are you going to wake up today?' Ana is here—I sense her close by. My hand is in hers until she slips somewhere far away, and I leave her once again.

. . .

'Hi, David. Wakey, wakey… It's freezing today. I nearly came off my bike this morning. It's so icy out there. I shall tell my boyfriend to give me a lift to work tomorrow. He's got a nice warm car with heated seats. Are you coming back to us today? My friends are praying for you, David…'

I return to the sound of a clattering trolley on rattling casters. Then a pain in my hand, a point is pricking my skin.

'Good morning, David. It's Tuesday. Rain all day, they said on the radio. My boyfriend gave me a lift. He's such a sweetheart…'

I wake, and someone is stroking my hand. Warmth. I can feel warmth wrapping around my fingers.

'Good news, David!' says Ana. 'Your parents are here to see you.'

But there is silence for a time, then footsteps, and someone is crying as they fall away.

Another day.

'Good morning, my love,' says a woman. 'It's Mum here. How are you today? Ana says you could wake up soon! That's so wonderful.' Her name? I know her, but—.

'Good to see you again, son,' says a man. 'It's Dad. I'm so happy you're improving, thank God. Slow but sure, eh? Your sister sends her love. I can't tell you how grateful we are… Can he really hear us, Ana?'

She is Sylvia. He is Michael.

'… The points were so badly pitted.' What is he saying? 'I

think I'm going to fit an electronic ignition. I don't know how much that will cost me...'

I wake, and I can feel my lips. They are so dry, and something is in my mouth. I'm biting something, a plastic tube, and it hurts to swallow.

'He's making advances every day. He's now responding to touch, and he's moving more.'

'Excellent, Ana,' there's an unfamiliar voice, rich and thoughtful. 'We will get him physio after the weekend. I see some muscle atrophy... staggering how his wounds have healed...'

I wake. The dying memory is of tranquillity, a safe place. And now something is new. I see light.

FOUR

Doctor Katherine Jacobs to camera:

So, this research is ground-breaking, and it could be lucrative for Hudson. Extremely lucrative. They poured vast amounts of funding into Oberon, urgently trying to speed the work up to reach the initial clinical phase. The urgency intensified when we heard that a similar project was underway in Germany. The technology wasn't the same, but it had the same aim.

Doctor Dean Dettori heads up Hudson in the UK. He's a brilliant scientist, and he knows it. Dettori is well-known in this field of science. The wealthy Italian is trying to make partner in the firm. He put tremendous pressure on us to bring forward the phase one trials. It's usually a lengthy process with a strictly controlled group of volunteers, using the actual drug and a placebo.

This is where things went wrong, and it became a red line for some of us. Further results from animal trials were coming back with some issues surrounding blood clotting in a small percentage of mice. Despite this, Dettori wanted to continue. Hudson Head Office wasn't happy and postponed the project, considering the blood clotting was too high a risk. Dettori was furious and went ahead with manufacturing a large batch of Y9-Alphapase and a placebo equivalent for the trials.

28th February 2022

Someone is ringing my doorbell. I jolt awake—there's daylight. I stand up, and I'm lightheaded. My mouth is bone-dry, and I'm finding it hard to swallow.

'No disrespect, but you look like shit, sir,' says McCall as she comes in. The first thing she sees is a bottle of single malt. 'I'll make us a coffee.'

I pull open the curtains, and I can see it's been raining overnight. The cordon tape is still there, fluttering in the wind. The scene guard officer checks her mobile, and a SOCO van has its doors open. As I remember the scene from last night, I feel sick and head for the shower.

'So, you know where I live now. We're even,' I say after my first sip. McCall makes a good cup of coffee, and she's made us toast with marmalade. I didn't realise I had marmalade in the house.

'I think the entire world knows where you live now.'

'How are you after last night?' My voice still sounds croaky.

'Good, sir. I can't believe I let Parkes find out where I live.'

'You didn't know who he was. He's locked up now and likely to be remanded. Any new developments?'

'Kate was a doctor. She's Doctor Katherine Jacobs.' McCall hands me a business card:

> *Katherine Jacobs MSc, PhD. FIBMS.*
> *Consultant Research Biologist*
> *Kajacobs-pharm@scimail-pharm.com*
> *Tel. 07700 901 061*

'A scientist! I'm flabbergasted!' I say.

'SOCO found it in a purse. There was a bank card, a credit card and a work ID card.'

McCall shows me the ID card, and it's a terrible photo of Kate. The card says Hudson Biotech in bold green letters.

'That doesn't tie up with her business card.' I see the date, valid until 09/2020. 'It's out of date. She obviously doesn't work there anymore. Any news on Vanessa?'

'No one has seen or heard from her. No one knows who she is.'

'I don't understand it.'

'Also, James has traced the taxi company that picked Kate up from the Wheatsheaf. They picked her up...' McCall refers to her iPad. 'They picked her up at 2035 hours and dropped her off at 2050 hours. They have CCTV inside the cab if we want it. The driver saw nothing untoward when he dropped her off.'

'So, we know she was alive after 8.50 p.m. and dead by 11.30 p.m. at the latest.'

McCall closes her iPad and sits forward to reach her toast. 'It must have been horrible to find her like that. Not a great welcome back to CID. How long had she lived next door to you?'

'About three months. I met Kate when she first moved in but ignored her at first until she needed help to put up a curtain rail. Soon after that, her friend moved in with her.'

'Walsh has already filled me in on what he asked you last night.' She takes a bite of toast. 'He's dished out the jobs first thing. He asked me to check on you. He said you never slept with her.'

I nearly spit out my coffee. 'Did he! Tell Walsh I'm okay.'

'Walsh wanted me to warn you about something, too. It's on the TV news already. And you're on Twitter and Facebook.'

'But I haven't given an interview.'

'It's just a photo of you and Walsh talking together last night, taken by your neighbours. They told the reporters that you lived next door to Kate. Walsh is furious.'

'Unbelievable! Bloody neighbours sticking their noses in.'

'Sorry, boss.'

Max is wagging his tail at me now and jumps up.

'He's such a friendly fella—the dog, not Walsh,' I say, rubbing his back. 'But I can't look after him.'

'I can help you with that.'

A couple in their mid-seventies open the door to their bungalow. I'm watching from the car as McCall tries to persuade her parents to look after Max.

There's an ache in my stomach, and I still can't believe Kate's gone. Then I see her sitting in the back seat, smiling at me. She doesn't look hurt now. I don't think my brain could have coped with that horrid image for much longer.

'We're taking care of Max for you, Kate,' I tell her. 'He'll be fine.' She's not listening. She's not here, of course. At first, the shrinks told me these are just hallucinations, mind dramas, a psychosis they couldn't treat, except with drugs. I don't want the drugs. I would have believed them, but then something like *this* happens: The car folds up around me like paper, and I'm standing somewhere else. There's warm sand beneath my feet, running softly through my toes. The shallow sea is a vivid turquoise, shimmering in the light, and the sky is a swirl of gold and cyan; the cosmos is revealed in a spray of a billion suns. I know this place—I've been here before. Kate is here, looking in wonder, lost in awe. She's surprised when she sees me.

'Hello, David,' she says. 'You look different.'

'Who was it, Kate?' I ask her. 'What happened to you?'

'I'm okay, don't worry. Just look at this place. It's beautiful!' Kate smiles, and her face is like it doesn't matter anymore. 'Follow the bird, David.'

She gives me one last wave and blows me a kiss. Kate turns around and walks away towards the gathering of the others waiting for her.

The door opens, and I'm back in the car. McCall returns without Max.

'Where did you go?' she says, getting back in the driver's seat. 'There, that's sorted. I told you they're suckers for furry friends. Where now, boss?'

'Take me back home,' I say. These sentimental visions don't help at all. 'I've got a doctor's appointment in half an hour.'

'Okay, boss.' She quietens her mood and leaves me with my thoughts.

We pull up outside my house, and there's the cordon, the scene guard, and the forensic search team poking around my garden looking for a murder weapon. They even have a spare key, checking my knives, my bins. My car is inside the cordon now. I can't face it.

'Actually, Helen,' I say. 'On second thought, I'll cancel my appointment. Take me to the station, will you? I can't deal with this.'

'Yes, boss, on our way.'

'And thanks for everything you've done this morning.'

She smiles as she drives us away.

Rachael Thorne checks her watch, and she has another ten minutes before she must go back to the ward. She is drinking coffee and chewing her way through an unappetising coronation chicken sandwich in the hospital restaurant. She beat the lunchtime rush, and there's now a queue of scrubs waiting to be served.

The TV is showing the news channel, with no sound. Rachael wonders why they do that—it's just a waste of electricity. Not even subtitles. Then she sees his face. It can't be him. They're reporting on something, a murder, perhaps? It's definitely him! She's walking towards the screen, staring intently. And there's the text beneath it, *Detective Inspector David Angelis discovered the body.*

'But he's dead,' she says to herself. She's feeling faint and stumbles back to her coffee.

A junior doctor is eyeing up her table. She's older and much scarier than him, and he backs away.

Rachael is on her mobile, and she's leaving a message. 'Hi, Jen, it's me. Watch the news and call me tonight. I'm finishing at 6. Love you.'

The briefing should have started five minutes ago, but Walsh is still on the telephone. Outside his office is a collection of detectives, including me, waiting to begin. I'm wondering what the collective term for detectives is. A posse? A squad? A case of detectives, perhaps? Police officers can't wait in silence—they must fill the silence with banter. It's an unwritten rule.

Walsh taps his window and beckons me over to his door with his phone stuck to one ear. 'David, take the briefing for me. I'm on a call with the senior command team. It's going to take some time. You okay with that?'

'Yes, sir.' I know more about the progress than he does, anyway.

I pick up a marker pen and rap it on a desk. 'Right! Listen up!' I shout over the laughing and name-calling. It's like being back at school. 'This is the briefing for Operation Greenwood only. If you are not working on this case, then you don't need to be here. I will catch up with you if it is urgent.' A handful of officers leak away, some looking somewhat disgruntled.

There's a whiteboard, there's always a whiteboard, and I'm standing in front of it. This one has a photograph of Kate pinned to the top. It's an enlarged driving licence photo, and she would hate it. Her hair colour doesn't look right for a start, and she looks miserable, which she never once did all the time I knew her. Next to Kate's photo, someone's drawn a big blue question mark and written Vanessa underneath it. They have given the question mark eyes and a smiley mouth.

'As you are already aware, this is Doctor Katherine Jacobs, date of birth 26th April 1989, known as Kate. The photo is a crap one, so can someone find a better one, please. I knew Kate as a friend and neighbour, but I barely knew her housemate, Vanessa. I will refer to Kate as Katherine for these briefings.' The reason seems obvious to me, but there are a few puzzled faces. 'Katherine Jacobs is a victim of an extraordinarily violent and gruesome attack, where the murderer has sliced open her throat, almost severing her head. There's a possibility that the killer sexually assaulted Katherine. I hope I don't need to remind anyone: do not share any crime scene photographs or pin them on this board.

'We don't know what time this attack occurred, other than it was after 2050 hours and before 2330 hours. The taxi dropped Katherine off at 2030 hours. At about 2240 hours, I passed her house and saw all the lights were off. I assumed she was asleep. I went straight to bed and Katherine's dog howling kept me awake. At about 2330 hours, I knocked on her door and realised that something was wrong. I asked a neighbour to call the police. We made a Section 17 PACE entry at 2337 hours, and we discovered Katherine Jacobs's body.

'Vanessa's location is still unknown, and we don't know her surname. The initial search of the property did not find any further details as to her identity. I last saw Vanessa two days ago, and I would describe her then as white, in her mid to late 30s, muscular build, about 5 feet 10 to 11 inches tall, with short dark hair. She sometimes colours her hair light blonde. Neighbours told us Katherine and Vanessa were last seen together at the property about 1730 hours after returning with the dog. I want to reiterate that we do not know if Vanessa is also a victim or the perpetrator. Or if she simply left the house earlier and stayed over somewhere else that evening. We know very little about her, in fact.

'Sergeant Harris organised door-to-door enquiries last night. James, over to you, please.'

I'm looking at the body language around me, and I'm getting nothing back from it. I know I'm coming across as stilted and awkward. They don't know me yet, and I don't know them. Talk about being thrown into the deep end.

James Harris is impeccably dressed and takes a lot of pride in his appearance. I'm wondering if he's going for an interview somewhere today. Standing next to me, I can see him puffing out his chest, moving his elbows outwards as he reads from a clipboard. Despite his polished appearance, Harris must be tired after being up all night. He's looking around, smiling through it, and waiting for everyone's complete attention. He's making the most of his height over everyone, but he's friendly and relaxed—unlike me.

'Knocking on people's doors at that time of night doesn't go down well,' says Harris, 'but we'd already woken everyone up with the lights and noise. As the boss said, we have a confirmed sighting of Katherine and Vanessa returning home after a dog walk at 1730 hours. They didn't see anyone else with them, and they looked relaxed together. Three of the neighbours heard Doctor Jacobs's cocker spaniel howling and barking on and off last night. A neighbour, living on the other side of Inspector Angelis, thought she heard a baby screaming for a few seconds.'

'What time was that?' I ask.

Harris refers to his notes. 'Around 2115 hours. A neighbour confirmed she saw you, boss, return home about 2240 hours or thereabouts.'

'Just to add, Katherine's car was still in her drive, and Vanessa doesn't have a car.'

McCall is writing these times down on the whiteboard. She's left-handed and holds the pen at a strange angle. She writes *Possible Window* on the board.

'So, this was 2050 hours to 2330 hours,' she says.

'James, did anyone have CCTV, doorbell videos?'

Harris glances at his notes again. 'One house, further along, had doorbell video footage but nothing out of the ordinary. It's only activated by a human passing it. It doesn't catch vehicles. There is no CCTV other than in a couple of back gardens.'

'So, that's a blank then,' I say. 'It's a possibility Kate knew her attacker. There was no sign of forced entry other than mine. We need to find her next of kin urgently before the press release names. Any other family, friends, social network? DS McCall, can you organise someone to do that? We need more background on Katherine and Vanessa. So, there's plenty to do. Has anyone found next of kin details at the address?'

There's an awkward silence.

'No, sir,' says Harris. 'There's very little detail about anything at the house to go on, just a few photos. I hate to say this, sir, but there's been a report on the news this morning. Someone has named the victim.'

'Shit! How did they get the name?'

'Nosey neighbours, sir,' says Harris. *'Possibly Katherine Jacobs*, they said.'

'For God's sake, they didn't have to broadcast it!'

'No, sir.'

'Helen, I'm going in to talk to Gary Parkes. I want to find out who he's working for. After that, we'll go to Katherine's house to search for any clues of next of kin. James, I don't doubt your efficiency. I just want to check again for my peace of mind. I'll be the one getting it in the neck.' McCall nods. 'And James, go home and get some rest. You must be knackered.'

I'm in an interview room with Gary Parkes. He looks and smells dreadful. I've gone through the necessaries with him, including his right to a solicitor—refused—and the caution through which he sang *God Save the Queen*. Now he's just staring at me, trying to intimidate me with his cocky, bad-arsed smirk. I'm not the one who wet himself.

'Why would I want to talk with you?' he says to me. 'I've got nothing to say to you.'

'Don't you want the chance to reduce your sentence?' I say. 'Helping us with our enquiries will do you a big favour. Tell me who you are working for, Gary.'

'You've got no idea. That's more than my life is worth. I'd be a dead man walking.'

'What is it with the false sense of loyalty? Whoever it is has done nothing for you. They've dropped you in it, and they're just walking away. The CPS is ready to charge you for multiple serious offences. I've spoken to the senior investigating officer, and he's happy to offer you this one chance. Don't forget, you are still under caution, Gary. This is your opportunity to do yourself a favour. Who are you working for? We can protect you from whoever it is. No one will know where you are.'

He laughs at me, but he's too late. Gary has conjured the memory, and now I see the man he works for. A man in his forties, well dressed, tall, good-looking, and wealthy. I just don't know his name.

'I know he's got money, Gary. He's not your normal thug, is he? What is his name?' Gary's boss is sitting opposite me now and is covering Gary's mouth to stop him from shouting his name to me. He's pushing his hand down Gary's throat, right down to his wrist. 'His name is?'

'Fuck off!' Gary shouts, 'Get me out of here!'

'No, that's not his name.'

Then I do the other thing I can do. I can *persuade* people to tell me the truth.

'He doesn't deserve your loyalty. This is the last time I'm going to ask you—name him.' Gary is feeling pressure in his head, an urgency, a fear. This isn't fair, but I'm not getting him to confess to something that isn't there. I suppose it is torture of a kind, mental torture that no one would believe if they challenged it in court. The video is recording us. I'm calm and polite, neither overbearing nor forceful. Yet Gary's head is being squeezed in a vice until he tells me the truth. And he *will* tell me the truth.

Gary begins to writhe in his chair. 'Dalton! Christopher

Dalton.' There's horror across his face as he realises what he's done. 'Shit! No!'

'Thank you, Gary. That's all I needed. We know who Christopher Dalton is.'

'What did you do to me?'

Parkes is sweating profusely.

'Me? Nothing. I'm just sitting here. It's all on video. You've been most accommodating. No one will know it came from you, Gary. You're safe and sound. Let's just hope Dalton can't put two and two together.'

Last year, I was returning a faulty kettle to a small store in town. It was May, cold and pouring with rain, like most of May had been. I was in a foul mood, waiting for the results from my inspector's promotion board.

The kettle was expensive, a good make, fast boiling with a blue light. The man in the shop accused me of dropping it and wouldn't accept it. Despite me banging on about my statutory rights, he still refused, and when he'd had enough of my face, he told me to go back to where I came from. He was referring to the colour of my skin, of course, and that really pissed me off—a red rag to a bull.

The shopkeeper turned his back to me. I didn't touch him—it was just a suggestion, a little persuasion. He walked over to the wall and head-butted it repeatedly until he could barely see through the blood running into his eyes.

I am ashamed of what I did, and it scares me, even now. My typical response to guilt and shame is to remove them from my memory. I have whole areas of the last ten years that are blank to me. If I don't remember them, then they never happened. But this remains unforgotten, and it serves as a warning to me, a shameful reminder.

The shop is closed up now—he went out of business. I never got the replacement kettle I wanted, and the sad irony is, the man was right. I had dropped the kettle on the kitchen floor.

'Christopher Dalton was a small-time criminal 12 years ago,' I say to McCall and Gregory. 'He sold drugs and imported dodgy goods. He dabbled in entertaining business executives from abroad by finding girls for them.'

We gather everyone in the office working on Op Greenwood. Sam Gregory is looking on PNC and local police databases.

'Dalton hasn't come to our attention over the last few years,' she says.

'As far as my memory goes,' I say, 'Dalton was untouchable because no one would talk to us about him. He's always kept well away from the coal face. He made a lot of money and unsavoury friends. I believe he's married now and lives in a big house on the road to Midhurst.'

'PNC has him for dealing ten years ago,' says Gregory. 'Common assault, handling. He's been inside for six months. Then there's nothing. Local databases mention he's an aggrieved party in a dispute in a pub three years ago and some ongoing disputes with ramblers on his property.'

I'm sitting on McCall's desk, and I can see her tilting her head as she's listening to Gregory. She realises that I'm staring at her.

'Helen,' I say, 'can you get someone to update the officer in charge of the Broyle Way case. We'll keep Dalton on our radar.'

'Yes, boss,' she says. I can see a slight increase in the skin temperature on her face. I wait until Gregory is on the phone.

'Is everything okay, Helen?'

She looks up at me and smiles. 'All fine.' But I can see she's struggling with something. For a moment, there's a figure standing over her. A man is shouting in her ear, pointing a finger. Then he turns to me and evaporates like smoke in the wind. She's quashed that feeling, that fear. She's in control again.

'I'll meet you back at Katherine's house, and we may need an extra pair of hands.'

DS McCall and another detective I haven't met before are outside the temporary front door of Kate's house when I arrive. The cordon is still in place, with a cold and miserable PCSO guarding the scene. My heart goes out to her—it looks like she's been forgotten.

'How long have you been here?' I ask her.

'Four hours, sir,' she says.

'You're a wonder. I'll see if I can get you relieved. What's your name?'

Her eyes light up. 'Angela. Thank you, sir. I'm off in half an hour.'

Along the line of the cordon are several bunches of flowers left by well-wishers and neighbours. The same neighbours who filmed Kate's murder scene, horrified and grateful it didn't happen to them.

We don't have the place to ourselves. There are still a few pieces of forensic work going on. Having no contact details for relatives is a concern, especially with the news gone out the way it has.

I hesitate before we enter. The other detective, Chinese, I'm guessing, is standing beside me. Her face is pale, and she's looking anxious. She knows it's messy in there. To me, she looks new in service, inexperienced perhaps.

'Who are you?' I ask directly. I didn't mean to sound short, but I don't want a distressed police officer on my hands.

'Po Cheung, sir,' she says.

'How long have you been with us, Po?'

'Three months.'

'You okay? Have you been to a murder scene before?'

'No, sir. But I have to get on with it. Anyway, the body is gone now.'

'Before you go in, could you make a note of any unusual messages left with the flowers at the front?'

'Will do, sir.' She goes straight out there, visibly relieved as she walks up the path.

McCall smiles at me.

'Do you know much about Po?' I ask McCall.

'She's from Hong Kong, moved over here as a kid. She's on a fast-track university scheme. She's hardworking, a bit too hard on herself, easy to manage, pleasant enough—more than I can say for some of her colleagues. Is there something wrong?'

'No, just being a caring boss. Let's get on with it.' We put on coveralls, gloves and masks and stop outside the dark hallway.

How do I describe what I can see now? I see impressions of the past everywhere I go, including here. They are the memories that places have, stacked in diminishing layers and replaying in a constant loop. Some places have stronger memories than others. I don't know why that is yet. Some people can pick up on it, chills, goosebumps, feelings of peace or foreboding. Then there are the other kinds of places. The Celts called them the Thin Places, where Heaven kisses Earth as they brush against each other. In these places, I see other things, other creatures that I can't easily describe. Here, though, I only see shadows of Kate and Vanessa. Many versions of them are here. They're moving around like ghosts between rooms, doing the same old boring stuff of life. I must remind myself that these visions are not their ghosts, just memories projected into mine. Yet, the night of the murder is a blur to me. It's too soon, out of focus, and too raw in emotion.

'You okay, sir?' asks McCall. She snaps me out of my thoughts. 'It can't be easy coming back here.'

'No, I'm all fine. Come on.'

After two hours of trying, James Harris couldn't sleep, so he's back at his desk, hoping no one will notice. He's remaining calm under pressure; it's usually what he does best, but there's a worry at home that's distracting him today. Then there's the desk job side of his work, which is driving him to despair. He's had to send back work to two detectives who should know better. Forms not completed correctly—statements not taken. Some of the door-to-door work on Op Greenwood hasn't been entered either. He'd much rather be out there now than sitting at a desk, but if he goes for the job at HQ he's seen, then he'll be doing nothing else. He'd be leaving CID behind and reviewing force policies and procedures. It's what Paul wants, keeping James away from harm, and the extra money would be helpful.

James sees a new envelope on his desk. It's a letter to be filed under Operation Whiteways, the cold case he's been working on. They found Colin Decker on the roadside after being beaten and run over. Nasty crime scene photos are in the file from December 2019. This date on the letter is May 2020 and is from Decker's previous line manager. They found it within a bunch of the other papers recently rediscovered. James's day is about to get more interesting, and he feels a rush of excitement that he wouldn't get if he was working somewhere else.

4th May 2020

Dear Sirs,

I am writing to confirm that I was Colin's former head of department at Hudson Biotech during the dates you requested. Please note that I am no longer employed by them. Whilst Colin was working for me, I found him to be an unassuming individual and one who held strong moral opinions. He kept his private life exactly that, and he did not mix easily with his colleagues apart from pleasantries. I had no concerns regarding Colin's role within our department, and I found him mostly amiable.

Colin had raised concerns with senior management regarding recent drug trials by Hudson. To my knowledge, these concerns remained unresolved before his death. I cannot remember any personal grievances he had against any other colleagues or vice versa.

I'm sorry, I cannot be more helpful than that.

Yours faithfully,

Dr Katherine Jacobs, MSc, PhD. FIBMS. Consultant Research Biologist

We start with the front room and will move through the house, leaving the kitchen until last. We need to find details of relatives or any photos, notebooks or diaries that give us a clue. I'm surprised how little there is here, and nothing seems to have been taken. There's a coffee table on its side, its edges covered in fingerprint powder, an expensive TV and sound system that I occasionally heard through my adjoining wall. I see little investment in this place and few personal touches—it's a home without a heart. There is one photo in a frame, lying face down. It would be easy to miss it. It's a photograph of Kate with a couple who could be her parents and another woman, perhaps her sister. I recognise the landscape in the background, the river, and the coloured houses on the other side.

McCall is looking at the table.

'An altercation between Katherine and Vanessa?' says McCall.

'Possibly,' I say. 'Look.' I'm showing McCall the photo and tracing the background with my finger. 'The views look like Dartmouth. It's either a holiday or where her relatives live.'

'I hope to God they never saw the news last night,' she says. 'They love it, don't they, *a local source says*, giving her name and everything.'

'There's nothing out of the ordinary here. It's clean and tidy. Has anyone got onto the landlord yet?'

'In progress. I've asked someone to get onto it.'

There's a drawer under the coffee table, and I open it carefully. Inside are some coasters and a set of keys.

We move into the dining room/office. There's a laptop charger but no laptop, a filing cabinet with a key in the lock. The filing cabinet looks a little out of place here. A set of medical and other science books are on the top of the cabinet, with titles that I'm struggling to read.

'James said nothing about the missing laptop,' I say. 'Have we seized it?'

McCall checks a list of items on her iPad, cursing that her

gloves make scrolling a little tricky. 'No, it wasn't here. We don't know if someone took it or if Vanessa what's-her-name has it.'

'That's what I used to call her.' I open the drawers of the cabinet, one at a time. They're all empty. 'No one thought to mention this either? There could be a motive here.'

We've moved up into Kate's bedroom. I see her everywhere here. She's putting on her makeup, pulling up her jeans, staring out the window. Then I see her with someone—they're naked, locked in an embrace—it's Vanessa. I turn away. So, she wouldn't have been interested in me after all. I read that completely wrong. I'm struggling to stay in here. Cheung joins us with a shortlist of names from the flowers.

'Can you and Po continue in here, Helen?' I say. 'I'll go to Vanessa's room.' She can see something's wrong.

'Okay, boss. I'll let you know.'

Vanessa's room isn't Vanessa's room. It's definitely unused. They haven't changed the bedsheets for weeks. There's a wardrobe with a few changes of clothes but no personal effects. There are no photographs, no paperwork, nothing apart from an old teddy bear in a dress, smiling at me from the bed.

McCall finishes checking Kate's room and meets me on the landing.

'I found an old ripped up bank statement in the bin,' she says, 'and a few of the usual things you'd find in a woman's bedside drawer—nothing out of place. There are two sets of pyjamas in Kate's bed, under the pillows. I also checked the bathroom. Two toothbrushes.'

I nod. 'Yes, Vanessa's room is virtually unused, just some clothes in a wardrobe. We'll head down to the kitchen-diner.'

Po is quiet but hanging in there.

'Well done, Po,' I say. 'I don't know about you. I'm finding this really hard.'

'Yes, sir,' she says. 'It's like walking into someone's life.'

Kate's house is a mirror image of mine. Her kitchen is more modern, much nicer, apart from the thick residue of bloody gore covering nearly everything. I'm struggling with this, and McCall knows it.

I'm trying to focus, to sift back through the shadows. I'm looking for the impression left by Kate's murderer. But it's all a blur, just a noise of shifting shapes. Perhaps I'm just too close, or maybe it's too soon. The memories that places have—I don't always get to choose what I can see.

My plastic box of flapjack is unopened on the side. That's stayed clean. Maybe she didn't like flapjack. Hanging over the sink is one of a set of green and white Gingham tea-towels I bought Kate for Christmas. She thought they were quaint.

I'm staying clear of the table, avoiding walking over the bloody footprints, now all labelled and photographed. There's a SOCO come in from the garden, watching where we're standing. I feel a telling-off coming, but it looks like we're doing okay.

'We're done in here,' he says to me.

'Thank you,' I say. 'Nothing else found for Vanessa?'

'We think we have two sets of different prints. But you'll have to wait and see.'

I'm looking at the fridge, the calendar. Kate has written my name on yesterday's date: 'David: 7.30'. I'm looking further back. There's our walk in the woods, but then there's more. Every day of the week in February has my name or initial on it. Against each is a brief note to herself, something that perhaps only she understood.

24th: David, N/I
23rd: David, 10 mins of para. act
22nd: D, call to parents, none
21st: D, call to work 7 mins, anxiety
20th: D, N/I
19th: David, disp. from view for 3 mins
18th: Prof. Allen, call 10.20 A.M. No chg./ D, low mood
17th: D, Pos. psych. episode. 35 mins/with para. act
16th: D, not in.
...

Then I flip over the sheet to January. Every day has one of these types of comments. I see Professor Allen on there, the dates of the meetings with my psychiatrist. I'm feeling something—there's anxiety building.

'She was researching *me*,' I say to McCall. 'Shit! She was watching me!'

McCall comes over, and she's turning each page of the calendar.

'It starts in November.'

'That's when she moved in. I felt like I was being watched this whole time. How did she know?' I have the thought at the same time as McCall. I'm out the front door and hop over the fence. The PCSO is trying to get my attention, but I ignore her. I'm still wearing my coveralls, and I'm in my lounge. I'm taking things off my mantlepiece, the vases, the clock. I'm examining everything. I look up to the ceiling rose, and there is something there. *The eyes on the ceiling.* It's a small black dot. I'm standing on a dining chair now, and I can see McCall behind me. She's removed her coverall and mask and watches me as I pull out the dot with my fingernails. It has a tubular body with a lens and a small antenna. I take ten minutes to find the others, which were hidden in every room.

'She was studying you,' says McCall. 'We just need to know why? Are you okay?'

'Not really. I didn't know. I mean, I sensed something, shadows lurking, that sort of thing. Perhaps she recorded video footage on the laptop that's missing. Did they find her mobile phone?'

'It was in the kitchen, smashed to pieces.'

I need some fresh air, but as I walk outside, I see an elderly couple talking with a pale-faced PCSO. Po has joined them. She looks at me in horror, and I recognise the couple standing in front of me.

FIVE

Doctor Katherine Jacobs to camera:

Dettori wanted to bring the trials for human testing forward. It was far too soon, but he considered the product too valuable to be scrapped and knew he had little time before Head Office would intervene. He wanted to publish a paper as soon as he had the results he was hoping for. Most of all, he wanted the glory and the recognition that this discovery would bring him. In April 2019, he convinced the board. Quite how he did that, I don't know. He tested Y9-Alphapase on his first human subject, Nathan Wheelhouse. He's a healthy young male with no previously known health problems. He was going to be in our base study, one of a small trial group. We didn't realise that Dettori had found this subject through a friend of his, a golfing buddy. Of all the stupid things to do. It was unethical not to go to the selection board—to do things properly. My team wondered if Dettori had other motives for choosing Wheelhouse, but we couldn't prove it.

Rachael Thorne has changed out of her uniform and has caught the bus home. There are three others on the bus, and she's sat at the back, well away from them. It's something she has had the habit of doing ever since the pandemic. She's still wearing a mask, but that's not unusual nowadays either. Her phone rings.

'Hi Jen,' she says. 'You got my message?'

'Yes,' says her friend. 'I've got the news on now. What am I looking for? You're being very mysterious.'

'Did you see the bit about the murder in Chichester?' says Rachael.

'It's gone past that bit now. What is it? Shall I rewind it?'

'Yes! Do it. Look at the photo of the policemen.'

'Are they dishy?' Jen laughs. 'Rewinding now. Hang on a minute. They're all a bit too young for me nowadays. I can still dream.'

Rachael waits, strumming her fingers on the chrome head-rest bar in front of her. 'Have you got it yet, Jen?'

'Right—got there. Here we go...'

Rachael can hear the replay on Jenny's TV and the reporter's voice.

'See him yet?'

'I've paused it on the photo of the two policemen. What am I looking at? There's an older fella... and a good looking... No! Rach, it can't be! It's him, but he died.'

'So, it *is* him then!'

14th February 2020

I know when my eyes are open now. I can see daylight—a huge relief. They've told me my eyesight is likely to return, and the awful fear is subsiding. I still see the faces, like pantomime characters, when people enter the room. The doctors say it's Charles Bonnet Syndrome, my brain compensating for the lost visual input. I don't know about that, but these nightmarish images are hard to cope with.

I'm told by Ana, in her thick Romanian accent, that it's Sunday morning. She brought me scrambled egg on toast for my breakfast, and she knows exactly how I like it, the egg slightly runny on white bread. Ana makes me laugh and is a first-rate nurse. I don't know if I would have had it in me to carry on if not for her. I look forward to when her shifts begin. She tells me she has a boyfriend, and I won't fancy her when I can see again. But I can see her soul, and she is a beautiful person. Before she goes home, she tells me she's praying for me. I'm not a religious man, but I appreciate it.

I'm listening to the news on the radio, and the virus spreading from China is worrying everyone now. It doesn't worry Ana, as her boyfriend says it's all a hoax.

I hear the door click open, and someone shuffles into my room and turns off the radio.

'Ana?' I say. But Ana wouldn't be silent. I see a vague impression of a girl. Her eyes are like saucers, and she's wearing a heavy chain. She's scared. 'Who are you?'

'Hello, Mr Angelis,' she says. Her voice is shaky, and she's breathing rapidly. 'My name is Amanda. I'm a researcher for a drug company.'

'Hello, Amanda.' I'm a bit of a captive audience, as I can't sit up. I turn my face to her voice. 'How can I help you?'

'I'm not sure you can help me, Mr Angelis, but I wanted you to know the truth about what happened.'

'I'm sorry, I don't understand. What are you talking about?' I'm smiling at her, trying to put her at ease.

'I don't have long, Mr Angelis.' Her voice sounds urgent.

'Go on.'

'After the attack on you, they brought you into the hospital. The trauma team stabilised you, but you fell into a coma. While in a coma, they gave you a drug that was part of a trial—not properly tested. They never sought consent from your family—they gave you the drug, anyway. But you need to know, no matter what anyone tells you—'

The door opens again. This time it *is* Ana.

'Who are you!' Ana says.

'I'm sorry, Mr Angelis,' says Amanda, 'you deserve to know. They're hiding something from you.' She thrusts a small piece of paper into my hand and runs out of the room.

'Who was that?' I ask Ana. 'I deserve to know what?'

'Ha!' says Ana, 'crazy girl. I've seen her hanging around this morning. I'll talk to security.'

I give the piece of paper to Ana. 'What is this?' I ask her.

'She's written you a note.' I can hear the confusion in her voice. 'I will put it with your things.'

'What does it say, Ana?'

'Never mind, she's a crazy girl. You can read it when you are well.'

28th February 2022

The two men walk into the club room together. The obsequious steward urgently finds them a table by the window overlooking the green and the lake. He takes their drink orders.

'Not such a good game today,' says Christopher Dalton. 'Perhaps you have other things on your mind, Dean?'

Dalton is a self-made man in his early forties. He's flashy, carries an air of success and confidence about himself that irritates Dettori. The nouveau riche, his wife calls it.

'This should have been the time when we went to full phase one trial,' says Dettori. 'I can't persuade headquarters. Instead, they want to continue with other projects, jumping on the Covid testing bandwagon. That market is saturated now, Christopher. My product is more than ready, but no one wants to take the risk. I've got so much of it ready to go, it's coming out of my ears.'

'You know I'm happy to try it. I've told you already—let me find the market for you. My understanding is your Y9, whatever you call it, creates its own demand.'

'This is where I could cross the line, Christopher. It's not addictive, but people can become dependent on it. If you don't get the dosage right, the body relies on it to keep it going. Nathan taught us that lesson. I'm happy to give it to you, but if you don't limit it, then it will take over.'

'You crossed the line a long time ago, Dean. As I said, it creates its own demand.'

'It changes the subject's physiology. Your body can depend on it for cell division. If you suddenly take it away after that, the body will age rapidly. The subject will experience a truly horrible death.'

'But a little of it will give people near enough superpowers!' says Dalton, raising his eyebrow.

'At the correct dosage, yes. But it's taken us time to get that right. We didn't get it right for Nathan. But he'll be okay if we can slowly wean him off it. I hope.'

'My wife would like to see those superpowers!' Dalton laughs.

'She certainly would. She'd be one very happy woman.'

'So, there's the market, Dean, and it's one where we can

keep control. If people have to keep taking it, who the fuck cares? We can supply for a price.'

The drinks arrive at the table, and the two men sit back and enjoy the view.

'Nathan has had a trying week too,' says Dalton. 'The unexpected resignation of one of our colleagues has left him in the lurch. Having to do everything himself.'

'Ah, yes, about Parkes. Is he going to remain tight-lipped? I'd hate for Mrs Dettori to find out about my use of your private services?'

'He knows what's good for him, Dean. I have contacts nearly everywhere to make sure he holds his tongue.'

'Good. As long as it keeps well away from me. But I am disappointed that those services will no longer be available, Christopher. It was money well spent.'

'Not to worry. There's plenty more where they came from. In fact,' Dalton leans in, 'we will be open for business again soon. This time...' He looks around and smiles. 'This time, even younger.' He laughs.

'Sick bastard.' Dettori picks up his glass and swills the wine in circles, observing its viscosity, its clarity.

'I never heard you object.'

Dettori reads a message on his phone, and a deep frown line contorts his face. Had he seen the news?

'Everything okay?' asks Dalton.

'Nothing to do with me anymore. Anyway, try the product, Christopher, and you'll make Mrs Dalton a happy woman, I'm sure.' He pushes his nose into the glass.

'Make it so, Doctor Dean. Make it so.'

'Okay.' Then Dettori raises his glass. 'Here's to a new you.'

I meet Kate's parents back at the police station with McCall. They're taken to a room used for taking witness statements. The room is bleak and formal, hardly a place to find comfort. They sit silently, both in blue waxed Barbour jackets, holding hands. Mr Jacobs thick, silver-framed glasses were smeared with dried tears. His thinning, grey hair is tousled, and his beard is speckled with pieces of tissue. Mrs Jacobs is younger, and there's still a hint of red in her greying hair. I can see Kate's likeness in her face. They are pale and broken people. Something has died within them, and they have nothing left but the comfort of each other's hands.

McCall and I sit opposite them, and McCall leads.

'Mr and Mrs Jacobs,' she starts carefully. 'I'm Detective Sergeant Helen McCall, and this is Detective Inspector Angelis. We are sincerely sorry for your loss and the terrible way you were made aware of your daughter's death. I can only apologise. Sadly, the media didn't think to consult us before speculating on names.'

Mr Jacobs looks up and slowly nods.

McCall points to a video camera near the ceiling. 'Mr and Mrs Jacobs, this conversation is being video recorded to help us get the best evidence and information we need. You're not under arrest, and you're free to leave whenever you want. If you feel it's appropriate, you can ask for free and independent legal advice. Is that okay?'

Mr Jacobs nods.

'Where have you come from today, Mr Jacobs?'

He gradually summons the strength to talk. It's like watching someone slowly inflate a tyre until he finally raises his shoulders.

'I'm Ted, and my wife's name is Edie. We drove down from Glasgow yesterday. Katherine was born there, as was Edie.' He tightens the grip of Edie's hand.

'How did you hear about what happened to Katherine?' I ask.

'From Elizabeth, our other daughter. She lives in Oxford. She couldn't face the journey.'

Sam Gregory appears with a tray of tea. 'Excuse me,' she says and glances up at the camera.

'Did Katherine talk to you about her friend, Vanessa?' asks McCall.

'No,' says Edie. 'Was she a girlfriend? We know she liked girls more than boys. I think she liked both, to be honest, but preferred girls.'

'Possibly,' answers McCall. 'We're struggling to find out anything about her, to be honest. Do you know any of Katherine's friends?'

'Only a few. Katherine was sweet on Amanda once, but sadly... well, Amanda had mental problems. There was a Colin from work. She didn't talk about him much, though.'

'Oh, there *was* a Vanessa,' says Ted. 'She was a work friend, too. Maybe it's her.'

'Katherine was closest to her sister, Elizabeth,' says Edie.

'Oh yes,' says Ted. 'Very close. They talked about everything.'

I catch McCall's eye.

'Do you think Elizabeth would be okay talking to us?' asks McCall. 'Could you give us her contact details?'

'I don't see why not,' says Ted. 'She may need a bit of help, though. Elizabeth has Down's Syndrome. And don't call her Elizabeth to her face—she prefers Lizzie. The number of times she tells us off.'

I'm somewhere else for a moment, and I can see Josh. He's standing with me. I want to reach out my hand to him, but he fades away.

'That's not a problem for us, Ted,' says McCall, smiling.

I bring up a photograph on my phone and show it to them. 'Katherine had a photograph of you in her house. I see you're standing together as a family in Dartmouth, I believe. Who's this other woman in the photo?'

Edie studies the image. 'Elizabeth took it. That was Katherine's friend, Amanda. We have a holiday home in Dartmouth. Katherine often goes down there to get away from it all.'

'Amanda took her own life, Inspector,' says Ted. 'I think they had separated by then. They met through work at Hudson's. Katherine left Hudson's after Amanda died.'

'I don't know who this Vanessa was, really, unless it's another one from Hudson's,' Edie says to Ted.

Ted shrugs his shoulders. 'Maybe Elizabeth knows.'

'This is going to be a tough question for you both. Do you know anyone who would want to harm Katherine at all?'

'Not in the slightest,' says Edie. 'She was kind, funny and very loyal to her friends and family.'

'Do you know who she was working for before she died?' asks McCall.

'Not really. Katherine said she was doing research for the Government,' says Ted. 'Someone called Lorna or possibly Lisa.'

I look at McCall, who has a frown on her face.

'Can we see her, Inspector?' says Ted. 'We want to see Katherine.'

'We need to check first, but yes,' I say. 'I was a friend of hers, Mr and Mrs Jacobs. It would be better if you were to identify her for us as I'm involved in the investigation.'

'Thank you for being her friend, Inspector,' says Edie.

'I promise you both, we'll do everything in our power to find Katherine's killer and bring them to justice.'

'I know you will,' says Ted. 'Don't forget her, Inspector.'

I nod and struggle to get out the words. 'I'll never forget her, Mr Jacobs.'

McCall and I watch them leave the building, hunched together as if walking through a storm. She gently squeezes my shoulder as they drive away. It's an act of tenderness that takes me by surprise.

'Are they going to talk to Lizzie after the identification?' McCall asks.

'Yes. That won't be easy.'

'I'll see if Lizzie can see me tomorrow. It's going to take me out of the office most of the day. Is that okay?'

'Yes, of course. I'm not sure a phone call would be appropriate.'

'That's what I thought.' McCall walks back to her desk, and as she leaves, I'm feeling her absence. It's a strange thing to explain to anyone. Her presence, her thoughts, her soul have moved away.

I'm leading an evening briefing as Walsh is out of the office at headquarters. DS Harris is in for his last late shift before rest days, and he's looking a little distracted. I can't see what's worrying him, as he's hiding it well. As tempted as I am to probe around, I respect his right to privacy.

McCall is back from the formal identification of Kate with her parents, and she's looking like she's been through an emotional wringer. You can't help but take on some of that grief. A sudden death in the family changes everything forever and goes on for generations afterwards.

'Thank you, one and all,' I announce, getting everyone's attention. 'Let's get on with this. I won't be here in the morning, so we'll do the briefing now.' I turn to the whiteboard and look at what new information we have. 'So, witnesses are still drawing a blank.

'We suspect that Katherine Jacobs and Vanessa were in a relationship. As it's likely Vanessa used to work with Katherine at Hudson, we're expecting to find out more about her soon.

'James, what do you have?'

'Sir, I had to confirm something,' says Harris, 'but it may be of significance or just coincidence. I found a link between the Colin Decker case and Doctor Katherine Jacobs.' We're all looking baffled now. 'Jacobs was Decker's manager when he was murdered. They both worked at Hudson.' There's a few raised eyebrows. 'And there's more. Digging a little deeper, I don't know if anyone remembers around the same time, the suicide of Amanda Wilson?' There are a few nods. 'She took an overdose of sleeping pills and vodka and lay down in the middle of the A27. It took them ages to find all of her. Doctor Jacobs was her line manager, too.'

'Well, we know they were lovers. We found a photo in Katherine's house, and her parents confirmed it today. Katherine's parents listed a Colin and Amanda as possible friends. The connection here is that they all worked at Hudson Biotech. That's great work, James.' He looks a little more cheerful now. Even a big brute of a man needs a pat on the back now and then.

'My team will dig around at Hudson,' Harris says.

'Good. You're off for a few days after tonight, so who's taking the lead on that? We need urgent information on Vanessa.'

'Sam and Po, you can get on that in the morning,' says Harris. There are a couple of nods at the back.

'Any forensics in yet, pathology? A bit early, I know, but...' I'm looking around in the silence. 'I'll take that as a no then.'

DC Dan Daley is checking for new emails on his phone.

He's in his mid-twenties and looks like a young Jack Black in glasses. He's the type of person who doesn't look right in a suit.

'Dan?' says McCall.

'Nothing in yet, Sarge,' says Daley.

'Keep on top of it for us, please.'

'Yes, Sarge.'

'Just a polite nudge,' I say to him. 'I know ours is not the only case they're working on.'

He gives me a thumbs up. A little odd, but I'll take that as a 'Yes, sir.'

'I'm arranging a visit to see Katherine's sister, Lizzie, in Oxford tomorrow,' says McCall. 'So, to follow up on what the neighbours saw at 1730 hours...' McCall looks at the whiteboard. 'Muhammad and Jack, can you do a bit of walking and talking in the local park. Speak to local dog walkers. See if anyone noticed Katherine and Vanessa or saw them speak to anyone as they walked the dog before 1730 hours. The dog is a small, ginger and white cocker spaniel. It will probably be worth posting the question on the local community Facebook group.'

DC Lang nods while DC Essam is Googling images of cocker spaniels.

The briefing is over, and the team has a buzz of excitement as things are moving on. McCall follows me into my office and looks worried.

'Sir,' she says. 'The calendar in Katherine's house. What are you going to do?'

'I'm not sure what to do, Helen. I need to talk to someone about it. Walsh is in meetings all day. It may become a conflict of interest if I'm caught up in any part of this investigation. It's so weird.'

'Earlier, you said something about shadows lurking, feeling like you were being watched?'

'Yes. I just couldn't figure out how. I won't focus on that now. Walsh will need to decide what he wants with that. We've got several lines of enquiry to follow. Let's hope something comes up that makes this clearer.'

'Okay, boss.' McCall is walking out of the office.

'And Helen... That was kind of you.'

'What was?'

'To check up on me. Thank you.'

It's getting late, the office is empty, and I should go home. But home isn't a great place for me right now, and I keep wondering if there was anything I could have done? How did I not know? Incessant, nagging questions. It feels like I'm chasing shadows.

I'm struggling with being back at work, and I feel like I'm a poor imitation of myself. Everyone assumes I'm in control, but I'm bricking it most days. I catch myself with my head in my hands, staring at my desk.

A woman is standing at my door. I don't know how long she has been there. She's tall, forty-something, with short, strawberry blonde hair and sharp, blue eyes. Her look is calm and confident. She has a face I half recognise.

'Can I help you?' I ask.

She smiles and steps into my office. 'Inspector Angelis,' she says, 'I'm Detective Chief Superintendent Laura Driscoll. I've been looking forward to meeting you.' She stretches out her hand.

I stand and briefly check her lanyard and shake hands.

'Ma'am? I'm sorry, you have me at a disadvantage.' I'm trying to read her, but I'm tired.

'It's okay, Inspector. You weren't expecting me. I'm here to offer you support.'

'Oh, okay. Thank you.' I'm aware I sound confused. She sits down on the chair in front of my desk, and then I sit. 'Can I get you a drink?'

'No, I'm fine, thank you. I'll call you David if that's okay with you. It's much less formal.'

'Yes, of course. I don't remember asking for support, not that I'm not grateful—'

'No, it isn't something you have formally requested.' I have a puzzled expression on my face that she finds amusing. 'But I'm right when I say you are struggling. Don't you agree?'

There's that feeling of anxiety. I look at her reflection in the glass of the office window, and she's there. She's not a concoction of my mind.

'Well, it's been a steep learning curve, but... have you spoken to my boss, Superintendent Walsh? I've been away for the last two—'

'I'm sorry, David, but I'm short on time. I know your recent history very well. I have spoken to Giles Walsh at length about coming to speak with you. I couldn't go into specific details with him because of confidentiality. I could reassure him you are not in any trouble.'

'Okay?'

'Let me speak frankly with you, David. Then we can avoid all the what-does-she-know questions you may have. I've read your medical and psychiatric reports, and I am in regular contact with your psychiatrist, Professor Allen.' What she means is cut the crap—I know all about you. She tilts her head and studies me for a moment. 'You're wondering if I'm real or not, aren't you? It must be terrifying, the things you see, not knowing if they are hallucinations or not. With your condition, David, you really shouldn't be working, but we need you. You are a talented man. It's remarkable how you pull off living from day-to-day, seeing the things you do. I can assure you, there's nothing sinister going on here. This is me, offering my help through this.' She pulls the chair forward. 'So, I'm just here to offer you a hand if you need one.'

'Thank you, ma'am. Yes, I'm having to re-adjust. As soon as I can work out what I need help with—'

'Please, David... Honestly, it's fine. If you need extra resources, I'm here to help. I will pop in now and again to see how the case is going. I can read the case notes on the system to stay updated.'

She stands, checks her watch, and makes her way to the door. I feel uneasy, though. There's a subtle message being sent here—the back of my neck is prickling.

'I'm sensing some doubt about me, ma'am.'

'I will be in touch again soon.' She turns, swings the strap of her handbag over her shoulder and leaves.

I'm home and eating crap again—a pizza delivery. I'm exhausted, overtired. I can't eat all the pizza, and there's another PCSO sitting in a car outside the house. I'm watching him as he browses his phone. I remember the scene guards I had to do. Mainly in the cold, the rain, the heat. Not nice. The worst one for me was doing the scene guard after a house fire. We charged a man with arson with intent to endanger life. The acrid stench stayed with me for days.

I box up the three slices remaining and make my way out to the police car. The PCSO jumps out of his skin and then winds down his window.

'Sorry to startle you. I'm DI Angelis.'

'Oh, hello, sir. You live next door, don't you?'

'Unfortunately, yes, I do. Are you hungry?'

There's a pause, deciding if he wants to be polite or not. That choice is redundant when I pass the pizza box through the window.

'Ah, cheers, sir!' says the PCSO. 'Yes, I'm famished.'

'Who are you?'

'Rob. Rob Kerr.'

'No worries, Rob. Seen anyone hanging around looking out of place?'

'Well, just one funny fella. It was difficult to see him, in his mid-twenties, perhaps. He had a bushy beard, army trousers. He was standing on the corner there for a few minutes, watching the house. I got out of the car to say hello to him, but he walked off. I couldn't exactly follow him, and this isn't really my area either.'

'Good spot, Rob. Write down his description for me and drop it into CID. How long are you here for?'

'Another two hours, then a PC should relieve me. Past bedtime for us PCSOs.'

I head back indoors in time to catch the landline ringing. It can only be one of two people ringing the house phone.

'Hello, Mum,' I say.

'Dad, actually.'

'Hi, Dad. This is late for you. Is everything okay?'

'Fine, fine. I'm just checking how things are for you now you're back at work. I think I saw you on TV this morning.'

'You may have done. Don't worry, everything's fine.'

'A girl killed, another disappeared. Doesn't sound good. Something to get your teeth into, though, eh?'

He can't help it, I tell myself. He doesn't realise who it was. It's not his fault.

'Well, Dad... That's right. In at the deep end. How's Mum?'

'Not bad. Her arthritis is bad today, but hopefully, the weather will get warmer and...'

'Yes. And the car?'

'Oh, yes. All is well. Greased the trunnions this morning. Thinking of getting electronic ignition. Fed up with adjusting the points.'

'Let me get you that for your birthday, Dad.'

'No, son. Far too expensive. Gem called. She asked if you knew about Alison McCarthy. She's dead, apparently.'

'Yes, Dad. I did, thank you. Quite a shock.'

'Any news on... you know?'

'Josh? No. Not a sausage.'

'Well. We're glad you're okay. Must dash—the News at Ten is about to start. Bye for now.'

'Bye Dad. Thank—'

He's gone.

It's never easy talking to him. He's a proud Trini, through and through, moving from Chaguanas, Trinidad to Worthing, England in the mid-1960s. He became a postman and stuck at the same job until he retired. Now he's a lover of classic British cars. I used to watch him tinker with them when I was a kid. He was out there most Saturdays, rain or shine. I would pass him a spanner or a feeler gauge, put my foot on the brake. I loved it.

I think of Kate's parents and of the bitter loss I can only imagine. I nearly put my parents through the same. The pain Dad went through almost broke him. So much so, he won't talk about it now. He just worries constantly. I want to get Kate and her parents justice. I'm going to find answers for them, so they can have the closure they deserve.

SIX

Doctor Katherine Jacobs to camera:

He gave Wheelhouse, the test subject, a small dose of Y9-Alphapase. He had some initial side effects of headaches and joint pain, but nothing serious. After twelve weeks, the subject had developed increased muscle efficiency and improved reaction times. He was faster, more alert, and we found minor cuts healed remarkably quickly. His senses became acute. This delighted Dettori, and he explored other markets, such as the military. He soon caught the interest of some sections within the MOD. I think Dettori tried to keep Hudson in Canada out of the loop.

We were all horrified by this. It was then we noticed Wheelhouse had begun to suffer from paranoia and had developed narcissistic and psychopathic tendencies. One of my staff, Amanda Wilson, didn't want to be a part of the programme anymore. She couldn't see how any good would come out of Oberon. She became depressed and threatened to leave. Amanda was a dear friend, and I know how hard this hit her...

> Nevertheless, the success with Wheelhouse encouraged Dettori, and he turned a blind eye to his deteriorating mental health. He wanted to test Y_9 on another human subject, but this time on a trauma victim, perhaps with a head injury. We all felt it was far too soon to do this. There was unlikely to be any consent from a new subject or their family, but Dettori argued that they would have nothing to lose. Colin was very much against it. He said it would make a bad situation worse.

'I am absolutely certain that is him,' says Dettori. He's in his darkened office with four other senior managers. They are all staring at a frozen TV image. 'The name isn't that common. He's a police officer, and his description matches the subject, too.'

Dennis Koziner, head of sales, has Angelis's file in front of him, and he reads the banner underneath the news report on the TV screen.

'Looks like he's had a promotion since,' he says, looking over the top of his glasses. 'I agree. He is the same person as our subject in this file.'

'So, what happened then?' asks Diana Jarvis. 'And how was it he was living next door to Katherine?'

'Vanessa, that's how,' says Dettori. 'She passed on Colin's files to Katherine, including information on the other subjects.'

'She told us that Angelis had died whilst in the coma!' says Diana, her cheeks flushing. 'And you just believed her, Dean.'

'I saw the report, Diana. Don't start the blame game with me.' Dettori's tone has turned icy. 'The facts are, we don't know now what part Y_9-Alphaphase had in Angelis's recovery.'

'So, Doctor Jacobs has been watching Angelis? Is that what you're implying?' says Dennis.

'Possibly,' says Dettori. 'What we know is this: Katherine was trying to blackmail me, and I'm sure as hell not going to take any blame alone here. The information Katherine was trying to use against us must have come from Vanessa. It was on Decker's laptop, which she stole from us.'

Oliver Downing, the financial controller, has been sitting back with his face in the shadows. He sits forward to speak, bringing his bald head under the spotlight, and presses his fingertips together. 'So, it was all on Colin Decker's computer, and he was murdered. Katherine had possession of the computer, and then she was murdered. Dangerous things these laptop computers. Who has it now, I wonder?'

'I don't know,' says Dettori.

'You realise everything is pointing at you, Dean?' says Oliver. 'Colin's murder and then Doctor Jacobs's. How long do you think it will take the police to come to you and start asking questions?'

'I had nothing to do with their murders, Oliver. What sort of person do you take me for? Did you know Vanessa is missing?'

'Missing?' says Diana. 'Well, that looks as suspicious as hell, doesn't it!' She breathes a sigh of relief and sits back in her chair.

'A very helpful scapegoat for you, Dean,' says Oliver, sitting back in the shadows.

'This is getting us nowhere,' says Dettori. He slams his pen onto the table and paces for a while. He stops and stands behind Martina. 'We can leave the police to work out what happened to Katherine. It's got nothing to do with us. Our concern is Angelis, who is ironically running this investigation. We need to find out why Katherine told us he had died, what happened when he came out of the coma, and have there been any long-lasting effects on his physiology?'

'At a quarter of a million dollars a dose, it would be good to know how you spent the money,' says Oliver. He sniggers to himself for a moment.

'Martina, you are quiet. Do you have any suggestions?' asks Diana.

'Not suggestions, but I have some information,' says Martina. 'My source told me there weren't any computers found by the police in Katherine's house. So, whoever killed her also took the laptop.'

'Source?' says Diana. 'You have a police source?'

'Nothing for you to worry about, Diana.'

'It must be Vanessa then!' says Dennis. 'Where would she have gone? Did she want all the blackmail money for herself?'

'Dennis,' says Oliver, 'you sound like one of those awful mystery programmes on the television. I'm sure Martina is skilled enough to handle her predecessor.'

'How about Vanessa's husband?' says Diana. 'How do we know she hasn't been in contact with him? Do we still have his loyalty?'

'I have that in hand,' says Martina. 'Any allegiance he has with his ex-wife will soon be broken.'

Dettori places a hand on Martina's shoulder and squeezes it.

'You see, Oliver,' says Dettori, looking at Martina. 'It's well worth paying for quality nowadays.' Oliver Downing doesn't respond.

'That's all very well,' says Dennis, 'but how are you going to find out what happened to Angelis in the hospital?'

'I'll request hospital records regarding the incident,' says Dettori.

'We can also try to talk to members of staff who were working there,' says Martina.

'Dennis, there are ways and means,' says Dettori, returning to his seat.

'Dean,' says Diana, 'if this gets ugly, then you will lose our support. We've backed you despite the ruling from Andrew Hudson putting a stop to this project. We backed you because we can see the huge benefits Y9-Alphapase can bring. But if the police start snooping around here, then we will know nothing, and you will find yourself on your own. I hope that's clear.'

'As always, Diana,' says Dettori. 'And when the profits come in, you'll be expecting all the benefits from those too, won't you.'

'Of course we will,' she says.

22nd March 2002

Nathan Oliver Wheelhouse takes the envelope from off the TV. He's left it there for days untouched. He tears it open and pulls out the card. *13*, it says on the front, with a picture of a cartoon football. Inside, his mother has scrawled a message: *Happy Birthday, Nate, love Mum x*. That's it.

Nathan lives on the 8th floor of Wellington House with his mother. She went to work last weekend and never came home. She always sings Happy Birthday to him and his sister, but not today.

Nathan looks over to the photo on top of the drinks cabinet —it's him and his sister. They should be celebrating together, but Social Services stepped in six months ago, so it's just him and his mum now.

Nathan can make himself a sandwich and use the microwave—so he's not hungry. He's washed up his plate, knife, and cup. The pile in the sink is his mother's crap—he's not touching her mess. There's no more milk, and the freezer's empty now.

The TV has been on the news channel all day. He's seen

nothing except that schoolgirl who's gone missing. He picks up a bag and puts a couple of his favourite tops in there, with that photo of them all together last year in McDonald's, his twelfth birthday.

Nathan puts on his coat, goes to his mother's bedroom, and lifts the mattress. She told him to look there if she never came home one day, so it's okay. Nathan takes all of it, stashed into two bulging envelopes, and stuffs them into his inside coat pocket.

Wherever she's gone, she's taken all her pills with her. Her silver locket on the chain is missing, too. She never takes that to work. He doesn't understand it.

Nathan sits quietly on her bed, and he can still smell his mother's perfume on the bedsheets. He will not cry. He can still see the bloodstain on the carpet—she never could scrub it out. That was six months ago when everything changed.

Nathan turns off the TV and puts the radio on. It's playing *She loves you,* by the Beatles. His mother loves the Beatles, and she told him once the radio is better for you than the TV. He closes the front door, leaving his key inside, and leaves Wellington House for good. There's a cousin who lives near Guildford—he may go there. Or he may try to find his twin again.

28th *February 2022*

Peter Grant opens his front door, and he's astonished to see Martina in a tight, low-cut, red dress, with a long slit running up her thigh. He is doing everything not to gawp like a hormonal teenager. He's guessing she's just on her way out on a date. She's dressed to kill tonight.

'Martina! You look incredible!' he says. 'Come in.' He runs in ahead of her, picking up a few cups from the living room table.

'Thank you. Scrub up well, do I?' she says, looking around the room.

'I wouldn't put it quite like that, but yes, you do. How can I help?'

'We both know what this is about.' She takes a seat on his sofa, drops a red shoulder bag on the floor next to her, and crosses her legs.

'It's all over the news. I hope it has nothing to do with the information I shared with you.'

'Nothing at all! I'm guessing when you didn't turn up, Vanessa panicked. Peter, the police are looking for her. It's not looking good. Or did you go to see her?'

'No, I couldn't face her, not after everything she did to me. Vanessa said that she had done something stupid, but I can't believe she meant...'

'Vanessa and Katherine were in a relationship. Something obviously went wrong between them, and they say more people are murdered by people known to them. Who else would it be?'

'A relationship? As in together!'

'You didn't know?' Martina looks unbelieving.

'Not with a woman, not Katherine. Vanessa told me she had met another man. Why would she lie about that? Unless that was just her covering her tracks again. As for stealing Decker's computer, shit! I thought I knew the woman.'

Martina's eyes flicker.

'You're sure she's left nothing here, a laptop hidden away somewhere?'

'Look for yourself, Martina, please do. I've got nothing to

hide from you. I mean, you've already been through my rubbish, anyway.'

Martina laughs. 'It wasn't something I enjoyed.'

'Where could she have gone? She hardly has any friends to speak of. I hope she doesn't think she can come back here.'

'Honestly, Peter, does it matter where she is? We both know she mistreated you. You have a new life now. You're a single man again and free to do what you want.'

'True. The police will find her soon enough. I don't want to know anymore.'

'Exactly.' Martina smiles, stroking her hair.

'Can you get Dettori off my back? There's nothing more I can do short of going to the police. If I hear of anything, then I will tell you. You know I will.'

'Dettori is being hassled by the management board. He has to be seen to be doing something.'

'About that PPE I was selling. Hudson had so much of it. I was broke.'

'Frankly, Peter, I don't give a shit about it. Dettori just wanted a bit of leverage.'

Peter is silently congratulating himself. He's played it cool; she's not suspected a thing. He's never seen Martina like this, and he's enjoying the signals she's giving off right now.

'You look like you're about to make someone's night. Can I get you a drink before you go?'

'Actually, I was hoping you were going to take me out to dinner. But you can cook for me here if you prefer. How hungry are you?'

Then the penny drops, and he's watching the split in her dress widening.

He's put a hessian bag over her head and tied it on. She can breathe if she doesn't panic, but that's extremely hard not to do. The strip of cloth is cutting into the sides of her mouth. It's too tight, and it's pulling back her jaw, making her gag.

Vanessa is sitting with her back against a brick wall—she can just feel it with her fingertips. Her hands are strapped back-to-back with cable ties. She's tried rubbing the ties against the brick, but she's mostly scraping the skin off her wrists. She doesn't want to struggle with them anymore in case they get any tighter than they are already.

She can make out a shadow through the hessian cloth, and someone is standing in front of her. He crouches so that his face is inches from hers. He hums a tune as he is staring at her. Then he sings, *She loves you*. Vanessa wasn't a Beatles fan before, and she likes them even less now. The man is insane.

'Found you, sweet pea,' he says. 'You couldn't hide for long, could you? Now, what am I to do with you? Let's start with the ground rules. There are always ground rules. Rule number 1: If you see my face—you die. That's an easy one, isn't it? Rule number 2: If you find out my name—you die. Rule number 3: If you try to escape—you die. Just to let you know, I am much stronger than you. Rule number 4: If you piss me off, you'll probably die as well. You can probably see there's a pattern emerging there.' His breathing gets heavier. 'If it wasn't for my strict instructions, I would have had you by now. I still might if I get desperate. And I've been feeling desperate a lot recently. I don't know what's got into me. So, rule number 5. I'll have you whenever I want you, and if you resist, guess what happens.'

The man walks away, and Vanessa hears a door opening, probably a fridge. He's opened a bottle and lifted the bag to just above her mouth. She can see black jeans and Nike trainers. He's tall and muscular. He pulls up her head and pushes the neck of the bottle over the top of the gag, pinching her lip. He slowly tips the sweet liquid into her mouth. She's struggling to swallow, breathing through her nose until she can't take any more and chokes.

'There,' he says, pulling down the bag. 'Who says I don't look after my guests?'

Vanessa tries to speak, but it's just coming out as noise.

'You're mumbling, Vanessa,' he says. He pushes her onto her side with his foot. 'I can't stand mumblers.'

Vanessa is wondering what he wants, and she knows who he is now. He must think she's stupid. She recognises his voice. Is Nathan working for Dettori or Dalton now? It has to be Dettori. Perhaps he wants the computer back? God, he's probably taken the one at the house! Hopefully, the password will keep him out for a while before he realises what she's done.

The last thing she can remember is walking out of the house with that bitch. She said that Dettori was in the car—he wanted to do a deal. This was his deal. What will Kate do? She'd call the police, call Angelis. Yes. The police would know what had happened.

'Now then, sweet pea,' says Wheelhouse. 'We know what you stole from Mr Dettori. You gave what you stole to the very delicious Doctor Jacobs. I feel horny just saying her name. Thanks to Doctor Jacobs, we have the computer back. But we think you've backed up the important files on there, using geeky computer magic. Am I right?' Wheelhouse takes her by the head and forces it up and down. 'Oh, I am right! Thank you, Vanessa. That's a very naughty thing to do, to copy other people's work. So, all we need now is the password of the computer so we can check.'

Wheelhouse lets go of her head and slides his finger between her breasts. Vanessa flinches and is glad she can't see his face. He slides his finger up, raising her chin.

'Ah! I hear you say. Why don't you just smash up the

laptop? That would do it. That's what I suggested, but a friend of mine told me not to be so stupid. She said they've probably backed up the important files to the clouds or to a stick. What the fuck does that mean!' Wheelhouse laughs. 'It means that you've put them into online storage somewhere, and you use that computer to access it. See, I can talk geek, too.'

Wheelhouse gets up and goes to the fridge. Vanessa can hear his trainers scuffing on grit—it's a concrete floor. They may be in a garage or warehouse. The fridge is only five steps away. Then she hears him sit—the creak of a chair. He's having a drink.

'So, we need that password. Do you know it?'

Vanessa shakes her head and shrugs her shoulders.

'I take that as a no. Oh, okay. Shall I let you go then? I know, I could ask the amazingly sexy Doctor Jacobs... But wait. I already did. She said you knew the password. Who should I believe? By the way, I don't know if you heard? Doctor Jacobs isn't very well. Someone, who shall remain nameless, decided she'd look better with her head removed. They didn't do a very good job of it, though.'

Vanessa is screaming and kicking at the pain, the hate, the vile, putrid man in front of her. Her tears are soaking through the hessian, and the cable-ties on her hands are pulling tighter.

'Not too happy about that then?' says Wheelhouse above the noise. 'That's okay. I'll leave you on your own to grieve for a while. Please accept my heartfelt condolences.'

SEVEN

1st March 2022

The morning is bright, and I'm enjoying a coffee in Hogs, waiting for McCall to arrive for a breakfast meeting before work. She's about to leave for Oxford to see Elizabeth Jacobs. I'm letting the sunlight through the window wash over me. I usually feel better once March is here, but I've had trouble sleeping. There's the appointment I have first thing, and it couldn't have come at a worse time. It's something I must do if I want to see Josh again.

McCall comes through the door with a smile that gives the morning sun a run for its money. She lifts her shades and gives a little wave with her fingers like we're old friends.

'It's never too early for a Meat Feast,' I say to her as she sits opposite me. I can smell her light perfume, and I realise that's just how she smells, and it's becoming familiar.

'I'll blame you when I pile on the pounds,' she says. 'I feel this is a bit naughty, escaping out here.'

'You need some sustenance before your trip, and I'm not on duty yet. So, the only one being a bit naughty is you.'

'You invited me!'

'You needed little persuading.' She just smiles at me, showing me the food in her mouth. 'I may have to reprimand you for that.'

Then there was a moment. A look that was held a little longer than it was meant to. But my phone buzzes and breaks it. I sigh a little too loudly.

'It's okay, boss. It may be important.'

It's Sam Gregory. 'Sir, are you free to speak? I know you're not starting yet, but I can't get hold of DS McCall.'

'Yes, it's all fine. What is it?'

'They've found a knife. It was in a rubbish bin at the end of your road.'

'Great! What sort of knife?'

'A large hunting knife with a serrated edge. It's an evil-looking thing. There's blood all over it.'

'Thanks, Sam. And that's getting sent to forensics on the hurry up?'

'Yes, sir. Already done. Walsh has cleared it.'

'Excellent. I'll speak to you later.'

McCall got the gist of that. 'In a bin? Why not take it with them?'

'Maybe they panicked?'

'A dumb move, really.'

'It's the mistakes that make our job possible.'

We talk about nothing important for a while. She doesn't know it, but it's what I needed. I can't say I'm really listening to what she's talking about, as I'm too busy watching her. She's animated when she talks, and her hands are constantly moving. I'm trying hard not to smile.

'So, Lizzie Jacobs,' she says. 'I'm going to have to take it softly with her. A support worker has agreed to sit in with me as an appropriate adult. I want to find out if Katherine talked to her in any detail about Vanessa, any worries she may have had. I hope she can cope with it. I've not dealt with anyone who's Down's before.'

'*With* Down's,' I say. 'Down's Syndrome isn't who they are. It will be fine.'

'Okay, thanks. I'll keep you updated. And thanks for breakfast.'

'Hey, we all need a treat. Your turn next time.' I hesitate for a moment as she cleans up her hands. 'Helen, have you heard of Chief Superintendent Laura Driscoll?'

McCall sits there for a moment. 'I can't say I have. Why?'

'She came to see me yesterday evening in my office. Offered me support. It's no problem.'

'I'd get all the help I could if it was me, sir. Did you tell her about the cameras in your house?'

I shake my head and wipe my chin.

'I can't go into it at the moment.'

'That's fine.' McCall looks at her watch. 'Look at the time! I have to go.'

'You've got plenty of time. Take care today, Helen, and enjoy the journey—say hello to Morse for me.'

She licks her fingers and waves. 'Thank you, sir.' Then she's gone.

One look at Cheung and Gregory and the receptionist at Hudson Biotech puts them in the lowest pecking order of importance amongst the calls she's receiving through her headset. Eventually, she can't ignore the huffing from the other side of the counter any longer.

'And who are you?' she says.

'I'm Detective Constable Cheung, and this is Detective Constable Gregory, Sussex Police.'

'Do you have an appointment with Ms Hannan?'

It irritates Gregory when she hears people say Ms with a buzz like a bee.

'No, but it won't take long.'

The receptionist gives a slight shake of the head, which riles Sam Gregory. She's trying to fix her with a glare, but the receptionist won't look up from her screen while she makes an internal call.

'Good morning, Ms Hannan, reception here, so sorry to disturb you.' She's doing an impression of a 1930s BBC announcer. 'There are two policewomen here who would like a word with you... No, they do not have an appointment. Yes, of course, I will, Ms Hannan...' She looks up. 'Ms Hannan will be down in five minutes, and she won't be able to speak to you for long. Take a seat.'

'Well done. That didn't hurt, did it,' says Gregory as she walks away.

Fifteen minutes pass, and there's still no sign of Angela Hannan from Human Resources. The reception area is doing its best to impress the two visitors but fails with Gregory. She thinks the Feng Shui water feature is far too up itself, and a coffee machine would have been a better use of the space. She tries to engage with Po, but she's passing the time reading messages from her fiancé on the phone.

Gregory watches the Hudson staff walking dreamily around the fountain and along the footpath. She's guessing they're all clever people, scientists, probably talking about all the subjects she hated at school.

A round woman wearing glasses too big for her face has appeared next to the reception desk.

'Are you the police?' she says, calling over.

Cheung gets up first and takes the lead. 'Thank you for your time, Miss Hannan.'

'Ms,' she corrects Cheung in a waspish voice, but Po ignores her.

It must irritate her too, thinks Gregory.

'Can we talk privately, please? It's regarding a former employee of your company and an ongoing murder investigation.'

That's done the trick, thinks Gregory. Ms Hannan leads them away briskly to an empty side office with a computer, and she logs into their HR system.

'What murder inquiry is this?' Hannan asks. Her cheeks have flushed. Gregory thinks she must be a fan of those real-life murder programmes they pump out for entertainment. Gregory never finds the heartache and wrecked lives very entertaining.

'You may have seen it on the news recently?' says Cheung. 'In Chichester?'

'No, I don't watch the news,' says Hannan, 'ever since Covid, it was so depressing.'

'The former employee is Doctor Katherine Jacobs.'

Hannan gasps. 'Kate Jacobs! Oh my God! Who would murder Kate? She is so, so lovely.'

'Was,' says Gregory. 'We don't know. That's why there's a murder inquiry, *Ms* Hannan,'

Hannan is too shocked to get the sarcasm.

'Do you know if Doctor Jacobs was well-liked here?' asks Cheung.

'Oh, yes,' says Hannan. 'She was very popular. A brilliant woman, but not at all up herself like some of them here.'

Like the Feng shit water feature, thinks Gregory.

'Why did she leave?' Cheung opens a notepad.

'I know it was a while ago, but I'm afraid that's confidential, Inspector.' Hannan folds her arms and leans back.

'I'm a Detective *Constable*, Miss Hannan, *not* an inspector.' Cheung's tone is cutting. 'Perhaps I haven't explained it clearly. Katherine Jacobs is dead—brutally murdered. I am part of a team of detectives who are urgently trying to find her murderer. To expedite our inquiry, we need information about Doctor Jacobs to build a picture of why she was murdered. Are you going to be an obstacle in our investigation, Miss Hannan, or are you going to be the person who helps us find the murderer?'

Gregory has to close her gawping mouth. She's seen a different side of Po today. Angela Hannan is flustered as she types into the computer to bring up the records.

'We still have them. We keep them on the computer for three years and then archive them. They're still on the database. I need some sort of request in writing to cover my back if that's okay?'

'Of course,' says Cheung.

'Katherine Jacobs was a lead researcher in an ongoing development project. She reported to Doctor Dean Dettori. He heads up Hudson in the UK. The notes say she resigned because of personal reasons.'

'What reasons,' says Gregory. 'Don't you have her resignation letter on file?'

'Strangely, no,' says Hannan. She searches for a few moments. 'The photocopy or file copy should be on the system. The line manager didn't upload it.'

'Do you know of any personal reasons?' asks Gregory again.

'Well, I know some,' Hannan lowers her voice as if someone could be listening. 'The rumour was she was in a relationship... with a girl!'

Shock-horror, thinks Gregory. 'What is your point?' she says.

'Well, it was a shock, with them both being so attractive and everything.'

'Are lesbians meant to be ugly then?' says Gregory.

Cheung intervenes. 'There is more to this, though, isn't there, Miss Hannan?'

'Yes, well. Kate's girlfriend was Amanda Wilson. She worked in Kate's team, as did Colin Decker. It all got very messy.'

'What got very messy?' Cheung is patiently drawing blood from a stone.

'Colin threw his toys out of the pram about something that happened at work. It was something to do with a drug trial that Dean Dettori was trying to put in place. That's all I know. It's company confidential after that, meaning I don't know. The rumours were that Colin was a bit mentally unstable—if you follow me. He would upset people he met all the time. The number of times I had him in here. He was on a final warning. The next thing I heard, he was dead—murdered!'

'We know about Colin Decker,' says Cheung.

'But it's still unsolved, though. I only saw the other day the leaflet through my door. I live quite near to where he was murdered. I reckon he probably shot his mouth off at someone he met in the pub or something.'

'How does this relate to Amanda and Katherine?' says Gregory.

'Well, shortly after that, Amanda walked out, calling everyone hypocrites. A couple of months later, someone said she killed herself. Very tragic. After that, poor Kate resigned. So, her personal reasons must have been not being able to cope without Amanda.'

They all draw breath after that, and Cheung is writing.

'Do you have anyone called Vanessa working for you or has worked for you in recent years?' asks Gregory.

'Oh yes,' says Hannan. 'There's only been two Vanessas that I know who have worked here. One retired last year, and the other left about three or four months ago.'

'Tell us more about the second one,' says Cheung.

DC Muhammad Essam wrinkles his nose. He isn't a dog person, but he's watching the dog walkers on the field this afternoon. He doesn't know the different breeds; he just knows he's uncomfortable around them, especially the more unpredictable and lively ones.

'There are plenty of the things here,' Essam says to DC Jack Lang, who is busy getting his notebook and folder out of the car.

'We look a bit out of place,' says Lang. He's talking about their CID suits and ties.

'Let's just get this done, and we can tick it off the list.'

They walk together onto the field, past the bowling green and cross a football pitch. They head towards a middle-aged woman with a cockapoo. She is eyeing them warily as they approach. Essam then realises they look like they're giving out religious pamphlets. Instead, they hold up their lanyards and show their warrant cards.

'Good afternoon, madam. I'm Detective Constable Lang, and this is Detective Constable Essam. We are investigating the murder that occurred in Alcott Gardens last Sunday.'

'Ah, yes. I'm Juliet Gibbs—I live over the road. How can I help?' she says.

'Would you have walked your dog in this vicinity on Sunday afternoon, any time before 5.30 p.m.?'

Essam is edging away from an over-friendly cockapoo. He's trying to ignore it, but it has dropped his ball at Essam's feet, hoping to play.

'He won't bite you,' she says to him. Essam laughs nervously.

'I know the woman and her friend you're talking about. It's so terribly sad, shaken the whole community. I didn't see her on Sunday. They used to walk their little spaniel down here, but Kate said she was being pestered by someone. A right creep by the sounds of it. She pointed him out to me once. A young man.'

'Pestered, you say? Did she go into any details?'

'Only that he'd been following her around like a lost puppy. She said she wouldn't go to the park again until he backed off. So, I guess she used to drive the dog somewhere.'

'How long ago was this?'

'About six weeks ago.'

'Can you describe the male?'

'Only that he was in his twenties, dressed in army type clothes—camouflage. He had a beard. I didn't get close enough to see him properly.'

Essam takes the woman's contact details and manages to kick the ball away for the dog without simultaneously kicking the dog. He has an aversion to dog slobber and refuses to touch the ball.

'Thanks for your help, madam. We may get in touch with you if that's okay. If you can think of anything else, please contact us, and ask to speak to the Operation Greenwood Team.' Lang hands her a contact card.

As the woman walks away, Lang makes notes.

'Do you have a fear of dogs, Muhammad?' Lang asks as he writes.

'No! I'm just not comfortable with them. Cats are okay if they are other people's cats. I don't have the lifestyle to look after pets.'

Lang shakes his head. 'That was a great start, anyway.' He's watching a man with a black Staffy, tying up a small plastic bag.

'That's what I'd hate the most, picking up their shit and putting it in a bag. What's that all about?'

'Stop moaning,' says Lang. 'Come on. Your turn to take *the lead*... the lead!' He laughs at his own joke.

'Terrible.' Even Essam's dour face cracks.

They follow the man, and he waits for them. Essam introduces himself.

'Police?' says the man. 'Is this about Kate's murder? About time we saw some police around here, though you don't look like proper police to me.' He takes another look at their warrant cards. 'Detectives, what are you doing here? I thought you'd be looking for a murderer.'

'We are making relevant enquiries, sir. Today we're talking to dog walkers,' says Essam. 'Were you walking your dog on Sunday afternoon at all, before 5.30 p.m.?'

'I was. Why? Do I need an alibi or something?'

'Did you see two women walking a brown and white cocker spaniel around this area on your travels?'

'You mean Kate and Vanessa?'

'Yes.'

'Why didn't you just say so? Yes, I did. It's such a bloody shame. This is what society has come to now. No proper police presence. You're too busy prosecuting car drivers instead of catching real criminals.'

Essam rolls his eyes. 'Sir, you said you saw them. Where and when?'

'Coming out of Alcott Gardens, roughly 4.45. They said hello. They were quite cheery, friendly.'

'How do you know them? They haven't been living here that long.'

'Kate was a regular at the Green Man. My pub. She stopped going a little while ago. Lots of people knew her, and she was a bit of a looker, too. Popular girl. Her friend kept herself to herself, though. There were rumours they were together if you know what I mean. Kept that all private, though.'

'You said that they were cheerful. Nothing seemed untoward?'

'Not at all.'

'Did you see anyone in the vicinity looking out of place?' says Lang. 'Perhaps hanging around or even following them?'

'Following? Oh, I know who you mean. No, not at all. That lad's harmless enough, by the way. Don't try to put the blame on him.'

'Who? What's his name?' says Essam.

'No, no, no. I'm not getting involved. Don't you go putting words in my mouth!'

'Can we take your details, please, sir?'

'Nope. I've got things to do.' The man turns his back and walks away with his dog.

'Tosser,' says Essam.

'It's still useful.'

'You're always so bloody positive, Jack. What's the matter with you? You're not normal.'

After another hour of following dogs and their owners, the two compare notes and return to their car. Essam still dislikes dogs, and Lang is feeling positive.

Julie Dalton is hoping for the time of her life this afternoon. Christopher has promised her something extraordinary for the bedroom later, after his bit of business with Nathan and that handsome doctor.

Her boobs look amazing in this dress, a style that Christopher really approves of. She doesn't look her age now, and with the mounting costs of looking younger, she's glad they have the money to keep it going for a few years yet.

The buzzer from the gate tells her that Christopher's guests have arrived. Nathan is part of the family now, so he's not really a guest, and the way he looks at her, well, that's a little something for when Christopher's away on business.

They're in the house now. She pulls down her dress a little tighter and checks there's no panty line.

'Jules!' calls Christopher from the hallway. 'They're here. Are you coming?'

'On my way,' she sings as she leaves the dressing room.

Nathan is sitting there in a tight black t-shirt and shorts. She finds him irresistible and would if he asked her. Christopher is watching her. He doesn't seem to mind her looking in fact, he gets a thrill out of it.

Doctor Dean is here, classier looking altogether. She thinks he's glancing at her cleavage as she welcomes him. He has a briefcase with him, and he's gripping it tightly.

'What have you got there, Dean?' she asks him. 'Anything naughty?'

'Not for you, Julie, regretfully,' he replies.

'Maybe another time, though, eh, Dean?' says Dalton, laughing.

Dettori places the briefcase on the table and looks at Dalton.

'Are you ready, Chris?'

'Oh, yes! No time like the present.'

'Are you feeling well? Taking any other medication? Alcohol?'

'No, all clear.'

Dettori brings out a document.

'Non-disclosure agreement.'

'Is this really necessary, Dean?' Dalton spends a few

moments reading it. 'I hope this doesn't jeopardise any future agreements.'

'For that reason, it's only Julie who needs to sign it.' He winks at Dalton.

'Sign it, Jules.'

Julie Dalton dutifully obeys. She trusts her husband completely.

Dettori opens the latches on the briefcase. Inside is a phial of clear liquid and a hypodermic syringe. He fills the syringe, taps it, and expels a small amount of the liquid.

'Can't waste too much of it,' says Dettori. 'You could buy a nice house with the cost of this dose. I've double-checked the serial numbers. The placebo is in identical bottles. We don't want to give you a dud.'

Christopher rolls up his shirt sleeve. 'You're not going to ask me to bend over, are you?'

Julie laughs. 'Not again, Dean.'

'You'll just feel a little prick,' says Dettori, playing along... And it's now in his system. 'You'll be as fit as Nathan here within weeks.'

'Oh, yes, please!' says Julie, clapping her hands in excitement.

Dalton stands up and takes a deep breath. 'We can have a drink to celebrate.'

'Not today,' says Dettori. 'Just to be on the safe side.'

Dalton rubs his arm. 'That was dead easy. We could do some great business with this.'

Julie goes into the kitchen and takes the hors d'oeuvres out of the refrigerator, with sausages and pineapple and cheese on sticks. She looks out onto the lawn and thinks that she's never been so happy as this. If they could see her now: those losers at school, those privileged bullies. She's beautiful, has more money than she'll ever need and a husband who adores the ground she walks on.

'Who's for a little sausage on a stick?' she shouts from the kitchen. There's no answer, just the murmurs of voices. Julie walks in with the tray and sees Dean and Nathan are leaning over the table. 'What are you two playing at?'

'Julie,' says Dean. 'Call an ambulance.'

Christopher is watching her, slumped against the chair. The right side of his face has fallen, and his right eye is closed. He groans, and his drooling mouth doesn't move.

The tray of hors d'oeuvres hits the carpet, and Julie's red dress is ruined.

Nathan quietly returns the syringe to the case and passes it to Dettori. There's a look between them that Julie doesn't see.

EIGHT

I enter one of the counselling rooms of Grace House, and Bella Brookes stands to greet me. She's not the doctor I told Walsh I was going to see but a counsellor. It's a Christian run centre, but it's not a religious propaganda machine. It's a relationship counselling service for men like me, with issues like mine. I sit in the hot seat and soak up the room. It's cosy and fuzzy in here, pastels and greys. As non-threatening as it could be.

'David, lovely to see you again,' Bella says. 'It's been a while, two years, isn't it?'

'Yes, something like that,' I say. Bella Brookes is still wearing the same blue dress, and her afro hair is the same length and style as it was two years ago. It's like they put her into storage just for me.

'Totally understandable with everything that has happened to you. But it's so good that you are coming back to us.'

'It's always been what I wanted, Bella. That hasn't changed.'

'Okay. Things have moved on since you've been unwell. Are you aware of that?'

'Vaguely, yes. Karen, you mean?'

'Yes, Karen. She's in a long-term relationship now. She tells me she's happy. How do you feel about that?'

'It's weird. I'm glad Karen's happy. I'm pissed that she never visited me, but she told me that's what she wanted.'

'Told you what, David?'

'That she wanted nothing to do with me again.' A chill runs down my spine. I'm trying not to read this woman—it wouldn't be fair.

'Let's remind ourselves of our goals. After all this time, they might have changed.' Bella Brookes maintains meaningful eye contact, glancing at her notes balanced on her knee.

'I can tell you what my goals are.' The word 'our' has rankled me. 'I want to see my son again, and I want a practical working framework with my ex-wife so Josh can see his father again.'

There is a pause while she writes a sentence. I don't know what she is writing; I thought it was bloody obvious what I wanted.

'David, I have spoken with Karen at length about this and the choices she has made. She wants her partner to be involved in this process as he now lives in the family home, becoming a parental figure to Josh.'

'Does she?' I'm remaining calm. I'm doing well.

'Are you prepared to agree to meet with both of them to discuss this?'

I just knew that was coming. It's the very last thing I want. 'Yes, of course. It's about doing the best for Josh, isn't it? What does Josh say he wants?'

Why has that question thrown her?

'It's difficult for Josh to verbalise his feelings, as you know David—'

'No, it isn't.' I'm remaining calm.

'His communication and cognitive skills are such that he will agree with any suggestion that is put to him.'

'That's bollocks.' I must stay calm.

'David, you must remain calm. It doesn't help your case. To have the non-contact order lifted, you must prove that you will not revert to conduct and behaviour you exhibited—'

'I know that, Bella! I'm not a child. Josh is perfectly able to express if he wants to see me again.'

'But how can you know that when you haven't seen him for two years?'

'That's not my fault, is it? And I *do* know. I also know that Karen wants him to see me, too. That partner of hers is the problem. I would like to talk to Karen without him there. I'm concerned that there's some controlling and coercive behaviour on his part in all of this.'

'David, how could you possibly—'

'I *do* know. You're just gullible and believe anything he tells you.'

I can see she doesn't like that, and that's the key that opens the image of him next to her. I was right; he's whispering lies into her ear. He's made allegations. Shit, he's made allegations!

'I think we need to end this meeting—'

'What has he said about me? What has he told you? And you won't allow me to defend myself?'

'This meeting is over, David. We'll meet again when—'

'No, Bella, you can just fuck off—that's what you can do!'

I broke the door handle when I left. I didn't stay calm.

Christopher Dalton is sedated. Julie is watching her husband through a window, numb with disbelief. He's hooked up to machines she doesn't understand, connected to tubes and bags of liquid. The light of her world is extinguished.

Dettori said it wasn't the injection. It was probably the

excitement; it was going to happen, anyway. Julie doesn't believe him, and she can say nothing. She can't tell them what happened; otherwise, Dettori would know, and she was afraid of what he might do.

Sitting a few feet away is Nathan Wheelhouse. He is looking at his phone. How can he stay so calm?

'Will he get better, Nathan?' she says. Her voice is faltering. She has nothing left in her stomach to throw up now. She is weak and sick with worry.

'I don't know, Julie,' Nathan says. 'Perhaps you should just go home—clean yourself up. There's nothing you can do here.'

'It didn't affect you, did it? This injection.'

'For fuck's sake, Julie! Stop talking about it here! It was nothing that Dettori gave him. Look at me. I'm fit as a fiddle, and I've had hundreds of doses of the stuff.'

'Dettori made it sound so easy.'

Nathan leaps up and gets in her face. 'I told you to shut up! It's got nothing to do with him.'

Julie cowers and sits back in her chair.

'What am I going to do without him? He's my everything?'

'He's not dead, Julie! Give him time to get better. Just stay calm.'

'Yes, you're right.' She's sobbing again. 'He needs me to be strong. But I can't look after him, Nathan. I'm not built to feed a grown man with a spoon, to wipe his bum when he needs me. He wouldn't want that either.'

'There's nothing you can do about that. You'll have to wait and see.'

'If he dies, then you'll be out of a job, Nathan. You'll have nothing.'

'No, I won't. If he dies, then I'll take over the business. It's what he would have wanted.'

'That will be my decision—not yours.'

'Really?' Nathan laughs. 'He would have made sure you're decently provided for. As far as business goes—keep well away.'

She can hear the menace in his voice. She just wants him to go. He's here to stop her from talking. He's as sweet as pie to the nurses, even flirting with a couple of them.

A nurse steps into the room and records the readings from the machines. Julie is watching for any encouraging sign, but she can see none. The nurse gives her a sympathetic smile and walks out again.

'Is this what you wanted?' she asks Nathan. 'So, you could take over?'

Nathan sighs and looks at her. He forces a smile and looks back at his phone. Then Dettori arrives.

'Any progress?' Dettori asks Nathan. Julie can see he's wearing an ID badge like he's a hospital doctor. He's got some front this man. Nathan shakes his head.

'Why are you here?' says Julie.

Dettori looks at Julie for a moment and walks over to the glass. He's silent for a while, watching Dalton being ventilated.

'I'm here because I care about what's happened.'

'You mean you want to control how this appears. Make sure it doesn't bite you in the arse!'

'Really, Julie? After all the time you've known me. Nothing will come back and *bite me in the arse*, as this had nothing to do with me. It's purely a coincidence. Anyway, you've signed the NDA. There's nothing you can say about it.'

'You take me for a bloody fool!' Tears are rolling down Julie's cheeks. 'It was your drug that did this.'

'What drug? I don't know what you're talking about. Do you, Nathan?'

'Not a clue,' says Nathan.

'They can do tests!' says Julie, jabbing her finger in the air. 'I'll tell them!'

'Now, that would be extremely stupid of you. If you do...' Dettori turns and bends down, with his face against hers. He makes a point of staring down her blouse and looking over her body. 'If you do, I will make sure that you lose everything—the house, the fast cars, the money. Yes, especially the money. You'll have nothing left, Julie. You will have to go back to the council estate from where you came and whore yourself out again, just like the good old days. It's probably the only thing you were ever any good at. You've still got a few good years left in you yet.'

Julie goes to slap him, but Nathan's hand grabs her wrist. His grip is powerful, and her wrist is hurting. Dettori nods at Nathan and steps away.

'You are an utter bastard, Dean!' says Julie. 'Nathan, I thought you were our friend?'

'I still am, Julie,' says Nathan. 'I'll make sure you're okay. You won't have to cope on your own, I promise.'

'I think it's time we were going,' says Dettori.

Nathan puts his phone away and follows Dettori through the door.

'I'll call you,' says Nathan finally as he leaves.

Once they've gone, Julie feels the darkness crawling its way back over her. There's a drink in her bag—the only friend she has left.

McCall has driven for two hours to the Redbridge park-and-ride in Oxford and taken a bus for another 25 minutes to Saint Clement's. She's put on her shades and soaks up the spring sunshine, with her jacket folded over the top of her Louis Vuitton shoulder bag.

The morning travelling has given her time to reflect on the last five days. Angelis is a real enigma. How he knew about

Parkes and the girls at Broyle Way is still a puzzle to her. There's something more to him than simple intuition. He seems to see things and know what people are feeling.

He's taken to being back at work well, despite the insecurities he's trying to hide. And she likes that about him. She really likes him, and her mind has been wandering in ways she would not want to admit to anyone. She doesn't want to go there. She doesn't want to be somebody's fool again.

It's a five-minute walk now, according to Google. She's glad for the leg-stretch and the fresh air. After one wrong turn, she finds the road she wants and comes to the front door of a massive house with a sun and a rainbow logo on the outside. She puts Angelis out of her mind once again and rings the jangling doorbell. A man answers.

'May I speak with Elizabeth Jacobs? I'm Detective Sergeant McCall. She is expecting me.' McCall holds up her warrant card.

'Oh yes, come in,' says the skinny tattooed man. 'I'll take you to her. I'm Jake, one of her support workers, her favourite support worker. She's not in a great place at the moment, losing Kate like that. She's heartbroken, truth be told. I'm not sure how she's going to react to you. But we'll give it a go.'

He leads McCall through the vast Victorian house, with the rooms having some similarity to her own. There's a lot of noise around, laughter, music, the smell of cooking. A man is chasing a young woman through the hallway, and she can barely run with the laughing. She stops and looks up at McCall.

'Hello,' she says, 'I'm Jane. You're so pretty!' She smiles at McCall and then suddenly runs off again before McCall can thank her.

'Slow down, Jane!' calls Jake. He's smiling and shaking his head.

'Come up,' he says. He's taking two steps at a time, but

McCall's skirt won't manage that. 'We're so glad you came. It's going to help Lizzie, talking about it. She wouldn't have spoken over the phone.'

They come to a lilac door with a smiling photo of a young woman in a frame. Jake knocks loudly,

'Lizzie! The police officer is here.' There's no reply. 'Lizzie, the police lady, is here... She's nice and extremely pretty.' McCall blushes slightly and smiles.

The door slowly opens. Lizzie is wearing a pink and grey onesie, patterned with white stars. Her hair is red like her sister's and styled in a bob.

'Hello Lizzie, I'm Helen. Is it okay to call you Lizzie?' Lizzie nods her head.

'Can Jake and I come into your room, please? I'm hoping you could help me.'

Lizzie steps back. Her room is mostly lilac and light grey. There are glow-in-the-dark stars on the ceiling, posters of some Korean boy band on the wall, next to a large TV, and a bed that McCall would have died for when she was a teenager. Lizzie is 19, and her expression tells McCall that she's lost her best friend in the world.

Lizzie and Jake sit on her bed while McCall takes the swivelling desk chair. She used to have one in her bedroom when she was a girl.

'Lizzie, you know I'm a police officer?' Lizzie nods. 'I'm a detective, which means I look into why something bad has happened and try to catch the person who did it.'

'I know what a bloody detective is,' says Lizzie. McCall blushes again. That told her.

'Right, that's good then. I'm trying to find who killed your sister, and I want to put them behind bars for a long time.'

'Good. I hate them!'

Jake rubs Lizzie's back for a few seconds.

'So do I, Lizzie. To help us find who this person is, we need to find out more about Kate and her friends. Your mum and dad told me you and Kate talked about everything. Is that right?'

'We did. Everything.' Lizzie lifts her head and pulls back her shoulders.

'Did Kate ever talk about anyone she was scared of?'

'Nobody. She was scared of nobody.'

'Did she ever tell you that someone was trying to hurt her?'

'No, she said she had her own special angel living next door.'

McCall has to pause a few beats. 'Ah, you mean David Angelis, her neighbour.'

'Yes, she liked him. She called him Mr Guinea Pig. She told me she gave him a Haribo. It's a secret!'

'Really! That's funny.'

'He was her experiment. She had to find out about him.'

McCall shudders, and the funny moment has gone.

'What experiment was that, Lizzie?'

'I don't know, do I.' Lizzie shrugs her shoulders. 'That's all secret-spy stuff.'

'Of course, it is. And what about Vanessa, her friend? Did they get on okay?'

Lizzie is frowning. 'She didn't talk about her that much. I didn't really like her—she's really bossy.'

'Did they ever argue, do you know?'

'Yes. Kate said Vanessa was a bit grumpy.'

'Did Vanessa ever hurt Kate?'

Lizzie thought for a time and looked like she was getting upset.

'No, I don't think so.'

'I'm sorry, Lizzie, to ask you all these questions. It must be hard for you.'

'It's okay. You can catch who hurt her now?'

'We are doing our very best.'

'Did Kate have any other friends in Chichester we can talk to?'

'Where's Max?'

'He's okay. He's staying with my parents.'

'That's nice. They don't let us have dogs or cats or parrots here. Can I see him one day?'

'I can arrange that for you, Lizzie—no problem.'

'There's Graham.'

'Who's Graham?'

'He loved her, but she said no.'

'That's interesting. Do you know where Graham lives?'

'No, but he works at the pub near Kate. The Green Man. Kate said he was a green man because she had a girlfriend.'

'Ah, he was jealous.' McCall is making a few notes on her iPad. 'I'm just writing that down, so I don't forget.'

'I've got an iPad, don't I, Jake?'

'You do, Lizzie,' says Jake. 'You only use it for YouTube and Facebook.'

'Yeah,' says Lizzie. There's half a smile on her face.

'I think I know where the Green Man is,' says McCall. 'Do you know what Graham looks like and his last name?'

'Kate said he's got a big beard and a big nose. She liked him because he was funny, but then he got too friendly.'

'Okay. Well, it will be worth having a chat with him, wouldn't it?'

'Yes, Kate said he's a prick.'

'I'll make a note of that especially. P-R-I-C-K, prick.'

'No other friends you can think of?'

'Not really. She was busy with her job. She wanted Mr Angel to be her friend, but she couldn't. She was my best friend... and now she's in heaven. I miss her so much.'

Lizzie leans into Jake, and she covers her eyes. Jake signals that Lizzie's had enough.

'I have to go now, Lizzie. Thank you so much for talking to me.' McCall looks at Jake. 'And to you, Jake, for arranging it. We'll work out how to get Lizzie to see Max again. You are a lovely man, Jake.'

Jake blushes, and Lizzie sits up—she's elbowing him.

Lizzie whispers too loudly, 'Get her number!'

'Actually, Lizzie,' says Jake, 'I already have her number. It's 9-9-9. Anyway. What would my real girlfriend say!'

As McCall takes the bus back to the park-and-ride, she thinks about Jake and his relationship with Lizzie and the others he cares for. Then her thoughts drift back to Angelis, and she thinks perhaps there are kind men out there, after all.

The GP quietly closes the door and leaves them alone in the room. Their world has blown apart. James is holding Paul so tightly he can feel the air squeezing out of his lungs. He doesn't know what he can do right now.

'Struggling to breathe here, James,' he says. James relaxes his hold and kisses him softly.

Paul puts the palms of his hands on the sides of James's face and gently brings him to look into his eyes. 'Look, my love. I'm okay. We're okay. Whatever happens next, we're going to be together. I won't let this beat me, especially with you by my side.'

James is struggling to speak through the tears. 'I don't want to lose you.'

'You're not going to, sweetheart. We can do this.'

'I'll find a way to fix this, Paul. I promise.'

'Come on, you big oaf. Don't make promises you know you can't keep. As long as we're together, we'll be fine.'

NINE

2nd March 2022

All the coffees on the tray look like treacle, and the one I chose is undrinkable. I'm still groggy from a bad night's sleep and I could have done with some caffeine. I'm about to lead the morning briefing, and I'm looking at the whiteboard. There have been changes. For a start, someone has written Grant as Vanessa's surname. Then there is the new column for Hudson Biotech, with Amanda Wilson, Colin Decker, Vanessa Grant, and Katherine Jacobs written underneath.

I'm about to speak when I see Laura Driscoll slip in at the back of the office, unnoticed by the rest of the team. The Chief Super nods at me, and it unnerves me a little to see her here, as I'm her focus of interest. I have to remind myself that she's looking out for me, but I can't help feeling there's some other agenda going on.

'I see there have been a few developments,' I say. 'Just to let you know, I am now officially leading Operation Greenwood.

So, all reviews and decisions regarding this case will come to me. Right, Po and Sam, what have you got for us?'

Gregory gives way to Cheung, who moves to the front as her voice doesn't carry well. She's deflecting attention away from herself by pointing at the board as she speaks, outlining the connection between Kate, Amanda Wilson, and Colin Decker. I'm sensing a vulnerability, but she's pushing through it.

'So, Vanessa's surname is Grant,' Cheung says. 'She's the former head of security. She left Hudson Biotech on the 1st of November last year. She wasn't well-liked by the sounds of things.'

'That's three Hudson employees now dead,' Daley says. 'That can't be a coincidence, surely?'

'Both Decker and Wilson had grievances against the Hudson company,' I say. 'We don't know why Katherine Jacobs left, other than for personal reasons, and one of those reasons could be to do with Wilson's suicide.'

'We know they were close,' says McCall from the back. 'Katherine had that photo of Wilson and her parents.'

'Thanks, Po and Sam. Regarding Katherine leaving the company, it's worth talking to Katherine's old boss, Dean Dettori, to see if he can fill in any details.'

I look over at Driscoll, and she nods in agreement.

'We'll follow that up, boss,' says Sam.

'We need to find any friends of Vanessa Grant and her ex-husband.'

'There are rumours amongst the Hudson staff she had an affair,' says Sam. 'Her husband is Peter Grant. He works in the Hudson IT Department. He handles computer repairs and upgrades. She may have left because she didn't want to see him at work every day.'

Daley is spitting out bits of a pen lid he's been chewing.

'Did her husband find out she was having a relationship with Katherine? Now, there's a motive if ever there was one.'

I point at Dan. 'Dan's right. Peter Grant could have a motive, especially if he found out where Vanessa was staying. What do we know about Peter Grant?' There's no answer. 'Nothing, then. Dan, run a check on him. Are there any other leads from anyone?'

'There is something else, boss,' says McCall. 'I found out from Lizzie Jacobs that Katherine had rejected the advances of a man who works in the Green Man pub, her local. She said his name is Graham. Lizzie said Katherine told her he was jealous she was in another relationship. She said he wouldn't leave Katherine alone.'

'Can you follow that up for us, Helen?'

'Will do, boss.'

'Sarge,' says Lang, standing next to McCall. 'That confirms something from a conversation we had. Muhammad and I spoke to a woman in the park near Doctor Jacobs's house. She was one of the dog walkers you asked us to talk to. She told us Doctor Jacobs was being stalked by a man in his twenties with a beard. Doctor Jacobs avoided the park because he kept hanging around there, trying to talk to her.'

'That was confirmed by a fella we met,' says Essam. 'He said Katherine Jacobs went to his local, The Green Man.' He checks his notes. 'He refused to give a name but seemed to know who this man was. He was quite riled when we asked questions about him—quite defensive, actually.'

'Lizzie also described him having a beard,' says McCall. 'That seems to point to the same person.'

'It's even more important to follow him up,' I say. 'Anything else?' There's silence. 'Okay, DS Harris is back in tomorrow, and I'll be on rest days, as is DS McCall—so DS Harris will be leading. Come on, let's get busy! I see there was a burglary overnight in Petworth. I'll allocate that to whoever made those terrible coffees.' A cheer goes up, and a ginger-haired detective behind me goes very pink.

As the team breaks off to their assignments, McCall comes over to me.

'Have you got a moment, boss?' says McCall.

'Yes, of course. Is everything okay?'

'While I was talking to Lizzie yesterday, she mentioned Katherine's comments about you.'

'Okay?' I'm waiting for something unpleasant.

'She said Katherine referred to you as her guinea pig and her experiment, which backs up what's written on the calendar.'

'I don't think guinea pig is an endearing term, do you?'

McCall's eyes are on mine. I think she's worried about me.

'There's something seriously screwed here, boss.' She swallows. 'Cameras spying on you, experiments?'

I shake my head—she doesn't see Driscoll listening in. But then Daley comes over to me, and McCall looks down at her iPad.

'Excuse me, sir,' says Daley. 'Peter Grant. Po got his date of birth from Hudson. There's nothing significant on PNC, just a speeding fine from years ago. I found nothing interesting on the local database either. He's reported a few dodgy photos he's found on company computers, but nothing relating to a criminal record or cautions for him.'

'Cheers, Dan. Helen, we should ask Peter Grant to come in. It's certainly worth getting his take on Vanessa's disappearance.'

'Yes, boss,' she says. 'I'll get Sam to see if he will attend a voluntary interview.'

'Sir,' calls Daley back from his desk. 'Some forensic results are in. They've just emailed them over.'

I go back to my office and close my door for a moment. I'm standing there, hiding behind the door, taking deep breaths. I need space. I need time. I close my eyes, and everything stops—frozen. I've stepped away, watching the world from a distant place as I turn and look around. I see the team slowed right down. There's no sound apart from my heart and the air moving in and out of my nostrils. I can smell a familiar sweet fragrance from a place I once visited; a walled garden full of wild honeysuckle. I could go there now if I wished, but I choose to stay here with my team. I can wander among them, and I see loved ones beside them. They are the people on their minds, their anxieties, pressures at home, loves and losses. There's even a small dog sitting on Dan's desk. It catches me by surprise and makes me laugh out loud.

I see Driscoll there, too. She is walking towards my office. I have a few moments before she reaches my door. She's walking with her shadows: agendas, orders, and secrets. As the door opens, I return.

I think she saw something, and her eyes flash, startled.

'Good morning, Ma'am,' I say. 'I assume you didn't want to be introduced to the team at this stage.'

'Good morning, David. No, thank you.'

'How can I help you today?'

'I understand you have discovered covert recording devices in your home.'

'Yes, cameras and microphones.'

'And calendar entries in Katherine Jacobs's home alerted you to them?'

'Yes.'

'I presume your perception helped you make that connection. Why didn't you tell me?'

I see a glimpse of Professor Allen standing beside her. He's been talking to Driscoll about me. I never liked him. He's only ever looking to further his career. So much for doctor-patient confidentiality.

'Tell you something you already know, ma'am? What's the point of that?'

'I see I owe you an explanation, David.' She takes a seat and straightens her jacket. 'We have been studying you closely, with help from a mutual acquaintance. A late mutual acquaintance, I'm sad to say.'

I'm feeling something like ice crawling up my spine. As I realise what this woman is saying, I see Kate once more. She's standing in the doorway, mouthing, 'I'm sorry.'

'Kate was working for you? You were spying on me? This is outrageous!'

'Yes, she was. You need to calm yourself, David. Please. You can do a lot of damage when you are angry.'

'But why? I don't understand.'

'We've known about your differentness, if that's a good way to describe it, for quite a while. Professor Allen brought it to our attention that you have developed unique skills. He was very concerned about what he observed. You could use those skills for good or for something more nefarious. We needed to know which side of the line you are falling, David.'

'So, what side of the line do you think I'm *falling?*'

'Ours, of course! But if you had gone another way, then it wouldn't be an exaggeration to say that you would have been a risk to national security. Hence my involvement. I work for the Domestic Counterterrorism Agency. I preferred Special Branch —less of a mouthful. We've never seen what you can do before. It is quite remarkable and has generated a lot of interest.'

Kate has gone; there's just the cool-headed woman in front of me now.

'You think I'm a security risk? You could have come to me. I respond well to honesty and openness. You understand I didn't choose what happened to me. I'm still coming to terms with it. How did Kate get mixed up with this?'

'We contacted Doctor Jacobs in September last year because we knew about her connection with you.'

'I only met her last November when she moved next door.'

'Actually, you met her before that, but you won't remember. She administered a drug treatment to you while you were in a coma.'

'She wouldn't do this.'

'It was part of a drugs trial called Operation Oberon. A failed and illegal drugs trial, I hasten to add, run by Hudson Biotech in the UK. Kate told us you were an ideal candidate. They based the drug on proteins enhanced by nanotechnology, designed to improve the survival rate of stroke and brain trauma victims and hold back the progression of Alzheimer's and vascular dementia. They promised it to be a miracle drug. However, Kate said there were big concerns about the side effects of the drug. It increased levels of overall strength and fitness tremendously, as well as sensory acuity.'

Amanda. The woman in the hospital tried to tell me about this. What did she say to me?

'That's a plus, isn't it?'

'Those side effects, yes. But they also observed increased paranoia, psychopathic tendencies.'

Amanda had something for me. What was it? Was that Amanda Wilson?

'And you're telling me they gave that drug to me?'

'She was told you died soon after the treatment. It's something I am investigating. Anyway, Doctor Jacobs didn't realise you were alive. We recruited her in exchange for immunity from any future prosecution. We asked her to gather information on you covertly. We needed to assess if there was any risk from you. Professor Allen made us aware of potentially worrying developments early on. In your discussions with him and through observing you while you slept, they gathered evidence of what we can only describe as paranormal behaviour.'

'Paranormal! Oh, come on!' I want to walk out of here—they know everything. Some of the team can see me gesticulating. I must calm down.

'No, seriously. I am usually careful with my choice of words. Paranormal is an accurate description of what they observed, David. You may not be aware of this activity. Your ability to vanish from sight isn't normal behaviour. You go somewhere, David. Do you know where you go? We don't.'

'I assumed they were more...'

'Hallucinations? The video evidence we have shows otherwise. Hallucinations are only in the eye of the beholder, David. Not on CCTV as well.'

Every time she says these things, it's like she's drilling into my head. They know more about me than I do.

'I wasn't happy to find the cameras installed in my house.'

'We felt it was a proportionate and necessary action. As well as watching you at home, Professor Allen also observed your ability to influence how others think. Also, he noted your perception of the thoughts and feelings of others. These are the most concerning aspects of your new skills. To change how someone makes subconscious decisions is exceptionally dangerous. You could get away with murder, and no one would know.'

'What are you accusing me of?'

'I am not accusing you of anything. However, if you had wanted to, you could have given your neighbours the memory of you coming home when you did that night. Or you could have stopped them from seeing you go into Doctor Jacobs's house. Do you see the point I'm making? No one could prove otherwise, especially in a court of law.'

'I never hurt Kate.'

'I believe you. Some sceptics wouldn't give you a chance. So,

I need to know that you will cooperate with me. I can keep you safe from false allegations as long as you are willing to work with me, David.'

I stand up and walk around the desk. I can feel my heart pounding in my ears.

'This is just ridiculous... I never asked for this.'

'Inspector, are you willing to work with me?'

'Yes, of course, I am!'

'Yes, ma'am, is the respectful reply.' She raises an eyebrow.

'Yes, ma'am, I will work with you.'

'Well, that's good.'

'How do I feed this into the investigation? I assume I can't talk about your efforts to find out if I am a security risk or not.'

'Absolutely not. The investigation into you and your abilities is Top Secret. If it ever looks like the reason for Kate's murder has anything to do with her investigating you, then I will step in. That's another reason for me to monitor the progress of this case.'

'Sergeant McCall has some awareness of what I can do.'

'That's okay. I doubt you have gone into too much detail with her, have you?'

'No.'

'McCall and Harris will inevitably notice something unusual about you. You can't help that. I may need to bring them into the circle of trust, so to speak. Look, just carry on the way you are. You are doing well. We are also investigating Hudson's illegal drugs trial activities. Just keep us in the loop.'

'Ma'am, someone must have lied to Kate about me dying after treatment. Who would do that?'

'Kate said there was a rumour—you somehow revived yourself. Rose from the dead, so to speak!' She finds that amusing and has a strange, hissing laugh. 'The stuff of legends.'

I really can't make her out, but that may be because I'm still shell-shocked. She pops her head out of the door and looks out towards the team, trying to find someone.

'But it would be good if you had someone else who you could confide in,' she says. 'It's quite a burden to carry on your own... Ah!' She spots McCall.

Driscoll opens the door and calls out. 'DS McCall, could you come into the office for a few minutes?' Helen has two full cups of coffee in her hand and makes her way over to us. 'What do you think of McCall?' She watches her dodge a group walking back to their desks.

'Think of her?'

'What I am asking is, do you think she is trustworthy? I've watched you with her, and you work well together. I'm sure you've used your skills to assess her by now.'

'She's a top-class police officer and a good sergeant. I would say she is completely trustworthy.'

'Good. Let me brief McCall for you. I think it would be good for her to know the full circumstances, and it should come from me.'

'Yes, ma'am.' Shit! I don't know what McCall's going to make of this.

Vanessa's been alone for a long time now—she doesn't know how long. Time is so deceptive. The last time she was with him was when he took her bottoms down so she could pee in a bucket. He enjoyed that. Now she is thirsty again. Very thirsty. She can ignore the hunger, but her mouth is dry, and she can't cry anymore.

A car has pulled up outside, and she can hear two voices she recognises. Dettori's Italian accent is easily recognisable. He's with Wheelhouse. She can't make out what they're saying, but

Dettori is angry about something. She knows Wheelhouse will be here again soon. He wants the password to the computer, but she doesn't know it. Not for the one they have.

They are out there for ages. Vanessa wants something to happen, to get this torture over with. She's resorted to talking to herself, telling herself it's going to be okay. But the fear keeps on returning, and it's getting harder to push away.

'Come on! You can get through this. You must,' she says. Her mouth is so dry. 'God, please help me! Get me out of here. Save me, please. I've been such an idiot.' Her prayers seem to fall away into the darkness. Vanessa thinks about the texts she learned as a child before her father lost his way. *Whosoever calls upon the name of the Lord shall be saved.* Romans 10, something or other. *The Lord will preserve you from all evil; He shall preserve your soul.* Psalm? She can't think.

The door opens, and he walks to the fridge. Vanessa hears a drinks bottle open.

'Sweet pea! It's me,' he says. 'The love of your life has returned. Do you need another wee, sweet pea? You know I like to help you with that. No? How about a drink? I bet you're thirsty.' Wheelhouse stands over Vanessa and holds the bottle in front of her face. Vanessa groans. 'So, you are thirsty. I know. How about you tell me the password of the computer and then I'll give you a drink? Someone just told me that the computer hard disk is encrypted. That means fuck all to me. He said, no matter how clever you are with computers, you still can't read the information on it. Not even MI5 could read it! Shit, that's clever. So, we need that password. I told them, you're thirsty, but they said you can't have a drink until you tell me the password. So, nod if you are going to tell me, then I can give you a nice drink.'

Vanessa sits perfectly still. She can tell by Wheelhouse's breathing that he's getting impatient. She hears a metallic click and then feels something sharp pushing through her hooded top. She doesn't move, even when she hears the cloth ripping as a knife cuts it off. Wheelhouse puts the knife under the shoulders, cuts off the rest of the hoodie along each arm, and peels the material away. She's now sitting there in just her bra and tracksuit bottoms.

'Very nice,' he says. 'I'll tell you what, sweet pea. You sit there and think about it a bit more, and I'll be back. Perhaps, we can have a play later? What do you think?'

He walks away and closes a door. Vanessa hears a latch falling, and she shakes.

McCall joins Driscoll and me in my office while I pull in another chair.

'Ma'am, would you like a coffee?' she says to Driscoll as I close the door. 'I'm afraid one of our officers has tried to poison us all this morning.'

'No, thank you, Sergeant. I'm a tea drinker—never liked coffee.'

'Helen, this is Detective Chief Superintendent Driscoll.'

'Good morning, ma'am. How can I help?'

'Helen, I've just heard a very positive review from Inspector Angelis about your abilities.'

'Thank you.' McCall looks at me. Her face blushes—she's not great at receiving praise.

'Superintendent Walsh knows I am here today. He thought it best to leave this to me. Helen, I work in counterterrorism, specifically concerning domestic security.' Driscoll motions to us to sit with her. 'This is about Katherine Jacobs and Inspector Angelis. You realise that with my involvement in the case, this won't be straightforward. My team was working with Doctor Jacobs on an ongoing project. She was working for us, covertly gathering intelligence about a specific subject.'

'And that subject was Inspector Angelis?'

'Yes. Well done. I forgot you saw the covert cameras, too.'

'Yes, ma'am. How is this going to change the case, and why involve me in this conversation?'

'Ma'am,' I say, 'I'm happy for you to disclose the personal details to DS McCall. Helen is going to find out eventually by working with me.'

'That's your choice, David. If you are sure?' says Driscoll.

She's raising an eyebrow at me, but I'm sensing that it will make this much more manageable for her. And I want Helen to know. I want her to trust me.

'Yes, I'm sure,' I say. I sense anxiety in Helen now. Her heart rate is increasing.

'Thank you, David.'

Driscoll leans forward to focus on Helen. I'm watching Helen as Driscoll tells her about what they've observed about me. She already knew about the incident in Brighton, and I've told her about what I called my *intuition*, but now she realises there's a lot more. She hears the phrase *paranormal activity* in there somewhere, and it's becoming a bit of a blur to her. Helen keeps snatching glances at me. She's frowning, trying to make sense of what she's hearing. A chief superintendent is telling her these things, not me. At the end of the briefing, she's staring into space, shaking her head.

'Ma'am, this is so...'

'Unbelievable?' says Driscoll. 'I think that, often. It's made me see things in a different light, too. I'm even talking in my sleep about it if I'm honest. My poor husband is worrying who this David is.' This was Driscoll's attempt to ease the tension. She hisses a snigger. 'But I can assure you, according to

Inspector Angelis's statement to me, he is only using these unusual gifts in a legal and honourable way.'

'Do you mind if I take a few minutes?' says McCall. She looks at me. 'I'm fine, honestly. There's just a lot to think about, sir. This must be really hard for you. I'm sorry.'

'No, go ahead,' I say. 'We'll catch up later.'

'I have to say this, Helen,' says Driscoll. 'This information is classified as Secret, an order from above, and you must not share it with anyone. Not even DS Harris.'

'Yes, ma'am. Of course.'

Helen thanks Driscoll and walks out of the office. Folding her arms tightly across her chest, she leaves the building, and I see her walk past Custody. She's going down the canal to clear her head.

'So now you have an ally,' says Driscoll. 'It's important to be understood. We won't tell Harris. I don't want this shared any further.'

'Ma'am, now that you know these things about me. What's going to happen?'

'This is all new ground for us, and we'd like to know how this happened to you. Was it something the drug did to you? It's the only contributing factor I can see. In the meantime, we will have to wait and see what happens next. But while you are a police officer, Inspector, I will need to monitor the situation.'

'Okay. No more surveillance, though, please. It's always my choice what I do with this. You will get the best out of me if I feel I have the freedom to choose what I do.'

'Of course, David. I'm sorry if it came across any other way.'

Is she being genuine? It's those who she works for who really worry me.

TEN

Rachael Thorne is standing outside the police station, and her stomach is churning over. She wants to see him for real first in the flesh to make sure. Then she can decide what to do. She can't just stand here, though. She looks so out of place. Now, Rachael's wondering why she's come at all. It's a foolish thing to do. Two years have gone by, and everyone is happy now.

A blonde woman comes out of the building and passes her—she's wearing a police lanyard. She looks at Rachael for a moment. Rachael turns away and goes back to her car. Not today—she's not ready.

Driscoll has gone, and I'm glad. She's done enough to upset the applecart for today, and I have to pick up the pieces with McCall, who is just returning after thirty minutes of fresh air. She's come back looking refreshed and returns to my office. She has something in a paper bag and puts it on my desk.

'I thought you might like this,' she says.

I peek inside the bag, and there is a split doughnut filled with fresh custard cream. She smiles as my eyes light up.

'Bless you!' I say. 'That's *exactly* what I need, my absolute favourite. How did you know?'

'Feminine intuition. Everything is still okay, sir. I don't understand any of it. Just don't try any mind control shit on me.' She's joking with me, but there's many a true word said in jest, according to Chaucer.

'I'll never do that to you. Even if I want a doughnut.' I'm glad she sees the funny side of it.

'Thank you, sir. If there's anything I can do to help, or...'

'I will.'

I'm reading the emails from forensics and the preliminary pathologist's report. The results for the knife found in the bin are not in yet—maybe tomorrow. The fingerprints around the home are Kate's and Vanessa Grant's. There's one other partial print on the charger plug—so far unknown. We have Vanessa's fingerprints on record after she was arrested after an alleged assault a few years ago. Mine are on the plastic container containing flapjack. DNA evidence is inconclusive, other than everything is awash with Kate's. They found some black fibres under her nails and no DNA or material on her clothing except dog hair.

Walsh phones me from HQ to find out my thoughts on Driscoll and to hear the forensic report.

'Driscoll's a strange one, don't you think?' says Walsh. 'I'm sure she's good at her job, but she's quite... menacing. Don't let her put you off, David. She's trying to do a delicate balancing act between protecting national security and looking after your wellbeing.'

'I'm still reeling and somewhat angry, to be honest, sir.'

'That's understandable. My feeling is that we're lucky to have you, and they should be too. Had you been someone without scruples, then God knows where we would be.'

'Thank you.'

I'm wondering now who *they* are.

'So, moving on to the pathologist's report...'

I give Walsh the outline of the fingerprints first and move on to the pathology. 'The report states the cause of death... which was obvious. There are no physical signs of sexual assault other than her knickers were removed. No one's but Kate's DNA was on them.'

'They could have removed them to humiliate her.'

'Or they were interrupted before they got the chance to rape her.'

'Shame there's not much for us to go on. There's nothing back on the knife yet?' I'm sensing frustration in his voice.

'No, sir. That's expected tomorrow. The murderer must have been forensically aware, which is why the knife being covered in blood and easily found makes no sense.'

'I was thinking the same thing. Well, keep me updated. Thanks, David.' He ends the call.

McCall is standing at my door, wearing her jacket. 'Hopefully, the knife will bring better news. I'm off to the pub to see a green man.'

'Enjoy,' I say. 'Have a double for me.'

I've booked myself on enquiries for an hour while McCall is out, but that's the last thing I'm doing. I'm walking in a copse near my home, following a path that runs parallel to a fallow field, which I suspect someone's going to build houses on anytime soon.

There's a seat here by a spreading oak, surrounded by chestnut trees, all thin and spindly after being coppiced for many years. There's a small plaque on the seat dedicated to the memory of Joyce Mayhew.

> *For Joyce Mayhew, who prayed here*
> *daily. 1 Thess. 5v17*

Well, if this seat was good enough for Joyce, then it's good enough for me. I sit, and I feel like my head's been battered with a hammer. Everything is imploding on me. There's the bizarre revelation from Driscoll, and the anger is still there about Josh. I really let myself down yesterday. I can't believe I told Bella to fuck off—it kept me awake last night. But Josh is my son, and I have a right to see him. It's all too much.

I wipe away the tears before they roll down my cheeks. I just hate the control these people have over me. I think of Karen and her terms and conditions for Josh. I could turn her away from that imposter she lives with. I could feed her paranoia and resentment against him. I could make her want *me* again. But then that's how this all started. That's how I lost everything. It was my paranoia, my resentment, my control. It really is my fault, after all. Shit, it really is.

A sudden breeze lifts and rushes through the budding branches above. A woman sits beside me, looking up at the branches, as I do. She is laughing and raising her hands as far as her frail frame can lift them. Then she looks at me. What is this, another layer of time I am watching? Is it the memory of this place? Her face is now young, in her twenties, soft and flawless skin and bright clear eyes. She is smiling at me, and then she stretches out her finger and touches my forehead. I can feel it! It makes me flinch. I blink, and she's gone. And I weep.

I text Bella Brookes:

> I'm sorry. All of this is my fault. I want to change.

The Green Man pub sits on the main road from Chichester to Bosham. It's on the opposite side of a lane, named after it, set back from the road. McCall quickly finds a parking space at the front of the pub and takes a moment to compose herself after the strange morning she's had. She must push on, and Angelis is occupying too much of her mind.

She enters the pub, and it's nearly empty, apart from two older customers. They are sitting alone, staring over their pints and contemplating. McCall thinks things must be pretty grim to want to be drinking on your own. Maybe it's the only place they can go for some peace and quiet.

There's a tall man with a big belly behind the bar. He's cleaning down the surfaces and polishing wine glasses.

'What can I get you?' he says.

McCall shows him her warrant card. 'Good morning. I'm looking for someone called Graham. Does he work here?'

The man stares at her for a few moments. It's like he's struggling to process it. 'Ah, you mean Swampy. Not many people call him Graham. Yeah, he works here in the evenings. He's not here now.'

McCall reaches into her bag and pulls out her mobile. She shows the barman a photo of Katherine Jacobs. 'Have you seen this woman in here?'

He's squinting, and again there's a delay. It's like she's interviewing him by satellite. 'That there's Kate. She doesn't come in here no more on account she's dead. She was killed last week. Very sad.'

'What's your name?'

'Kevin Lampard.'

'I'm DS McCall, Kevin. I'm aware she's dead because I'm investigating her murder.'

'Oh, you're the police then?'

McCall smiles through gritted teeth. 'I showed you my warrant card.'

'Oh, that's what it was. I don't have my glasses with me—can't find them anywhere.'

'How often did Kate drink here, Kevin?'

'A couple of times a week. On her own at first, but then she came with a friend. They ate here sometimes. Kate was a pretty girl, like you. Some of the lads got a bit excited and took an interest. But she was clever, you see. In a different league.'

'Was Graham interested in her?'

'Oh, yes. Swampy couldn't keep his eyes off her. He kept asking her out, but she wouldn't have any of it.'

'Have you got an address for Swampy?'

'He lives just down the road in the house opposite the millpond. You can't miss it.'

'Thank you, Kevin. You've been really helpful.'

Kevin crouches down behind the bar, and McCall sees a pair of glasses balanced on the top of his head.

McCall gets back into the car, drives a mile further into Fishbourne, and turns into Mill Stream Road. She parks up and sees a house opposite the pond. The small garden at the front is overgrown with nettles, and there's a pile of rotten logs by the front door. McCall bangs the knocker, making more of the green paint flake off.

A bearded man opens the door. He's in his mid-twenties, wearing camouflage trousers and a green t-shirt. It's clear to McCall he's never been in the army, but he's dressed like he's about to enter the jungle. When he sees McCall, he puffs out his chest and gives her a smile he's obviously rehearsed.

'Are you Swampy?' she asks.

'I am, sweetheart.' He looks her up and down. 'How can I help you?'

She can see a sheath on his belt and a bone knife handle. McCall steps back and shows the man her warrant card.

'I'm DS McCall, Sussex Police. I'm investigating a serious crime that occurred about a mile from here. I think you may have known the victim.'

'You mean Kate, don't you,' he says. 'Come in if you want. It's tidy, but the cats are a bit fierce. They catch the rats.'

McCall takes one look at the hallway. 'No, thanks. I'd rather stay out here.'

'Scared of me, aren't ya. I don't know why. I'm friendly.'

'When did you last see, Kate, Swampy? Is it okay to call you Swampy?'

'Well, that *is* my name. I bet Kev told you where I live. I saw Kate the day she died. She weren't too happy with us.'

'Actually, Swampy, I'm wondering if we could do this down the police station. It's just easier to record the conversation.'

Swampy frowns, and his bottom lip goes out.

'No, no, no. What do you take me for? Flashing your

eyelashes at me like I'm some dumb arse, asking me to come down to the station. You'll fit me up before I know it.'

'Swampy, it's not like that. We can arrange a mutually agreeable time for you to come in. We need to paint a picture of Kate's movements, the friendships she had.'

'Why me, though? Who's been saying stuff about me?'

'There have been allegations you were following Kate after she turned you down.'

Swampy gets into McCall's face. 'Go on! Fuck off from here! I'm not talking to you.'

McCall steps back and feels for the spray in her pocket.

'Calm yourself! Step away.'

Swampy moves towards her and unclips his knife. McCall draws her spray and aims for his eyes. He falls onto his knees and screams.

'My eyes! Help! I'm blind!' He shuts his eyes tightly, and his nose pours with snot.

McCall's on the radio. 'I've got one in custody. Can I have a van? He's been sprayed.'

She snatches the hunting knife from his belt and tosses it behind her.

'I weren't going to stab you, stupid cow! It hurts!'

'Remain calm. It'll wear off soon. Swampy, Graham, whatever your name is, I'm arresting you for being in possession of a bladed article in a public place and assault on a police officer.'

ELEVEN

I'm catching up with case reviews when my desk phone rings. I'm grateful for the interruption.

'Great, thanks. We'll be over to get him shortly.'

I walk over to McCall, who is back at her desk. It looks like she's writing an arrest statement for Swampy, the alias for Graham Thomas.

'Peter Grant is here,' I say. 'How did it go with your green man?'

'I arrested him,' she says. 'He threw his toys out of the pram when I tried to talk to him about Kate. I sprayed him.'

'Is he the bearded man?'

'Well, he's got a beard. I arrested him for carrying a bladed article, assault police and being a nob. We'll ask him about the stalking in interview, see where it leads us.'

'Good job. Let him stew a bit. Let me know once you've finished your statement. Then, you and I can talk to Grant.'

'Actually, I'm nearly done here. I'll get Muhammad and Jack to interview the lovely Swampy. I don't want to be his next sex fantasy.'

Grant has been waiting for ten minutes. I'm watching him through the glass door panel to see what I can pick up from him, but anyone can see he's nervous. He looks more like an estate agent than a computer geek. He's bronzed, slicked-back black hair, greying at the sides—no wedding ring. Despite that, I'm seeing him as a small boy; his eyes downcast, his chin tucked into his chest and arms tightly folded. There's a naughty boy if ever I saw one. As I walk in, the boy vanishes and Grant looks up at me, feigning confidence.

'Mr Grant, I'm DI Angelis. Thank you for coming. If you'd like to follow me...'

Grant walks a few paces behind me as we enter the old police building. He's limping slightly and keeps catching his breath. I find a free interview room, and he sits down gingerly. I see an expensive watch and nice shoes. The tan can only be from a foreign holiday. I'm wondering where an IT technician gets the money to pay for it all. It's all for show— he's a man living beyond his means.

'Mr Grant, thank you for attending the police station this afternoon,' says McCall. 'This interview is being video recorded. To remind you, this is a voluntary interview. You are not under arrest, and you are free to leave. Also, you are entitled to free and independent legal advice should you require it. You told us you did not want a solicitor. Is that still the case?'

'Yes, I don't need one, do I?' says Grant.

'Should you change your mind, Mr Grant, let me know. I am Detective Sergeant M2609 McCall and also present is...'

'Detective Inspector A2470 Angelis.'

'No one else is present in the room. This interview is being conducted in the interview rooms at Chichester Police Station, and the time, by my watch, is 1409 hours on Wednesday, 2nd March 2022.'

As McCall cautions Grant, I'm watching for anything unusual. I sense a hint of something wrong with him. Apart from the increased stress levels of being in here, there's underlying guilt and anger, but nothing on the level of a brutal murderer.

'Is this going to take long?' asks Grant. 'I've only put on an hour for parking.'

'Mr Grant,' McCall begins, 'Tell us what you know of your wife's whereabouts.'

'I don't know where she is,' he says. He's stretching his neck from side to side, like a boxer about to go into the ring.

'Okay, so when did you last see your wife?' McCall again.

'Over three months ago, the day she left me.'

'Was that at the beginning of November last year?'

'It must have been, yes.'

I'm smelling something rotten.

'Tell me the circumstances of why Vanessa left?' says McCall.

'I'd rather not,' says Grant. 'She found someone else. End of story.'

'Have you had any conversations since?'

'No.'

Why is he nodding? McCall has seen it, too.

'Where were you last Sunday, 27th February, between 8.30 p.m. and 11.30 p.m.?'

'I was at home, watching TV. Alone.'

'So, no one can confirm that?'

'Only Amazon. I ordered a new oven light about 10 o'clock.' Grant shifts in his chair.

'What were you watching on the TV?'

'I can't remember. I must have fallen asleep.'

'Has Vanessa ever told you where she was living or about her plans for the future? Perhaps in writing, social media, text message?'

'No, not at all.' Now I see something. His left eye begins to twitch, and then a long black creature, something like a millipede, appears from around the back of his head. It's crawled along his jaw, over his mouth, and is trying to push itself up into his nostril.

It's my turn. 'Are you quite certain, Peter? Think back. Anything via a friend, perhaps? Or maybe a letter, just to let you know she was okay?'

'Still no.' He can see my mistrust, and he's playing with his watch strap.

'I have information to the contrary, Mr Grant,' I say. McCall gives me one of her looks, but she's learning to trust me. 'Frankly, I don't believe you.'

Grant stares down at the table and is struggling to find words.

'Well, Mr Grant?' says McCall.

'I don't know who you have been talking to. Okay, Vanessa wrote me a letter, but I don't have it anymore. She said she wanted to apologise and said she's done something stupid.'

'So why did you just deny that?' I say. 'Why was that difficult?'

'Look, I don't know. I want nothing to do with this. Vanessa wrote she would tell me all about it if I went to see her at Katherine Jacobs's house. But I didn't want to see her again. She's screwed up my life big time. I'm in arrears with the mortgage and struggling to pay the bills. I told Martina Hayes about the letter.'

'Remind me who she is?' I ask. He looks up at the ceiling

and sighs. It's then I see red marks and bruising below his shirt collar. I catch McCall's attention, and she sees them, too.

'She's the head of security now at Hudson. They wanted to speak to Vanessa, too. Vanessa stole a laptop containing confidential files from them. I hoped that's what she meant by stupid, nothing worse.'

'How did you get the red marks on your neck, Peter?'

His hands go to his collar, and he blushes. For a moment, I see hands with long red fingernails around his neck. A woman is kissing and biting him.

His eye twitches again. 'Oh, this? I think I'm allergic to my washing detergent. It's nothing.' There's a pause, and he looks uncomfortable.

'What happened after you received the letter, Mr Grant?' asks McCall. 'Did you go to the house?'

'No, I certainly didn't. I've moved on from Vanessa now. Martina told me Vanessa and Katherine were in a relationship. Maybe Katherine found out about the stolen laptop and confronted her? Look, I have a horrible feeling that someone is trying to frame Vanessa. She's always had a temper, and she's strong too, but she's not a murderer.'

'So, to confirm,' says McCall, 'you are suggesting that someone is trying to implicate Vanessa in Katherine Jacobs's murder?'

'I don't know,' says Grant, 'but it's possible, isn't it?' He's digging in his nails into his wrist. He doesn't know what he thinks.

'Does she own a hunting knife, Mr Grant?' I say.

'No! She's not afraid of a bit of blood, but... a knife?'

'Where do you think Vanessa is likely to have gone?'

'Who knows,' says Grant. He's unconsciously scratching his head like something's bitten him. The black creature crawls over his hands and buries itself under the skin in his wrists. 'She'd probably just run somewhere far away from it all. Somewhere she knows.'

Welts have appeared on his wrists, and his scalp is flaking.

'Why didn't you come to us before?' asks McCall. 'You must have known the police would want this information?'

'Yes, I know. I should have.'

McCall looks back over her notes. 'Can I confirm for the recording, you are telling us you weren't aware of the relationship between Vanessa and Katherine until Martina Hayes told you about it?'

'No. I knew nothing about it.'

'You are extremely anxious, Peter,' I say. 'You're trying to hide something from us. What is it?'

'Not at all! Look, I have come here voluntarily. I've done nothing wrong. This was a mistake. Please. I have had enough. I want to go. You said I'm free to leave.'

'You are,' says McCall.

'Peter,' I say, as I feel his anger bubbling, 'I'm going to request authorisation to view your mobile phone records. Not just your phone calls, but also where your phone was on Sunday evening. How do you feel about that?'

The bronze tan drains from Grant's face.

'What are you playing at! You have no right,' he says.

'What's wrong, Peter?' I lean forward. I'm not intimidated by his tantrums. 'If what you told me is true, then there will be no problem. Will there be a problem?'

Grant is welling up.

'Mr Grant?' says McCall. 'Is there something you want to tell us?'

'Okay. I went to see Vanessa that night. I wish I hadn't.'

'Where did you meet her on Sunday evening?'

'I met her in Alcott Gardens, at Katherine's house.'

'What time was this?' McCall is pushing him.

'I was there just after 9. Vanessa opened the door. She was pleased to see me. She took me into a room, an office. She said Katherine was in the garden keeping the dog out the way. I don't like dogs.'

'How did Vanessa look? What was she wearing?'

'She appeared anxious. She was pale, and she had lost weight. She was wearing a grey tracksuit thing, a hooded top and bottoms. Very casual for her.'

'Did you see Katherine Jacobs?' I ask.

'No,' Grant looks at me. 'But I heard her talking to the dog. She was calling out to it. I think she called it Max.'

I give him a moment. He's clearly feeling the pressure. He takes the moment to sit back and take a deep breath.

'Why did Vanessa want you to visit her?' I say.

Grant wipes his eyes and his nose with a handkerchief.

'She said she stole that laptop from Hudson. It had files on it containing information about a dodgy drug trial they were doing. The laptop used to belong to someone called Colin Decker. I remember him from a few years ago. I thought the laptop was lost, but Vanessa found it. She told me she had shown the files to Doctor Jacobs, and she was very interested.'

'Where is the computer now?' I say. 'There was nothing found in the house.'

'I have it. Vanessa asked me to look after it for her. She said that she didn't want it falling into the wrong hands. Vanessa was going to take it to the police, but Katherine had other ideas.'

'Other ideas?'

'She wouldn't say, but Vanessa wasn't happy. Anyway, I've always got laptops that need repair or data wiping in the boot of my car. They're all securely encrypted. As all Hudson laptops are identical, bulk buying and all that, I swapped it over for one that had a fault, one that kept overheating. Nobody apart from Vanessa knew I swapped them.'

McCall is rubbing her eyes, trying to work this out. 'So, Mr Grant. You swapped over the computer in the house with an identical computer that was faulty. And you now have the computer that Vanessa took from Hudson?'

'Yes.'

'So,' McCall continues, 'the problem is, Mr Grant. The computer you left with Vanessa is missing. Why would Vanessa have taken it with her?'

'She wouldn't have taken it. She knew it was faulty. Maybe someone else took it?'

McCall is looking at me. I can sense frustration and disbelief in her. I must admit, this does all sound farfetched.

'Why didn't you tell us this in the first place?' I say. 'It could be important to the investigation.'

'I didn't want you to know I was there that night. I agreed to take the computer because Vanessa was afraid someone from Hudson would come for it. I knew it was stolen. I didn't want Vanessa to get into trouble, even after what she did to me. I was trying to protect her.'

'Someone might suggest you have tried to conceal or dispose of important evidence from police enquiries.'

Grant slaps his palms on the table. 'I wasn't concealing anything!'

'So, you knew Vanessa stole the laptop, and you agreed to get rid of it for her?'

'Not to get rid of it. Look after it for her.'

'Didn't it strike you that this would look suspicious?'

'I don't know! Look, do I need a solicitor? I'm not happy with the way these questions are going.'

I look at McCall and nod.

'Maybe you do,' I say. 'Peter, I'm arresting you on suspicion of perverting the course of justice and handling stolen goods.

We'll need the location of your car and that laptop. Hopefully, we can bottom this out.'

The metal hatch snaps shut on cell number nine. Peter Grant lets out a long sigh. If he closes his eyes, he can imagine he's back home, looking over the garden again. But he can't fool himself for long—he knows where he is. It reeks of disinfectant, and it's a degree below being warm enough. They've given him a thin polyester blanket, crackling with static electricity, and there's a blue foam mattress to lie on. The blanket is large enough to hide beneath from the camera in the corner. Holding up his beltless trousers, he walks over to the source of light, a square of translucent glass cubes, teasing him with shades of blue and green from a world outside.

This, again, is her fault. Every time he trusts her, she smacks him in the face with something. She has implicated them both now. So, now he can only wait for the wheels of justice to turn. There's a duty solicitor on the way, and Peter knows they have 24 hours to charge or release him. They'll have the computer soon, and they'll want the password. He'll put himself first from now on—no one else. Even that vicious tart, Martina, couldn't get it out of him. He'll tell the police anything they want to know.

'Listen up!' I say. Those not on calls begin to gather around. McCall stays at her desk while contacting the Neighbourhood sergeants to get some bodies together for a search team.

'We have arrested Peter Grant for perverting the course of justice and handling. During an initial voluntary interview, he told us he had visited Vanessa the night of Katherine Jacobs's murder. Vanessa asked him to look after a laptop computer she had stolen from Hudson Biotech. He is alleging it contained sensitive information that Katherine Jacobs wanted to use to blackmail Hudson. Peter Grant knew the laptop was stolen, and he swapped over the computer for an identical one in the boot of his car. It's enough for us to arrest him, and we'll do a Section 18 search of his home address and his car. This raises the question of why was the replacement laptop missing? It is unlikely Vanessa Grant would have taken it with her. Any questions?'

'I presume he's not telling us where Vanessa is?' asks Daley.

'Either that, or he doesn't know, Dan.'

'Shall we get a statement regarding the computer from Hudson?' says Cheung. 'Sam and I are going there.'

'Don't let them know anything yet. He may be lying about the computer being in the car, which is an idiotic place to keep computers. Not exactly data protection compliant. Once we have it, it's going to Digital Forensics. Hudson hasn't officially let us know a computer has been stolen. That information needs to come from them, otherwise, they'll know that Grant has been talking to us.'

'We're assuming Katherine is alive when he was there?' says Daley.

'He says he went there after 9 p.m., and he heard Katherine out in the garden with the dog. It's all too vague. So, we won't assume that just yet.' McCall is off the phone, and she gives me the nod. 'The car is in the multi-storey in Avenue de Chartres. So, I need someone to drive it back here for us to search. DS McCall is getting a search team together for Grant's house. Okay, over to you, Helen.'

'Jack, where are you?' says McCall. Lang was hiding behind Essam. 'Can you go over to meet with officers at Grant's address now. The lovely Swampy can wait.' She hands Lang a search form I've just signed and Grant's front door keys. Lang gets his coat on, and McCall drops Grant's car key into Essam's hand. 'It's on the top floor.'

It's a relief that something is moving at last—it will keep Walsh off my back. I'm watching McCall talking to a civilian investigator. I've never seen him before. He looks very much at home here, an older man with thinning silver hair, probably ex-job. McCall calls me over.

'Sir, this is Bob Lister. He's been digging around Christopher Dalton. Something interesting's come up.'

Lister looks up at me over the top of his glasses and then back at his notes. I'm getting a sense of shrewdness and wisdom from this man.

'Sir, I've been following the fall-out from Broyle Way and Parkes's arrest,' Lister says. 'A contact of mine told me Christopher Dalton was a member of the Summersdale Golf Club, Gold Membership no-less. He used to meet with a lot of his old cronies there, doing so-called business over lunch. I spoke to the club and to some of the staff there. Dalton is a close associate of Dean Dettori, the head of the European division of Hudson Biotech. Staff said that Dettori was frequently in meetings with Dalton. They played a lot of golf together.'

'Hudson is certainly in the middle of everything,' I say. 'Do we know if Dalton was offering Dettori any of his seedy hospitality services?'

'Possibly,' says Lister. 'Several local businessmen met with Dalton at the club. The chair of the Boldham Youth Carnival Committee was one of them. Officers caught him on their body-worn video outside Broyle Way when Helen raided it. He scarpered when he saw the police vans. The latest development is that Dalton has had a severe stroke, and he's currently in Saint Richard's Hospital. Another contact told me Dalton's very ill and isn't expected to recover. His wife, Julie, is at his side.

Dettori has visited him on two occasions, using his doctor's credentials.'

'You have a lot of contacts, Bob.'

'When you've been doing this as long as I have...' he says with a wink.

'Why haven't we met before?'

'I only work two days now. I've already done my thirty years, so this is my hobby. After I retired, I became a lay minister, but I still like to offer my time here to help. So, with that, looking after Mrs Lister and the garden, I'm a busy man.'

'Bob, that's really helpful. Keep on digging. Thank you.'

'And David Michael Angelis was pronounced dead at 12.37 p.m. on 11/12/2019,' says Martina. She looks up from the A4 sheet of paper and shakes her head. 'He was in a coma for five days, and then he just died.'

'Just died. So, how the fuck is Angelis walking around and breathing?' says Dettori. He leans back in his office chair and rubs his temples.

'The woman I spoke to said they took him down to the morgue. He was waiting there for over an hour. Then he just started breathing and moving—'

'You realise how absolutely ridiculous that is?'

Martina perches on his desk and stares out of the window at the fountain. She presses her calf inside his thigh.

'Perhaps the drug was still working somehow?' she says. 'Perhaps his heart had slowed down like he was in hibernation or something.'

'Is that your considered scientific opinion, Martina?'

Martina moves away. 'You tell me what happened then, Doctor Dick!' She doesn't enjoy being ridiculed.

'I'm sorry. You could be right. Angelis certainly couldn't have been dead, could he, and resurrection isn't on the list of known side effects. Who did you speak to at the hospital?'

Martina, a little less offended now, moves closer again to Dettori. 'A nurse called Jennifer Bailey, and a hospital porter called Korbi Watts. Bailey was there with another nurse when Angelis died. Bailey and Watts took Angelis down to the morgue.'

'Was there an investigation into this giant cockup?'

'The hospital was told to brush it under the carpet, and they took Angelis to Southampton hospital. No one told his parents their son had died. Angelis doesn't know either.'

'Hence why they shut us down so quickly, without an explanation. It's all very suspicious. It's like someone spirited him away.'

Dettori stands up and looks out of his window. He can see two women walking towards the reception together.

'Katherine was studying Angelis,' says Martina. 'Why? She had nothing more to do with the project. And Vanessa couldn't have told her about Angelis, as she knew nothing about him. There was nothing in Decker's files about Angelis being alive. Decker would have assumed he had died, too. How did Katherine find out Angelis was alive?'

Dettori looks at Martina, and his eyes light up. 'You are absolutely right! Vanessa couldn't have known anything about Angelis unless Katherine told her. So how did Katherine get involved in all this? There's another agency at work here. There has to be.'

'That's the point I'm making. I'll look into what Katherine was doing after she left here. Hopefully, I can trace some of her contacts.'

'Thank you, Martina. HR received Peter Grant's resignation letter today. Well done. I won't ask how you convinced him.

I appreciate your hard work. Drop by tonight. Mrs Dettori is staying with her mother. I have something for you.'

Martina pretends to smile sweetly at Dettori, and she leaves him in the office alone. Dettori can feel his stomach turning as he thinks about the control slipping away from him. Dalton's stroke is always in the back of his mind, but he had to get him out of the way.

But what if Andrew Hudson was right? What if this project is too dangerous? He's seen Nathan turn into a vicious monster over the last two years, and now Martina is losing that pleasant reserve she once had. He could leave right now, run back to the remnants of his family in Venice. He has more money than he needs. Forget about Oberon and Y9. Nathan would undoubtedly die, and Martina? He's guessing she would probably age prematurely and curse him for the rest of her short life. But the most important thing to him would be shattered too, and he couldn't bear to let that happen. Seeing his precious reputation destroyed would be the end of him.

11th December 2019

I'm looking out of the side room window, and I'm aware of the commotion behind me, but I don't want to watch. That's not me anymore. Nevertheless, I have a sense of calm. It's a relief to see and move again, but I don't recognise my body or this strange perspective. This side room overlooks a small garden, with a sculpture as its centrepiece. It's a bronze of a man sitting on a bench, and his hand is open in front of him. He's receiving an invisible gift in the palm of his hand from a female figure standing over him. I go outside to see them, and I'm standing over them. I can see the alloy in such detail: the traces of the sculptor's finger marks from the mould, the microscopic layering of copper and tin.

The surrounding grass is breathing, gases exchanging, sugars forming. I've never seen grass this way, and I can hear and feel it growing in the soil. I look over to the window of my room, and the doctors and nurses are still working on the man. But it's all in vain—it's over.

I seem to float away when the world folds up around me, and I'm now in another place. There's a dark, cyan sky, painted with stars in swirls of gold and silver. The turquoise sea laps the orange shoreline. Along the shore, I see shapes moving in the distance, gathering together.

Am I breathing? I just can't tell. But I'm not afraid. Not anymore.

'Hey, David,' says someone standing beside me. It's a creature that looks something like me but neither male nor female, powerful with shimmering pale skin and bright eyes.

'Hello,' I say. I want to laugh. The sound of my voice has changed. 'Where are we?'

'You're waiting, my friend,' the creature says. 'Everything will be clear soon.'

'Am I dead?'

'How can you be dead when you are talking to me?' The creature laughs. 'Please wait with me.'

As I wait, I crouch and pick up a handful of sand and watch the grains fall softly through my fingers, again and again. I love the soft texture, the sensation as it runs over my skin.

A woman is with us, and the creature bows gently towards her. Her face is fierce and beautiful, her skin is black, her hair intricately braided with colourful beads, and she wears a crown of delicate white blossom. She comes close to me, and I smell sweet perfume, like jasmine and orange, vanilla, and ginger. She takes my head in her hands and kisses my forehead.

'Hello, David,' says the woman. I feel like I know her. 'Welcome! Do you like this place?'

'Yes, it's amazing.'

'It is. But even this is not your new home,' she says. 'It's just a place you can enjoy while you wait.'

'Thank you. You know, I think I may be dead.' I laugh. 'It's all slipping away from me now.'

'You are not dead, lovely man. You cannot die!'

The woman and the other creature are laughing together. It's such a sweet musical sound.

'I don't understand. Everyone dies.'

'Not you, David Angelis! That's such a great name. Don't you remember the promise I made to you?'

'No. I don't know what you mean.'

'You will remember, David. One day, you will remember. I miss you so much. I enjoyed our talks together. We are friends.'

'Am I going somewhere from here?' I'm looking at the gathering in the distance. 'What are we doing now?'

'That is up to you,' the woman says. 'Choices, choices. I've got something for you.' She opens her hand, and I see a piece of fruit in her palm. 'You have a free choice. You can take this fruit or leave it. If you take it, you will go back to your life, but you will return with a gift to help others, especially that wonderful boy of ours. We love him so much. If you choose to leave the fruit, then you will go home with me now, as I once promised you.'

I look at the fruit in her hand. It's red, like an apple, succulent and sweetly fragranced. 'It's so beautiful here, and you're beautiful, too.'

'You think this place is beautiful! Just wait until you see your home, David! Ha! And this,' she looks over her body, 'this is just a simple veil I wear. But when you come home, you'll see me face to face! Oh yes! That will be a good day!' She does this little dance, moving her arms and hips. 'Our friendship will be complete.' She laughs again, an infectious joy that causes the stars above us to dance and swirl in different directions.

'I want to go home with you. There's nothing like this on Earth.'

'Our Earth is just a taste of things to come, David. Another veil over the reality to come.'

'If I go back, you said I can help people?'

'Yes, and you'll have the chance to mend a few things that are broken, too. What do you want to do, David, my lovely friend?'

'If I take this fruit, will I see you again?'

'Yes, you will see me again soon, I promise. Since you love this place so much, you can come back here whenever you wish.'

'If you take the fruit,' says the creature, 'then you will see as we see. But be wise and look to love, heal and mend.'

'This is a hard choice, but for the sake of those I love, I choose to take the fruit, to love, heal and mend the things that are broken.'

'Then let it be,' says the woman as she blows me a kiss.

My eyes are open, but I cannot see. I'm scared. I have this overwhelming feeling of loss and homesickness. I feel a cloth over my face, and I'm cold. I try to speak, but my mouth doesn't move. After a few moments, my body shakes, and the fabric slides off me.

'Oh my God! What is that!' comes a voice in the distance. 'Help, we need help in here!'

TWELVE

Sam Gregory and Po Cheung follow a stick of a woman through the reception doors. It's their favourite receptionist returning from lunch. Gregory goes back outside for a few moments and returns.

'We'd like to speak with Doctor Dean Dettori, please,' says Cheung in her most polite voice.

'Ah, hello again,' says the receptionist. 'Is there any point in asking if you've made an appointment?'

'Yes, we have,' says Gregory. The receptionist still shakes her head.

'Take a seat,' the woman says.

'Supercilious cow,' Gregory mutters under her breath while doing a PNC vehicle check on her police mobile. Then she smiles to herself.

'What is it?' whispers Cheung.

Gregory walks up to the reception desk. The woman does everything she can to ignore her until Gregory coughs loudly at her.

'Yes,' she says with a sickly smile.

'I saw you coming out of the driver's seat of a vehicle in the car park,' says Gregory. 'The white BMW.'

'What has that got to do with you?'

Gregory holds up her warrant card. 'I've already told you, I'm a police officer. Your front offside tyre is bald, and your MOT was due a month ago. Three points on your licence for the tyre, and I can report you for having no MOT. It's probably worth an insurance check to see if you're still covered with no MOT. I could get a traffic officer down here—what do you think?'

'I didn't know.' The receptionist's cool composure is slipping. 'I just don't get the time. If you were in my shoes—'

'Just get it sorted, Mrs Harriet Unwin. And while you're at it, get that pickle out of your arse and be nice, eh?'

Gregory makes her way back to Cheung, looking self-satisfied. She's just about to sit down when Dean Dettori appears.

'Police,' Dettori says, putting his hands up in the same way Gregory's dad used to. 'You've got me. Take me away... Officers, follow me.'

Gregory and Cheung smile to humour him and follow him up two flights of stairs that lead to his office. Dettori does his best to cut an impressive figure with Gregory. Not only has he got the Italian good looks, but he's also blatantly wealthy and intelligent with it. Gregory glances over at Cheung, who isn't giving away anything.

'So, you made it past the company rottweiler,' says Dettori, and Gregory laughs. 'How can I help you today, officers?'

'Doctor Dettori,' says Gregory, 'thank you for taking the time to see us today.'

'Call me Dean. It's the least I can do to help.'

'So, you know we are investigating the murder of a former employee of Hudson Biotech, Doctor Katherine Jacobs.'

'Yes, I saw it on the news—so awful! Kate was really lovely.

A much-respected member of our team here. I just don't know how anyone could do that to her.'

'Everyone we've met here says she was lovely,' says Cheung. 'Do you know of anyone she didn't get on with so well?'

'No, not at all. We were all sad to see Kate leave Hudson.' Dettori's leaning back in his leather chair, hands on the back of his head. Gregory can see that his self-confidence is putting Cheung on edge.

'What were the reasons she gave you for leaving?' says Cheung.

'You know, I can't remember that far back. Something personal, I think. You'll have to check with HR.'

'We did, and they told us you hadn't uploaded her leaving letter.'

'Bloody computers. My dear Nonnina is more tech-savvy than I am, and she's 87. I'm a medical man. Computers are just a means to an end.'

'I understand Hudson is a biomedical research company,' says Gregory. 'Can you tell me more about what you do in the UK?'

'Yes, of course. Here in the UK, our focus is on researching drugs to treat Alzheimer's and other progressive neurological disorders. Some of it is hush-hush, as you Brits say. Our state-of-the-art laboratories make us world leaders in this research.'

'And this is the research Doctor Jacobs was involved with when she worked with you?'

'Yes.'

Cheung continues. 'A short time before Doctor Jacobs left Hudson, there were two deaths of employees on her team. They are seemingly unrelated, but it now looks rather suspicious, considering all three deaths were within two years of each other. Tell me what you think about that, Doctor Dettori?'

'You're absolutely right. Statistically, it looks suspicious. The girl who killed herself on the road, what was her name?'

'Amanda Wilson.'

'Ah yes. Amanda's suicide. Colin and Kate were murdered. Kate left a long time ago. Colin had a history of winding people up the wrong way, and Amanda... well, her mental health wasn't good, as far as I remember. She left a suicide note, I believe. So, I see it all as unconnected and purely coincidental.'

'Was there something that Doctor Jacobs was working on that would have put her in danger?'

Dettori looks up to the ceiling as if trying to remember. Gregory notices a slight change in his expression. 'While she was here, do you mean? She was the lead for one of those hush-hush research projects I was telling you about. We don't make chemical weapons if that's what you're worried about. It's important research that benefits humankind.' Dettori makes an unmistakable look at his Rolex. Time to go.

'Just one more thing, Dean,' says Gregory. 'Vanessa Grant. What can you tell me about her?'

'Oh her! Hitler's daughter, we called her. She and the rottweiler got on well. She left the company a few months ago after she walked out on her husband. I guess she didn't want to meet him here every day—guilty conscience, I suppose. She was a nasty piece of work, though. I wouldn't want to meet her in a dark alley.'

'Were you aware of her romantic relationship with Doctor Jacobs?'

'Ha! Really? Girl-on-girl sort of thing?'

Sam Gregory tenses. 'If you mean they were lovers, yes.'

'Never knew that. Well, wonders never cease, do they!'

'Was Vanessa in any kind of trouble when she left Hudson?' says Cheung.

'Trouble? What kind of trouble?'

'It's just a routine question, Doctor Dettori,' Cheung says. 'Did she leave on good terms?'

Dettori is drumming his fingers on his desk and looks at his watch again.

'Good enough, yes. It was her choice to leave.'

Gregory looks at Cheung, who nods.

'Thank you for your time, Doctor Dettori. We'll likely have more questions another time.'

Dettori nods and then leans forward in his chair.

'Your Inspector Angelis. It would be good to meet him personally,' he says. 'Tell him I'll happily do a tour around the place for him. Tell him he can just drop by.'

'Do you know each other?' asks Cheung.

'No, not at all. I saw him on the TV news. I'm just happy to help any way I can.'

As they walk to their car, Cheung turns to look at the water fountain and the grounds. She shudders.

'Nice place to work, but he gives me the creeps!' Cheung says.

'He's so smarmy,' says Gregory. 'All those good looks wasted because he's a prick.'

'What's all that about Angelis? It sounded bizarre.'

'He's trying to be all buddy-buddy. People like that are usually as guilty as hell.'

Lang is calling me. It's been two hours since he left to join the search of Peter Grant's house.

'Sir,' he says. 'We've found something.'

'Go on.'

'In Grant's laundry bin, there's a heavily bloodstained tea towel.'

'Describe it.'

'Green and white squares.'

'Gingham?'

'Er, yes. That's it. Oh, shit!' Lang goes quiet for a moment. 'It's got a clump of red hair in it—it stinks! I feel sick.'

'Bag it up, quickly! Then you can throw up. Well done, Jack.'

He ends the call.

McCall is standing at my door with a what-was-that face.

'Lang's found a blood-soaked tea towel in Grant's laundry bin. It's got red hair on it. I think it's one of a set I bought Kate for Christmas.'

'Shit!' says McCall.

'I know. I wonder how Grant will try to account for it?'

Essam is standing behind McCall now, waiting. I sense he's a little nervous about me. I try a friendly smile, but it seems to make it worse.

'Excuse me, Sarge,' he says to McCall. 'We have recovered three laptops from Grant's car. Two with chargers in bags and one just floating around in the boot.'

'Great,' says McCall. 'We'll get them sent off to Digital Forensics. My money is on the one without a bag.'

Essam is still there. He's looking sheepish.

'Is there something else, Muhammad?' I ask.

'I'm not sure if I should have done this or not...' he says to McCall.

'Okay?' McCall pulls a face.

'There was a satnav in the car. It's the same as mine. I looked at the history, and it's got Peter Grant making a journey to 24 Alcott Gardens from his house on the night of the murder.

It records he arrives at 9.03 p.m. I took a photo of the screen.' He shows it to McCall and me. It looks like that's the last time he's used the satnav.

'So that supports he intended to go to see Vanessa,' says McCall.

'And... There's a dashcam in his car. I've copied off the files on the memory card. Three of the files show the journey to Alcott Gardens. Then, it shows him leaving... It's on my computer if you want to see it.'

We walk over to Essam's desk, and there is a video still on the screen. I'm standing close to McCall, and my hand brushes against her waist as we move to get a clearer view of his screen. The still is of Kate's front door, illuminated by the headlights of Peter Grant's car. Vanessa is at the door, seeing him off. The timestamp says 9.27 p.m.

Essam presses play. We see the car reverse, and Vanessa lifts a hand to wave him off. Max, the cocker spaniel, appears at the door, and there behind Vanessa is Kate.

McCall and I are stumped, and we watch the last video once more.

'There are other videos, numbered sequentially,' says Essam. 'Each one has a date, too. After the journey back from Alcott Gardens, Peter Grant goes home. The next file in the sequence is the next day, where Grant goes to Hudson Biotech in the morning. There aren't any missing files. Grant has the technical know-how to change the names and dates on the file-names, but there's also a timestamp on the video, which is much harder to change and easier to spot if he tampered with it. Digital Forensics can confirm this.'

'Well done, Muhammad,' says McCall. 'But what about the bloody tea towel? Why is it in his laundry bin? Did he return to Alcott Gardens later and kill her? Perhaps by taxi, or someone else took him?'

This isn't right. It can't be that complicated. Has Peter Grant really created an elaborate alibi by using his dashcam?

'Helen,' I say. 'We'll further arrest Grant on suspicion of murder and get him to account for the tea towel. He'll have a solicitor by now too, but we won't disclose the dashcam footage.'

'Yes, boss,' says McCall, but her face looks doubtful.

'I agree. It makes little sense. So, Grant went home and ordered his little oven light from Amazon. I want to get in there with him again. I'll question him about the tea towel. It's just too convenient we found it. If it was me, I wouldn't leave it in a laundry bin with the rest of my washing. Gross! It feels like someone has planted it there.'

'I'm writing up my handover for James, who's back in tomorrow. I'll see if Bob's free to help you if you're happy with that?'

I agree.

I'm preparing for Grant's second interview, and Sam Gregory appears at my door. She can see that I'm up to my eyeballs.

'Sorry, sir. I forgot to say. Dean Dettori sends you an open invite for a guided tour of Hudson. It was a bit menacing, in a Bond-villain sort of way, but I said I would pass it on. You just need to turn up.'

I laugh. 'I may well take him up on that. Thank you, Sam.'

Priory Park is busy this afternoon with after-school mums and their children. The sunlight carries a little warmth today, and it is cheering them all. Karen watches Josh as he sits in the sand near the swings. He's on his own and happily playing in the sand. Josh is clearly enjoying the feeling as the sand trickles over the skin between his fingers. He's tilting his head, watching the falling grains closely as they fall to the ground, and then he repeats the process again and again.

Karen is thinking about the phone call she had an hour ago with Bella Brookes. Bella told Karen about the text from David, his expression of wanting to change. As much as Karen wants to believe it, she can't. She knows him too well. Yes, he has changed since he came out of the hospital, but he is the proverbial leopard. His spots are immutable.

But then there is Josh. He talks about his dad all the time, and he's obsessed with the police, too. Ian says Josh needs his dad. Ian is the polar opposite of David. He'll always put others first.

Josh looks up. It's almost as if he knows she's thinking about him. Karen smiles.

'Are you having fun there, Josh? Don't you want to go on the swing?' She already knows what his answer will be.

'Nah, thanks, mum,' says Josh. 'Go home now?'

Karen closes her hand and makes it nod up and down.

'Yes, Josh. Ian is making tea tonight!' She is signing to him.

'Oh, no,' says Josh, but he's joking.

I'm back in the interview room after further arresting Grant on suspicion of murder. Bob Lister, my intriguing new discovery, is sitting with me. We are waiting for Grant and his solicitor to be brought in, and Lister is exuding calm and professionalism while he's digesting the key points so far.

Bob has a certain grandfather quality about him. My grandfather was a rogue, according to my mother. He left my grandmother with two children and went off with his agent. He was an actor I've never heard of.

Bob has a silver fish emblem on his jacket lapel. I remember those when I was a teenager at school. The girls of the Christian Union had them on their blazers. They didn't care about the ridicule. I realise my mind is wandering—I'm tired.

'Where did you work before coming here, Bob?' I ask.

'I was in the Met,' Lister replies as he reads the notes. 'I was a DI and then a DCI of a major investigations team for twenty years.'

All I can do is nod—impressive. I was twelve years old then, and two when he joined up.

The door opens, and the custody staff brings in Grant and the duty solicitor. The solicitor is Lorraine Lane-Lewis. A jolly, forty-something woman with long black hair and lots of make-up. I've had dealings with Lorraine before. She's firm but fair, not anti-police, and good at her job. She's had an hour with Grant, and I've disclosed the tea towel found in Grant's dirty laundry.

I start the recording and go through the preliminaries. Grant rests his head on the table as if he doesn't care anymore. He is now looking dishevelled.

'Peter,' I say. 'About 90 minutes ago, I further arrested you on suspicion of murder. During a search of your home, officers found a heavily bloodstained tea towel containing a large amount of hair and scalp tissue. The tea towel is one I recognise as one of three from Katherine Jacobs's kitchen. It's identical. I strongly suspect, Peter, that the blood, skin, and hair are from Katherine Jacobs. Please look at the photograph my colleague will put in front of you. It's labelled as exhibit JL/02 and is a photograph of the blooded tea-towel.'

Lister slides the photograph in front of Grant, but he's ignoring it. 'Come on, son. Sit up and look at it!' Lister's not taking any nonsense from Grant. It does the job.

'Remember, Peter,' says Lane-Lewis, 'you don't have to answer any of the questions.'

'That would be very unwise, Peter,' says Lister. 'We need an explanation of how that blooded tea towel came to be in your laundry bin. It's an incriminating object, don't you think, Peter? Has your solicitor explained what adverse inference means? What a jury may infer if you remain silent? Has your solicitor prepared a statement for you?'

'As you know,' says Lane-Lewis, 'my client does not have to—'

'She put it there,' says Grant. He holds up his hand to stop Lane-Lewis. 'It's probably why she came round.'

'Vanessa, your wife?' says Lister.

'No! Martina Hayes.' Grant can't look anyone in the eye. 'I thought she wanted sex, but she was just teasing me. She... She hurt me.' Tears are falling from his cheeks, and he wipes them away with his sleeve.

'Is that how you got the bruising around your neck?' I ask.

'And the rest.' Grant lifts his shirt, and he's black and blue. He stands up and turns around. Deep red gouges are going down his back. 'She walked over me, literally, and ran her nails down me. I made the mistake of saying Vanessa had stolen Decker's computer. I couldn't have known that it was Decker's, you see. Not unless I had gone to see Vanessa that night. Martina beat me until I could hardly breathe. She's so strong—I couldn't stop her.'

'When was this?' I say.

'Two days ago. Monday evening, sometime after 7 p.m.

'She must have put the towel in the laundry basket while I was unconscious. She planted it, and I think there's proof.'

Lister looks at me and shrugs. I'm focusing on Grant now. The room goes dark around me, and it's as if Grant is sitting under a spotlight on a stage. From the shadows comes a woman,

Grant's memory of Martina. She's wearing a red dress and has long talons for fingers. Her face has large, bulbous black eyes and bright red lips. She looks at me, and I see blood dripping from her mouth. She suddenly sees Lister and recoils back into the shadows.

Lister is looking at me, wondering why I'm not speaking. The vision has gone.

'Why didn't you come to us sooner?' I say. 'I'd like to get your injuries photographed.'

'I was ashamed, that's why!' Grant is falling apart in front of us. 'I'm so stupid. I didn't see it before.'

'What is the proof you have, Peter?' says Lister.

'The red bag. The towel must have been in her red bag. You see, I installed a video doorbell after Vanessa delivered her letter. I wanted evidence if she came again. But it must have recorded Martina arriving and when she left. It shows her going across the road and dumping her bag in the skip over the road. I was wondering why she did that. It must be because—'

'DNA traces left from the tea towel,' says Lane-Lewis.

'Thanks, Lorraine,' I say. 'I've worked that out.'

'Then I suggest you get your officers down there and retrieve it as soon as possible, Inspector,' she says. 'It will add to the proof that my client is innocent and has been framed. I mean... would you put a blood-soaked tea towel in with your laundry? Come on!'

'I'll send someone down there.' I'm failing to disguise my dislike of being told how to suck eggs.

'I can access the video footage from my phone and show you,' says Grant. 'It's on an app.'

We suspend the interview there while Bob goes back to get Grant's phone out of Custody. While we are waiting, I'm seeing Grant deteriorating before my eyes. He's a broken man.

'Do you need a drink, a comfort break?' I say to him.

Grant shakes his head. I can't help but feel sympathy for him.

'What's going to happen?' he asks.

'I want to look at this video footage with you and Ms Lane-Lewis. Then I will talk to the Crown Prosecution Service. I can't talk about it any further until we are recording again, Peter. But I will see you are treated fairly. I promise you that.'

Bob returns, and we resume the interview. Grant shows Bob how to use the doorbell app. Within a few moments, we crowd around the small phone screen in Lister's hands. We are watching Martina Hayes leaving Grant's home, walking over to the house opposite and placing a shoulder bag into the skip containing the remains of an old kitchen. The image is in shades of grey, being in night-vision mode, but you can clearly see her covering a bag with broken pieces of kitchen cupboards and plasterboard.

'Peter,' I say, 'after viewing this, I'm going to release you pending further enquiries. There's more for us to do.'

'Quite right, Inspector,' Lane-Lewis chips in, with just enough of a gloat for me to see.

Bob and I are heading back to the office. I sense Bob has something on his mind—a question is hanging over him.

'He was well and truly stitched up,' says Bob.

'Trying to keep it all secret didn't help him,' I say. 'Didn't his mother tell him that honesty is the best policy?'

'Psalm 139 verse 2.' Bob winks at me.

'And that is?'

'You discern my thoughts from a distance, to paraphrase.' Bob stops and looks me in the eye. 'That's like you, isn't it.'

Bob smiles and walks away.

Essam walks back into the office with me. He and Lang have just interviewed Graham Thomas, alias Swampy, and he's looking serious. Essam always looks serious.

'Muhammad, how did it go? Anything?' I say.

'No, boss,' Essam says. 'He has a verifiable alibi for the night Katherine Jacobs was murdered—he was working in the pub. The possession of a knife charge won't stick, as he claims he was just using it to gut rabbits in the kitchen. He took it outside by accident. Assaulting DS McCall was more promising, but the CPS don't think there's enough there to take it forward.' Essam drops into his chair, looking exhausted. 'He kept going on about bloody Furzzle. I thought, who the fuck is Furzzle? It's his dog. He was more worried about his bloody dog. What is it with people and dogs?'

'Time to go home, Muhammad.' I pat him on the shoulder, and he nearly smiles.

The office is clearing, and a reduced late shift is slowly taking over the computer terminals. The light is fading, and we're beginning to see our own reflections in the tinted windows. McCall has logged out of her computer and joins me, standing close to me as I stare out of the glass, looking at the top of the cathedral spire lit by blue floodlights.

'We still haven't found Vanessa or any more witnesses,' I say to McCall. 'And now I'm just plain confused by it all.'

'I know what you mean,' she says. 'There are officers in Norwich Street recovering the bag from the skip. James can look into that tomorrow.'

'This Martina Hayes is certainly pushing her way into the frame. I feel bad leaving James to handle all this on his own.'

'He's more than capable, sir. We were coping before you arrived.'

Ouch. I felt that. McCall blushes.

'I'm hoping we'll get the forensics back from the knife soon,' I say, and McCall nods and stares into the distance. She looks pale and preoccupied. 'Are you okay, Helen?'

McCall looks at me in the eyes. She's trying to say something but keeps bottling it. 'Sorry, I didn't mean... I'm just tired. I'm looking forward to rest days.'

'That's okay. But there's something else.' I know I shouldn't pry, but I will. As I turn towards her, my shoulder brushes gently against hers. 'Is there anything that—'

'Don't, sir. Please... I love my job here. And I promised myself, never again.' She holds my gaze for a few more moments. 'Have a good break. You deserve it.' McCall puts on her coat and walks out of the building.

I'm at home, the TV is on, and my curry order has arrived. The cold beer is officially open as rest days begin. It's then I realise, as I'm looking around me, I have only one friend outside of the job. I must call Terry—why haven't I called him? What's wrong with me? This isn't a pity party. I know I keep everyone away, and that started shortly after I married Karen. I didn't want friends—I just wanted Karen. I didn't want her to have friends, either. I did everything in my power to stop that. All she needed was me, just me. And then Josh arrived: the competition; a baby with a disability that needed extra attention, which should have been mine. My monster became fully formed then, and I paid the price for it. I lost them both before I could harm them any further. So, I choose to be alone in case that monster returns. That is why I turn away from friendship even when it's offered to me on a plate. That's why it took so long to trust Kate. Shit, that's a bad example of a friend.

But today, with Helen, I just wanted that chance to be a good man once again. Perhaps she can see that monster with her own sixth sense and is keeping well away. I don't know. But I have screwed up with her.

Another beer would be good right now. To drown out the voices, the visions, the guilt, and the loneliness.

Christmas Day, 2019

The carols have finished; it's not long after midnight on Christmas Day. The old mission church was heaving twenty minutes ago, but now it's just Mr and Mrs King in the office, counting the offering, and Michael Angelis is on his own, his head bowed and shaking with tears. His son is still with them by God's grace, but his life hangs by a thread. No one can see Michael as he sits in the shadows. The lights are dimmed, the bells no longer ring. It's just Michael alone with God.

'My boy, my boy!' he says. His voice choking on his tears. 'Oh God, what would you do if your son was dying? God help my boy. Don't take him away.'

He can see David's face, ten years old, peering over the top of the steering wheel. 'Which one do I press, Dad?'

'The middle one, son! No, the middle one!'

David wanted to be a police officer since he was 12. David and Michael used to watch *The Bill, A Touch of Frost,* and *Inspector Morse*. They fired David up; he wanted to save the world. When he finally joined, Michael lost him to the job. They hardly saw him; he was always busy, constantly tired.

Michael sighs and pulls out a handkerchief. He hears Mrs King laughing in the office—they're packing up for the night. He ought to go home. Sylvia will be on her own and worrying. Michael stands and waits for the blood rush to calm down. He puts on his trilby and turns up the collar on his overcoat. He looks one last time at the wooden cross on the platform.

Michael is surprised to see a woman sitting behind him. She's black, with braided hair and has her eyes closed. She opens her eyes and looks up at Michael, and smiles. She has kind eyes and a warm smile.

'Happy Christmas, Mr Angelis,' she says to him.

Michael doesn't know her—he's a little puzzled. 'Happy Christmas to you.'

The woman holds out her hand to him, and Michael takes it. It's tender and comforting.

'He's in God's hands, Mr Angelis. Safe and sound, and dearly loved. God has a purpose for him. Be patient. All is well.'

'Thank you, sister.' He knows she means well, but how can she be so sure? He feels a warmth come over him, and his spirits are lifted. 'Perhaps, you're right.'

The woman digs around in her bag, pulls out a red apple, and offers it to Michael.

'For your journey home, Michael Angelis. Happy Christmas to Sylvia too.'

He takes the apple and polishes it. Nodding, he tips his hat in thanks and walks home to Sylvia.

THIRTEEN

3rd March 2022

A rest day for Helen McCall, and she sits in the Cathedral Cloisters on one of the stone benches beneath the arched window traceries. It's chilly but bright, and the stone is draining the heat from her bum through her jeans.

Helen is in a reflective mood this morning. She can sense something of the cathedral's reverence seeping out into the cloisters to where she is sitting. She's only stopped there for a minute. She's mentally and physically exhausted, and her tummy is cramping. Helen is watching the couples, the families, students, and tourists coming in and out of the café or turning left towards the Bishop's Palace Gardens. At this very moment, though, she's missing her parents. They would love to have gone for a coffee or walked around the gardens with her. A sigh escapes as she wonders if she only ever speaks to them when she wants something.

She had little sleep the night before, which isn't helping her think things through. She's also started her period, which isn't helping either. David Angelis is the subject that banged on and on in her head throughout the night. What has he done to her? She vowed to herself there would never be another Stephen in her life. It was a work romance that went to a marriage proposal, that went to two years of being deluded enough to believe Stephen was one of the faithful ones. He hit her, but she was the one who had to move away to a different town, losing the house, moving back to her parents, and now she is in the beautiful Bognor Regis. David is an inspector, too. What are the odds? Never again—she shudders.

What is he, anyway? All this mind-reading mumbo jumbo. All her years of cynicism and unbelief of anything supernatural cast long shadows of doubt. There must be another explanation for the things she has witnessed him doing. Otherwise, the world as she knows it would be upside down.

Somewhere a child is crying, and it brings her back from her thoughts. Helen picks up her bag and walks through the cloisters and outside towards the entrance of the cathedral. She stops in front of the large, smoked glass doors and wants to go in. She thinks there may be something inside to help her, but she can't bring herself to go in, in case there is something in there that actually can.

Her phone pings with a message from James Harris: *Do you think the boss would mind me calling him when he's off?*

No, he'll be fine, she replies. And I don't mind either, she thinks to herself.

This job just invades everything, every day—there's no letup.

'Shit!' she says under her breath, just as a woman goes in through the cathedral doors. Helen can't go in there now.

She needs to move. She walks past the Bell Tower and then sluggishly up the steps towards a busy West Street. Helen pauses. Every fibre in her just wants to go home and curl up in bed, but she wants to think this through. She'll just sleep if she goes home.

Helen meanders east towards the Market Cross. The sunlight reflects brightly on its Caen stone arches, forming the famous octagonal shape with the four distinctive clocks.

Her legs feel heavy and tired, and she needs to rest again. At the Cross, Helen sits inside an arch, upon another cold stone seat. From within the arches, she can see the shoppers in North, East and South streets. They look like they're moving in a dream, drifting along the pedestrianised roads without a purpose that Helen can make out. The city is nowhere near as busy as it was when she was a child. The stores failing after Covid removed several of the big names. There are some signs of renewal now, but it's going to be gradual. Helen still thinks the place went downhill after Woolworths closed. She laughs to herself at that thought as she realises how old she's getting.

Then she sees Angelis. Her stomach turns. Yes, it is him. He's walking away from her with someone. They walk along East Street together, him and another woman. Is she younger than him? She's tall and slim, with long red hair. Maybe he prefers red hair. Kate had red hair. She can't hold back the wave of gut-wrenching sadness that overpowers her.

'Yes, of course. I'm so stupid,' she whispers to herself. What else did she expect?

Nathan Wheelhouse is really pissed off and maybe out of a job, so he's seeking comfort. He parked in the bus bay alongside Avenue de Chartres and is now watching the college girls go by. He wants to take one of them. Any of them would do, preferably tall and skinny. It's a fantasy he has; he's never acted on it so far. It would take a bit of planning, not a rush job. There's still a part of the old Nathan that would stop him. It hates what he's become, but the old Nathan is dying. It's being starved to death, getting weaker every day. Any day now it will die completely.

He has an idea. The fun he has in his lockup can wait a little longer—she's not going anywhere. He starts the van and heads north out of Chichester towards Midhurst. Once he gets a few miles north of Singleton, he takes a right up a steep slope until he gets to some iron gates. They open once he enters the door code.

Julie Dalton has a whiskey glass in her hand when Nathan walks in. She's still in her dressing gown and looks at him through a veil of the constant stream of alcohol.

'What am I going to do, Nate?' she says. 'How am I going to run this place? It's all that doctor's fault. I should sue him, call the police!'

'Don't talk like that, Julie!' says Nathan. 'Christopher knew exactly what the risks were. It's no one's fault. Don't call the police. That would open a big can of worms. You'll lose this place for sure.'

'How? It's mine now Christopher's gone.'

'They'll look into his finances, Julie! You know, as well as I do, not everything he did was legit. In fact, you don't know half of it.'

'Really?' Her voice is more of a whimper now. 'I just wish he didn't get that jab.'

'Doctor Dettori said the stroke was probably coming, anyway. It was just a coincidence. You'll be fine, Julie. I'm sure he's left everything to you. You don't have to get involved with any of his business dealings. It's time to look after yourself. It's what he would have wanted. I can take over the complicated stuff. You don't have to worry about anything if you sign it over to me.'

'I don't know about that. I'll have to think about it. I'm actually quite switched on to the finances, Nate. I know a lot more than people give me credit for.'

'Good for you, Julie.'

'Yes, good for me, eh? I'm 43 years old, Nate. Who would want me now? I don't want to be on my own. I've never been on my own.'

Nate walks over to her and takes the whiskey glass out of her hand. 'You won't be alone, Julie. You've still got your friends. You've still got me.'

She's aware of how close he's standing. He's looking over her body.

'No, Nate. I won't. Christopher isn't even cold yet.'

'Sorry, Julie. I thought that's what you always wanted.' He turns away and walks towards the door.

'It's okay,' she says. 'I'm just all over the place. I don't know anymore, and it's—'

Nathan quickly steps back. He grips her hands and effortlessly pulls them both behind her back. He's so strong, she can't stop him as he takes her to the floor. She can smell his sweat, which drips from his neck onto her face as he climbs on top of her, and not even her screaming takes away the terrible pain as he enters her.

Karen has chosen this place. She feels safe here, and it's in public just in case I kick off about something. I don't blame her at all. I order Karen a coffee from the counter.

'You always did like this place,' I say.

'I can't be long, David,' says Karen, refusing to be drawn

into reminiscing. 'Bella recommended limiting this to 15 minutes. Just to let you know, the first sign of any argument from you, then I'm leaving.' Karen is calm and direct. She looks incredible, and that hurts.

'That's clear. I'll get straight to it then.' I swallow hard. I've rehearsed this, but I'll say it as it is. It's time for honesty. 'I'm an arsehole, Karen. I have only just realised it. I know you've told me countless times, but now I'm calling myself an arsehole. I've been a total shit over the years, and I'm sorry. I really am sorry.'

'Yes, you have been. And now you want me to forgive you and let you see Josh. Is that how this works?'

'No.' And this part burns. It breaks my heart in two. 'Take your time on that. I miss Josh like crazy, but I've been a crap father and a crap husband. I tried to control you—I'm sorry—I see it now. Yes, I really want to see Josh. But not right now. No, take your time. When you're ready.'

Her jaw drops. I stand to go.

'What! Is that it?'

'Yes, I mean it. I'm glad you are happy now. I really, really am. You've found someone who treats you as you deserve. And you look great on it. I lost you because I'm stupid... No, take your time. I need to earn that trust—I get it now.'

As I walk away, I'm fighting back the tears, and I won't let them come until I'm sitting in my car, and I drive away.

'Sarge, we've got results back for the knife,' says Daley from his desk, chewing a chocolate bar.

'One moment, I'll come over,' says James Harris. He finishes typing a sentence and gets up with some effort. Everyone has noticed how tired he looks. He's lost his usual sparkle, and there's a constant frown line scaring his face. People are treating him carefully and keeping their distance.

'They've confirmed fingerprints from the knife handle match Vanessa Grant's,' says Daley, reading the email. 'There's DNA from material caught in the serrations with a conclusive match for Doctor Katherine Jacobs. There's some trace DNA of Grant, too, from the handle. Not a lot, but enough to identify her. We've got her then, Sarge.'

'It certainly looks that way. Martina Hayes's bag will be interesting if we can get that back quickly. There was definitely some red staining in there. I'll let the boss know about the results.' He moves to the front of the whiteboard and draws a thick red circle around Vanessa's photo on the whiteboard. Martina Hayes's driving licence photo has also appeared on the board.

'Listen up!' he shouts, and the Op Greenwood detectives quickly gather around him. 'Vanessa Grant is now our prime murder suspect. The hunting knife found is our murder weapon, with Doctor Jacobs's DNA found on the blade's cutting edge. Vanessa Grant's fingerprints are on the handle and some trace DNA. We must now concentrate our efforts on finding Vanessa Grant. Martina Hayes's involvement is still uncertain. I'll get some publicity organised for social media regarding Grant, and we'll need to chase up the CCTV of Fishbourne and Chichester railway stations to see if she left by train. Po, call around the taxi firms and ask if any of them picked up Grant that night. Dan, you and I will recheck Peter Grant's dashcam video and see who he passes near Alcott Gardens.'

I'm not sure why I am here again, but I'm walking through the copse once more, and I find Joyce Mayhew's seat. Apart from the occasional rasping call of a rook, it's quiet. I feel like I've just given up everything I care about. I'm rereading the small plaque. *Prayed here daily*, it says. I wonder where that got her. I used to pray when I was a teenager. My parents said it was just a phase I was going through, but I fancied this girl in the Christian Union, the ones with the silver fishes. Her name was Alison McCarthy. I was 16 and about to take GCSEs. I couldn't have picked a worse time to put my heart on a sleeve. I went along to the Christian Union meetings just to be with her. They were very excited to have a heathen in their midst. I fought them over evolution, other religions, world suffering—everything, but Alison was just kind and patient. She invited me to church, and I began to pray. I even *became a Christian*, whatever that meant. We went out together for three years. Her family didn't approve of me or my background. Eventually, they won. They stopped her from seeing me when she went to university.

I heard Alison died of cancer last month, and I still wonder why that could ever happen to such a lovely girl as her. Someone told me that God wanted her more. I don't think her children agreed with that.

Now I see Joyce Mayhew again. She appears in the layers of time, and there are many versions of her here. It looks like she really did pray here every day. I focus on a younger Joyce. She looks a little like Alison McCarthy did back then, even down to the slight crook in her nose. I'm watching thousands of Joyce's now, praying. It's bringing back a memory, a feeling I once had. There's that smell of jasmine again, citrus fruits. The memory passes. Then there's a moment where I swear Joyce is looking at me. She has in her hand a red apple, and she offers it to me.

My mobile rings. The vision passes. It's James Harris, and he tells me about the forensic results on the knife.

'It all happens on rest days,' I say to Harris on the phone.

'That's an excellent result. Now we just need to find Vanessa Grant. I assume you've got the taxi pick up angle sorted?'

'Yes, boss. Po is ringing through a list as we speak. Then we'll check the railway station CCTV.'

'Of course. Sorry, James. I know you're more than capable.'

'I've been missing things recently. I nearly forgot—Christopher Dalton died last night in hospital. They're saying it was another stroke.'

'That's a shame. I was looking forward to locking him up.'

'I thought you'd like to know.'

'That's not a problem. I appreciate it.'

When the call ends, I'm on my own again. I'm thinking about Josh, Karen's new life, and then I'm thinking about Helen. How did I mess that up so badly? I must have totally misread it.

It's time to go back to my house, which I have been trying to avoid. I think I may have to move somewhere else. There are too many ghosts there.

3rd March 2022

McCall is standing at the door after ringing the bell. The dog is barking. She's guessing her parents are in the garden, as they're taking so long to answer. She leaves the door and heads to the side gate. She never goes in this way. It's always been through the front. Why doesn't she go in this way? She's not just a visitor —she's their daughter.

McCall closes the gate behind her, and an over-exuberant

spaniel greets her. He's jumping and licking her, squealing with excitement. Helen walks down the path, and there, in the greenhouse, she can see her parents potting up plants. Tears are falling down her cheeks, and she's frozen to the spot. Her mother looks up to see what Max is so excited about, and when she sees Helen there, her face breaks into a wide smile. She takes off her gloves and walks towards her.

'Helen is here!' she says. 'Darling, Helen is here—look.'

As she gets closer, she sees her daughter's tears and thinks for a moment. But that instinct that mothers often have kicks in. She says nothing and hugs Helen as tightly as she can while Helen sobs over her shoulder.

Daley has all the dashcam files copied by Essam, and he's ready to go through them with DS Harris. But he's staring at his computer screen, far away in his thoughts. He's been like this all day. Daley decides he will talk to McCall when she is back from rest days. He's never seen the DS like this before.

'Sarge, I have the footage ready to roll,' says Daley.

DS Harris looks over at him and remembers what they need to do.

'Yes, Dan. On my way,' he says.

'Sarge, is everything okay? I don't mean to be nosy, but...'

Harris smiles at him. 'No, Dan, everything is not okay. But thank you for asking. I appreciate that. I've got some personal stuff going on. I'm sorry if I'm a bit out of it.'

'Honestly, I was just worried. I'm sure you know who you can talk to. Let me know if I can do anything to make things easier for you here.'

Harris is fighting back the tears. It wouldn't be good to blubber in front of his team.

'You're a good man, Daniel. Thank you. Let's have a look at this dashcam footage.'

Daley has chosen three video files before and after Peter Grant visits 24 Alcott Gardens. They're spotting the parked cars along the journey, illuminated by the car's headlights. It's tedious searching, sometimes going frame by frame. Daley is making notes of the number plates of vehicles within half a mile of Alcott Gardens. Then, as Grant leaves the address, the car swings around the corner where there's a turning into garages. There is a black BMW just on the edge of the headlights.

'Just there!' says Harris.

Daley pauses the video. He goes back a fraction of a second, and the image is clearer. It's an executive style car, expensive. And right behind, in the shadows, is a white transit style van.

'Sarge, I'm getting a feeling about this.'

'So, am I. There's only a partial index on that BMW. Let's do some checks. I'm intrigued by that white van, too. There are gardens backing onto that area. Once you've got that list of vehicles, you and I will knock on some doors and see if they have CCTV or witnessed anything.'

After trawling over another twenty minutes of footage, the best lead they found was the executive car and the white van. Daley is going through a printed list of partially matching vehicles. He works better with tangible copies of words in his hands. It's the same reason he doesn't get on with Kindles—he prefers hard copies of books. His girlfriend, in the small, framed photograph on his desk, is the complete opposite.

'Sarge, this has to be it,' Daley says, turning around. He looks up but realises he is talking to himself. Harris is drinking a coffee, staring out of the window on the other side of the office.

Harris's watching the digging machines being unloaded onto the old police field. The land has been sold and it will soon be built on.

'It's sad to see those fields go,' Harris says as Daley stands beside him. 'I remember the police open days, the football matches. I met my husband on an open day five years ago this summer.'

'Lots of good memories, Sarge. What's his name?'

'Paul. My team were doing a public order demo, and Paul had been watching me. He came up to talk to me afterwards. Do you believe in love at first sight, Daniel?'

'I do. Me and Melissa. We met in Glastonbury. I fell over her tent pegs and knocked her flying. That's all it took, apparently.'

'What have you got for me?' Harris finishes the dregs of his coffee.

'I've got three vehicles that are local to this area. But... most interesting is this one.' He points to a number plate highlighted in green. 'It's owned by Hudson Biotech. It's one of their pool cars.'

'Bloody marvellous! Well done, Dan. Let's go to Alcott Gardens, knock on the doors of those properties backing onto the garages. It's worth a try. Where's Sam?'

'She's scoping out Martina Hayes's flat. She's just building up some intelligence on her for when we go in and arrest her.'

'That may not be necessary...' His voice trailing off. 'Anyway, get your coat—we're in your car.'

Julie Dalton pulls at the cables around her wrists, but it's futile. She's only wearing her silk dressing gown now, but he's ruined it. She hurts so much down there—she can't bear to look. She's wet herself several times, but that doesn't seem to stop him. He's in the kitchen helping himself to food out of the refrigerator. He's kept her tied up, and she's thirsty. She's too tired to scream, to cry, almost to breathe.

'I do like these American-style fridges,' Nathan says to her. 'I've always wanted one. My family was poor, Julie. Not like you now. I have so much going for me, and I have nothing to show for it. We come from the same roots, you and me. But you got lucky with Christopher. The punter who just kept giving.'

'Let me go,' she hisses.

'No, Julie. I can't do that. I've been working for your husband for years now. He got me to do things for him that no one should have to do for their boss. I got nothing out of it for me, though. Just one of his skivvies, going nowhere, doing his dirty work while he got richer and richer. Great boob job, by the way! I hope you feel you've got your money's worth today.'

'Let me go! I won't tell anyone if you get let me go.'

'That's a good idea, Julie. I need to leave now. I've been here long enough. I have someone else desperate for me to get back to them. Bear with me one moment.'

Nathan goes out the backdoor, and Julie frantically pulls on the cables tied to the chair. Her wrists are bleeding now, and everything hurts. But Nathan is back. He has something in his hand. The next thing Julie knows is she's being splashed with cold liquid—its fumes are suffocating. Her eyes! She can't see—the pain is unbearable! When the boom comes, the heat, the black, acrid smoke, she knows what he has done. If it wasn't for the agony, she would feel relief.

I've been doing household chores, including a lot of cleaning. I've realised I'm trying to wash away something that's happened beyond my walls—it won't work. Since I've been thinking about moving, the place is not a home anymore—no matter how spotless it is. I have a kitchen cupboard door to fix, but I can't be bothered. I'm about to search for a new house on the Internet when my doorbell goes.

'Where have you been, fuckwit?' It's Terry.

'Ah, mate!' I say. 'Come on in.'

Terry walks into my front room. He doesn't look happy, but I know he's putting it on.

'So, exactly why haven't you got back to me? I'm meant to be your mate. You even called me mate when you answered the door, but you're not acting like my mate. Because a real mate would have answered my copious messages.'

'I didn't, not answer. I didn't receive. Show me the number you sent the messages to.' He digs around on his phone and shows me a phone number. 'That's not my phone number, fuckwit. Why are you sending text messages, anyway? Who sends text messages nowadays? Use Messenger.'

'Oh.'

I laugh, as does he. Terry gives me a hug and sits on the sofa.

'Shit, my friend. You've been through it this last week. I even saw you on the TV!'

'So I gather.'

'I'm sorry about your friend. I saw the boarding next door. Awful.'

I go to the kitchen and get a few packs of beer.

'Are you staying over?'

'No. I have to be over in Bristol tomorrow. Got a job with a BBC wildlife programme. They want drone shots over a river somewhere.'

'Nice work if you can get it. So, tell me, Terry, are you still a virgin?'

'How very dare you! You know I'm not a virgin.'

'Sex with yourself doesn't count, Terry.' He laughs and kicks back, but I'm sensing something wrong.

'What is it? What's bothering you?'

He shakes his head and sits forward.

'You can't turn it off for a minute, can you. I should have known.'

'You know I can't.'

'I'm worried about you, that's all. First, we lost Joey three years ago, then we nearly lost you, and now Alison McCarthy's gone. It's just so depressing. I was wondering how you were going to cope going back to work after all this time.'

'I'm okay, mate. I had to hit the ground running, but it's okay.'

Terry swigs his beer and looks around him.

'This place is looking kind of empty. You know you can always come and move over to Portsmouth with me. You could transfer. I don't like the thought of you being on your own. Especially, with... what's just happened.'

He's genuinely worried about me. I'm touched.

'Cheers. I'm thinking of moving house. It's all a bit too awful here. It's only ten feet between where I'm sitting and where Kate was murdered.'

'That's a horrible thought—definitely move. Be closer to your mates. Robbo is always asking how you are, and Tanya's got very hot all of a sudden. She's divorced and lonely now. So...'

I laugh. He always makes me laugh.

'I haven't seen Tanya since school,' I say. 'She had glasses, braces and spoke with a lisp.'

'Not now, my friend. I saw her at Alison's memorial a few weeks ago. Tanya was looking amazing.'

'Alison's memorial? I didn't know about that?'

'Oh,' Terry looks awkward. 'I thought they invited you. It was on a Facebook group. Look.'

Terry swipes on his phone and hands it to me. There are the photographs from the memorial. I recognise the faces of past school friends. I swipe over to pictures of Alison's parents, her kids. They look lost amongst it all.

'Those poor girls,' I say. 'What's going to happen to them?'

'Their Aunty Laura is looking after them, Alison's sister.'

'I remember she had a sister, but I never met her, though. She'd moved out by the time Alison and I got together. She told Alison she wasn't happy about us.'

Terry swipes over a few more photos. 'Yes. Here.' And there she is, talking to Alison's girls, Laura Driscoll.

'Shit!' I'm struggling with this. 'That's Chief Superintendent Driscoll.'

'No way! You know her?'

'I do, Terry. I'm working with her now.'

'Ha! I tried it on with her, but her husband stepped in.'

'Terry! You didn't?'

'I did. I didn't know Aunty Laura was married.'

Unbelievable. I'm wondering if Driscoll knows? She must do. I swipe over once more, and there's a collage of photos on the wall. A collection of Alison's friends and family arranged ad-lib and pinned to a corkboard. There, right in the centre, is Alison, with an elderly woman. I know her.

'That's Joyce Mayhew,' I say.

'It's Alison's grandmother. They were close.'

When worlds collide, you can't help but sit up and take notice. Something, someone, is grabbing my attention, and my mind is running away. I talk to Terry. I tell him about Helen, about Kate, and what Laura Driscoll told me. He listens. Having a friend who really knows how to listen is a precious gift. At the end of it all, he opens another beer.

'Davey, boy. There's something or someone much bigger than us at work here. I think we need a curry.'

Music to my ears.

Terry's sleeping over on the sofa tonight. Getting through a six-pack on his own means he's in no state to drive. God, he's a breath of fresh air. It's late now, and I cover him with a spare blanket as he drifts off to sleep.

My head now thinks about Driscoll and the secrets she's keeping. She must have known who I was. What is her agenda with me?

FOURTEEN

7th March 2022

My mobile is ringing. It's 6.20 a.m., and I rub my eyes to clear the blur. The phone is telling me the number has been withheld. If it's a scam call, I will not be happy.

'Angelis,' I sound gruff.

'Hello, it's me, Josh.'

I'm struggling to hold it together. 'Josh! Hey, young man. How are you?'

'I'm okay. I'm in my PJs. Mum pressed the numbers for me.'

'Can you say thank you so much to Mummy for me?' I have to clear my throat.

'Mum!' Josh is shouting off the phone. 'Dad says thank you so much for me!'

'Mummy said it's okay. You sound different.'

'I've just woken up, Josh. I haven't had my cup of tea yet.' I'm wiping away my tears.

'I don't like tea. Ian made Mummy tea in bed.'

'Lucky Mummy! Is Ian her friend?'

'Yes. She likes him a lot. Ian sleeps on your side.'

'That's the best side, Josh.' I'm okay with that. It's all okay.

'I'm going on a trip to the woods, and Tilly is coming.'

'Who's Tilly?'

'Tilly looks after me when Mummy is at work.'

'That's amazing. I wish I had someone like Tilly.'

'You can't have my Tilly, though... Oh. Mummy says breakfast is ready.'

'Ah, that's okay. Can you call me again?'

'Yep. Sure. Love you, Dad. Bye!' He's gone.

'Love you, Josh.' It's too late.

I'm in the office early, and I'm still on a high after speaking with Josh. It's only me and the ginger coffee-killing demon here so far.

'You're in early,' I say to him as I approach his desk. 'Tea, coffee?'

'Good morning, sir,' he says. 'Well, if you're sure. Could I have a tea, white, no sugar? I don't drink coffee.'

'That explains a lot. Who are you?'

'PC Robert Hagan, sir. I'm on secondment for four months.'

'Ah, I remember those.' I'm sounding like an old wise police officer now. 'What are you working on?'

'I'm reviewing CCTV and looking at ANPR records for the Dalton fire a couple of days ago.'

'Dalton?'

'Yes, sir. A fire has gutted Christopher Dalton's house. The Fire Service has confirmed it as arson. They found evidence of an accelerant, and someone turned off the sprinkler system. They think they've found the remains of a body in the kitchen.'

'Think?'

'The extreme heat has taken most of it. We're assuming it's Julie Dalton, Christopher Dalton's wife. It's not confirmed yet, but she is missing, and she was there alone after her husband's death. It could have been a bizarre suicide, I suppose. Lots of forensic work's ongoing.'

'Thanks, Robert. I'll take a trip out there later.'

'Also, sir, the pathologist's report is in and is on your desk. There's a question mark over Christopher Dalton's stroke. Someone is querying about Dettori's involvement. I have emailed a copy to you and DS Harris.'

McCall arrives in the office, puts her bag down, and her attention goes straight into her emails. She's ignoring me. I'm seeing a brick wall going up around her, and I'm confused. As the rest of the team come in, she's welcoming and friendly with everyone except me. Something is going on here. I've done something wrong.

The whiteboard has changed, and lots of arrows are pointing to Vanessa Grant's photo. There's a lot of activity on the go and a new buzz of excitement. Below her name are others: Peter Grant, Verity Kidd, Geoffrey Kidd. Peter is the ex; who are the others? Martina Hayes's name is underlined.

When James comes in, I'm shocked at how gaunt he's looking. There's a little stubble on his face and head. I'm feeling a burden on him as I watch him, like he's carrying something, and it's hurting him, big time.

I signal to him to start the briefing, and the others pick up on it. McCall is standing at the back. She still won't look at me.

'Good morning,' Harris starts. He sounds less than enthusiastic. 'We have the governor back today from rest days and DS

McCall. It's time to fill us all in on developments. So, we know that Vanessa Grant left the house with someone.'

'How do we know that?' I say.

'Dan went through the dashcam footage of Peter Grant's car journey to and from Alcott Gardens. He caught a short clip of a black BMW parked up around the corner by some garages—it's less than a second long. The BMW is pretty much in the shadows. We have traced it to a car owned by Hudson Biotech. Behind it was a white van.

One house, number 66, has CCTV covering their garage. It's not great footage, but it activated when two females walk over the BMW. One of them is likely to be Vanessa Grant. We can't make out the other female. There's a male with a beard in the back of the car, wearing dark clothing. The driver looks very much like Dettori. The two women go out of sight, and the CCTV cuts out.'

'Great work, Dan, James. I'll come over later, and you can show it to me.'

'Dan went around the back of the garages while I did door-to-door.'

'There's nothing obvious there at first,' says Daley, 'but I did bag up some chewing gum, found where the BMW was parked.'

'We're still not sure if they forced Vanessa or not,' says Harris. 'No local taxis picked up anyone from Alcott Gardens that night. The type of executive car seen is one of Hudson's pool cars, for picking up customers from airports.'

'Hudson Biotech has a lot of questions to answer,' it's Walsh. He's come out of his office.

'We've traced Vanessa's parents,' says Jack Lang. 'They're separated and both living in London. They are... Verity and Geoffrey Kidd. He's a disgraced vicar, by all accounts. Neither of them has heard from Vanessa for months, but they aren't a close family. Sam, who's off today, has asked them to call us if they hear anything.'

'Lastly,' says Harris, 'we're grateful to neighbourhood officers who recognised the white van. It's one they've clocked before. They told us it belongs to a local builder who's having a fling with the woman at number 62. The van was there overnight, so we don't need to chase it up any further.'

'A fling?' I can't help but laugh. I haven't heard it called a fling for a while. 'So, we've managed to discount the white van. I can see you've all worked hard on this and put in some long hours. Our priority is still to find Vanessa Grant, especially with news of the knife. The part Martina Hayes has played is a mystery.'

'When are you going to bring her in?' asks Walsh. He's pushing for quick results.

'Knowing she can be extremely violent, I would suggest an operation with a firearms unit and a dog. Sam has been sussing out where she lives. Stopping her at her home is a too high risk, as it's near a school and facing buildings. I'm suggesting we bring her in tomorrow. Perhaps take her from work or a hard stop on her car.'

'Sounds good to me,' says Walsh. 'Carry on.'

'I think we're done for now. James, when you're free, could you come and have a chat in my office, please?'

'Yes, boss,' he says, looking puzzled.

Harris is struggling to know where to start. He's fighting back the tears, so I lean across and close the blinds.

'Take your time, James,' I say. 'I haven't known you for long, but I think it's obvious that something is wrong. I don't want to pry, but if there's anything I can do.'

'It's Paul, sir, my husband. He's been diagnosed with early-onset Alzheimer's. We don't know how long he's got before it gets bad, but they've done brain scans, and it's unmistakable. He could have three years, or he could have 20 years. My world has fallen through, sir. So, that's why I'm struggling.' The big man's tears are falling now. 'It's so unfair—we had everything going for us. Now there's the prospect of long-term care and suffering, and God knows what else. I'm not sure I can get through this for him.'

'What do you need, James?' As he's sitting there, I can see his memory of Paul sitting with him, with his arms wrapped around Harris's shoulders.

'I don't know, sir. I really don't know, apart from I need to work. I've booked counselling through the job. But while Paul doesn't need me at his side, I would like to work.'

'Only you can decide that, James. If anything changes or you need compassionate leave, let me know. You come across to me as a hard-working and dedicated police officer. I admire your commitment. Just don't be too hard on yourself. Family is more important than anything, especially in this job.' I can hear myself say it. I never used to believe that. This job was more important to me than family once.

'Yes, sir. Thank you.'

'It must be hard for you investigating Hudson in these circumstances.'

'You mean their Alzheimer's drug trials. I would have jumped at signing Paul up for that. Ironic, doesn't cover it.'

'Other companies are working on it, legally. If there's anything you need, please let me know. Get yourself signed up with some of the national support organisations, too.'

'Yes, I will thank you.'

All morning I've been wondering what's bothering McCall. I sense people are hurting everywhere I go. It's background noise, like the rumble of traffic. I've learned to push it away, but sometimes I can't. I just wish the gift or curse I received had the power to take that hurt away. I have this memory: *to love, heal and mend what is broken*. What is that? It just evades me. I just wish I could mend Harris's situation.

I reach McCall's desk, and she's still blanking me. That wall she's building is getting taller.

'Helen, how were your rest days?' I ask. She's staring at her computer screen and doesn't answer for a moment.

'Fine, sir,' she says. 'Excuse me, I need the toilet.' She hurries away. For a moment, I see someone following her, a memory ghost; someone she once knew. He's shouting at her, taunting her.

I can't do this today.

'Good morning, sir,' says Cheung. She is altogether much more cheerful than her boss.

'Good morning, Po. How is it going? You and Sam have a lot on your plate. How are you coping?'

'Okay, sir. I'm looking forward to a couple of days off,' she says. 'Sir,' she looks in the direction where McCall just left, 'I'm worried about DS McCall. She's not herself today.'

'I know, Po. I'll have a chat with her shortly. You do right looking out for her. Leave it to me.'

'Thanks, sir.'

'What are your thoughts on Vanessa Grant? Where do you think she is? She's not gone to family, has no friends that we know about.'

'If I were planning a murder, then I would have pre-planned an escape route or an alibi. Vanessa doesn't have an alibi, so I'd have a bolt-hole prepared somewhere far away if it was me.

Vanessa and whoever she was with in the BMW probably travelled there together.'

Something has struck me. 'Po, you might have something there!'

'Really?' She looks pleased with herself.

McCall is back at her desk and frowning.

'Helen, do you remember when we spoke to Kate's parents? We talked about that photograph in Katherine's front room. They confirmed they took it in Dartmouth, didn't they?'

Helen shrugs. 'Yes.'

Again, she won't look at me. It's annoying me now.

'Do you think that's far away enough, Po?'

'I'd say so!'

'Po, are you happy for a drive today? It's probably going to take you four hours or so each way. I'd get the local police to do it, but we know what we're looking for. You'll need some support for an arrest if she's there. There's a stay overnight if you want one?'

Po is already up and getting her things together.

'Helen, could you quickly call Ted and arrange it? We need a key. They probably have a key-safe outside the door or use a neighbour.'

She rolls her eyes. 'You can see I'm snowed under here.'

Her attitude is really pissing me off now. I see that memory again. He's standing over her and staring at me.

'Just come into my office for a moment.' She's looking at me now. I can see she's hurting—it's undeniable. 'Helen? My office, please.'

She's standing in front of my desk, arms folded. Her face is red, either with embarrassment or rage.

'Shut the door,' I say. McCall is reluctant—she knows trouble is coming.

'Can this wait?'

'There are two ways I could go with this, and I'm debating which one is the best.'

'Just get on with it!'

'If you don't start showing me respect, Sergeant, I'll have you up for a disciplinary! Is that clear?' She is starting at her feet now. 'I said, is that clear?'

'Yes, sir.' McCall is crying. For goodness' sake, she's the second sergeant I've made cry today. I must be a great manager.

'So, there's that way, or there's this way—Helen, what has got into you this morning? I'm worried.'

She pulls out a tissue from her pocket and sobs. I'm uncertain what to do. I'd love to comfort her, but this is work—this is professional.

'I'm sorry. I've had a shit few days. I'm feeling sorry for myself, that's all.' The wall is coming down.

'I'm sorry you've had a shit few days. Can you tell me why that is my fault? What have I done?'

'Nothing, sir. Just nothing.' There's another memory revealing itself. She's trying to suppress it, but it's really hurting her. There I am, in that memory, and I'm walking away from her —with Karen. She saw us together. And she's assumed...

'Helen,' she's looking at me now. 'The woman with the red hair is my ex-wife. Her name is Karen. I was meeting her to talk about seeing my son again.'

She's pretending she doesn't know what I'm talking about, but she can't hide it from me. She knows she can't.

'That's your mumbo-jumbo shit working again, sir?'

'Yes. My mumbo-jumbo shit. I told you, I can't turn it off. I'm sorry if I upset you in any way, but none of it was intentional. I have a backstory, Helen. We all do.'

'Yes, we do. I'm so sorry.' Her tissue is disintegrating.

'Wait there.'

I rush out and get some tissues from Po. I know she will be discrete. Helen sits down and slows her breathing, brushing the hair back from her face.

'You must think I'm an idiot,' she says. 'I promised myself I'd never fall for someone I work with again. I'm such a fool. I was hurt so badly and despite this practised hard exterior, I'm as gullible as they come.'

'You told me you were married before?'

'Yes. An inspector in Hastings. It went badly wrong. He was handy with his fists at the time and a control freak. He eventually lost his job because of it, but they made me transfer here first. I didn't mind too much. I was closer to my parents.'

'I'm sorry to hear that, but I'm glad you moved over here. I married young, 21 years old. I didn't know which way was up, let alone ready for marriage. We met when I was 20 and were engaged for 3 months. She's the only woman I've ever been with.'

'Really!' A beginning of a smile is forming on Helen's face.

'Yes, really.' I laugh. 'We had Joshua within 12 months. He's ten now.'

'So, you don't see him often?'

'No, but you need to know, Helen, it was my fault. I'm ashamed to say this, but I was once that control freak your ex-husband was. I never hit Karen, but I was so paranoid about losing her. She was gorgeous, and lots of other men were attracted to her. I was jealous for no reason, and I became this monster. A total nob. The only way I could cope with it was to make this job more important than my family. I wanted them in their little box, something I could come home to. I eventually lost Karen and Josh. So, I won't lie to you. It was my fault, but, and they all say this, I'm not that person anymore.'

'Are you still in love with her?' That was a difficult question for her to ask.

'I'm in love with something that's gone, that won't come back. She's happy now, and we have both moved on. It's taken me longer if I'm honest. In some ways, my injury broke me away from that. It changed me.'

'Thank you. I appreciate your honesty. I hope you get to see your son soon.'

I nod. 'Me, too. I miss him, but he called me this morning. First time in ages.'

'That's good news... So, what happens now?' She's looking out of the gaps in the blinds at the busy office. 'You know stuff about me, how I feel. I don't know what you're thinking. You can be honest with me. How do you feel about me?'

FIFTEEN

McCall and Cheung are beginning their journey to Dartmouth. They've taken an unmarked car, and they've prepared overnight bags in case they will have to arrest Vanessa and interview her locally. Cheung is driving as her boss looks washed out today. Cheung's glad to have her company—a late decision by McCall.

'Devon and Cornwall police are providing us with two officers when we get there,' says McCall. 'If she's there, then we just nick her on suspicion of murder. There are grounds with her fingerprints and DNA found on the knife.'

'I've spoken to the neighbours,' says Cheung. 'They said they have seen no one at the property recently, but they could have missed her. Edie Jacobs says the property is let out for short stay holidays from April, but not at the moment. There's a keysafe by the front door, and I have the code.'

'That's great, Po.' McCall's put her shades on and is resting her head, staring out of the window. Po leaves her to rest, and soon she only has the satnav for company.

McCall wakes with a start, and she tries to gather her bearings. 'Sorry, I dozed off. Where are we?'

'Just another three hours, Sarge. Let me know if you need a comfort break.' McCall doesn't answer. 'Is everything okay, Sarge? I hope you don't think I'm nosey. I'm worried about you today.'

McCall turns her head towards Cheung. 'Actually, Po. I am absolutely, bloody amazing.' The colour has come back to her face. McCall's face is shining, and she pretends to punch Cheung's arm. 'I've spent the last few days worrying about nothing, and I've exhausted myself. Thanks for asking.' She laughs and goes back to staring out of the window, humming a tune to herself.

I turn my car into the steep drive, and I can see the telltale stream of water draining away from the scene, down towards the main road. There's a fire investigation unit at the scene and men in hi-vis and hard hats walking around with clipboards and video cameras. There's also another police unit here, the inevitable scene guard. Another stalwart PCSO protecting the cordon. It's Rob Kerr again.

'Sir, we meet again,' says Rob as he greets me. He gets the scene log ready to write my name in.

'You must have pissed off someone, Rob. Another scene guard deployment?'

'Yes, sir. Perhaps I haven't brought in enough cakes for the section. Are you going in, sir?'

'No, Rob. I've just come to get a feel for the scene. I won't interrupt these guys.'

'They're saying it's arson.'

'So I hear. Is this your patch?'

'Yes. I'm based in Midhurst normally.'

'Did you know the Daltons?'

'I met him a few times. He used to complain about ramblers walking over his property. He thought he could control the right of way, and money could buy him certain privileges. I don't normally speak ill of the dead, but he was as corrupt as they come. The Golf Club Mafia, they call it around here. Him and that Wheelhouse, Gary Parkes, and the other minions.'

'We should have gone straight to you, Rob, for the intelligence.'

'Yes, sir. We have the inside knowledge.'

'Did you ever meet Doctor Dean Dettori?'

'He was here when I visited Dalton once. A smarmy git, if you know what I mean. I'd describe him as a Golf Club Mafia associate. He threatened me once. I caught him pestering a young girl that Dalton had brought up to the house. I was here to talk about so-called trespassers, and the scumbag was trying to put his hands up her dress. She didn't want to press charges and ran off. Dettori said he'd find out where I lived if I took it any further.'

'Nothing worse than a rich bastard.'

'Yes, sir. Very much so,'

'Thanks, Rob. You've been really helpful. I have an invitation to his workplace. I may just pay him a visit.'

I walk away and take several steps back to view the burnt-out shell. I'm sensing a bad feeling here: despair, hopelessness. I see a shadow of a woman rushing through the blackened remains, a lost soul searching for something it can no longer hold.

I shudder as someone stands beside me.

'Do you want a tea, sir?' asks Rob. He has a flask and a cup in his hand.

I smile. He's a good man.

'Bless you, Rob. Cheers.' I take his small cup and join him. We survey the ruins of the once-mighty Dalton house for a while longer until I leave to confront Dettori.

'Do you have an appointment?' says the receptionist. She's doing that weird coy smile thing. Telling me she fancies me. There's a queue of people waiting to be seen. All in suits, like me. Sales reps, pharmacists, photocopier engineers.

'He's invited me personally,' I say.

'Your name?'

'Angelis. Detective Inspector Angelis.' I show her my warrant card, and her face drops. I don't think she fancies me anymore.

'Oh. I see. You're sure you had an appointment?'

'No. But he wants to see me.'

'I don't think so, Inspector. Next, please.'

'Are you a close friend of his?' I lean over the counter.

'Of course not. Next, please!'

'Then how do you know? He said he wants to show me around.'

The woman is getting frustrated. She doesn't want to be beaten, but Dettori's arrival ends the conversation.

'Inspector Angelis, I presume,' says Dettori, walking from behind a screen. He holds out his hand.

'Doctor Dettori. One of my colleagues told me you have given me an open invitation to visit you.'

'Absolutely!'

'Mrs Unwin here has tried to obstruct us every time we come. I'm beginning to take it personally.'

'Apologies, Inspector. We will have words again, won't we, Mrs Unwin?'

Mrs Harriet Unwin has gone red.

'You wanted to talk to me.'

'It was a tour of our facility I was offering.' Dettori has a fixed grin on his face.

'I don't have time for that, but I have a few questions.'

'Follow me.'

We walk into a small office and sit opposite each other at a desk. Dettori is fussing with his tie, and I immediately sense the shroud of falsehood covering this man. He is hiding more than he can deal with.

'I've heard a lot about you, Inspector,' he says. 'I read about that terrible assault on you in, 2019 I think it was, just before Covid hit us. That was a truly remarkable recovery.'

'Thank you. I had great support.'

'And now you're back at work and moved up a rank. I can't imagine many other people doing that so quickly. It's quite remarkable. What do you attribute your rapid turnaround to?'

'Doctor Dettori, why do I sense you know a lot more about me than I do about you?'

He clearly flushes. This man has so many issues it's easy to read him.

'I don't know what you mean, Inspector. Your story was well publicised. Your officers came yesterday and asked questions about Doctor Jacobs. I simply thought it might help your enquiries if you saw the company she worked for.'

'Bollocks. That's an English word you may be familiar with, Doctor Dettori. You are hiding something. Your drug trials, your connection to Christopher Dalton and his cronies. You are in deep, deep shit, Doctor.'

There's an immediate change in his demeanour. Gone is the sickly grin. I see a dog coming out from behind him. It's vicious and bad-tempered, and precisely what I suspected.

'You are throwing my goodwill back in my face. If you

realised what you owed me, Inspector, I think your tone would be very different.'

'Owe you? Ha! I don't owe you anything. Ah, you're talking about the unsanctioned drug your organisation gave me when I was in a coma. You ordered it, Dettori. I owe you, do I? We are very close to getting a full picture of the company you keep and what you have been doing.'

'Are you threatening me, Inspector?'

'God, yes! More of a promise, actually. If I find you were anything to do with Kate's death, I will personally send you to hell and back. Do I make myself clear?'

The dog is snarling, and Dettori is glaring at me. He is clenching his fists now.

'Your threats can lead you into a lot of trouble, Angelis. I have more influence than you know.'

'Do I look scared? I don't think I do. But you do. Your heart rate and blood pressure are right up there. Careful, you don't want a stroke, like your friend Dalton.'

'Sto bene grazie, Angelis. How about your team? Are they all well? Your sergeants? McCall, Harris? Don't neglect them. We wouldn't want either of them falling by the wayside.'

I focus on his dog of a temper that's about to explode. I push in against it, and it whimpers off behind him and vanishes. Dettori gets a sharp pain in his head. He screws up his eyes. He knows it's me doing this.

'Thank you for your time, Doctor.' I stand. 'We are so onto you. Don't go anywhere. We'll be coming for you soon. I'll find my own way out.'

McCall and Harris? How could he hurt them? I won't let him. He'd better not go anywhere near them.

I walk past the receptionist, and she looks up at me like a scolded dog. I glimpse her wrist, and there's a purple mark surrounding a red ring, scabbed over now, but clearly, the serrations were made by teeth. It stops me in my tracks, and I look at her. Her eyes meet mine for a moment, and she looks away, pulling down the sleeve of her blouse.

'Who did that to you?' I ask. 'That's a bite mark.' She's trying to ignore me, pretending I'm not here.

'Leave me alone,' she says.

I see a young man is hanging off her—he's blind. His hair is long, and he has the fuzzy beard of an adolescent. He's aggressive, pulling at her, punching her, rocking backwards and forwards. She's tired—exhausted.

She looks up at me. Her eyes are flitting across my face. She's been found out; something deeply personal is uncovered. She blushes.

'Your son?' I say, looking at her wrist. 'You don't have to cope on your own. There's help out there.'

'He's a good boy, Inspector. He doesn't mean to hurt me. It's frustration.'

'I know. But if you fall apart, Mrs Unwin, then who will look after him? Get some help for you.'

She nods, but I'm not sure she heard me. Perhaps something useful has come out of this visit, and now I have Dettori in my sights.

I've bought lunch in the city, and I've turned to walk towards the Market Cross. I need to chill after visiting Dettori. To get him out of my system. I shouldn't have done it, but I've put the fear of God into him.

I check the time and see that Helen's been gone for an hour

and a half. I'm wondering if she's okay. She was exhausted when she left, but she wanted to go with Po.

As I'm walking, I sense someone is watching me, following me. It's not some kind of paranoia—this is real. I look behind me, and there's a woman with a buggy, looking at herself in the reflection of a shop window. Someone is giving a lost tourist directions to the cathedral, and two men in yellow jackets are re-setting loose cobbles in the road. I can't relax—I need to shake off this feeling.

I make it to the Cross and take a seat under the east-facing arch to eat my sandwich. I can see down three streets from here. When I was a probationer, I used to stand a few feet in front of where I'm sitting now. It was a great vantage point, and people could see a police officer patrolling in plain sight, flying the flag.

Now when I come here, the history of this place opens up to me. When I focus, I see layer upon layer of time and space that surrounds us. Encapsulated within these temporal layers are thousands of lives, walking together, blending into one another. It's like watching them through multiple layers of film. Different styles of clothing, hair, old vehicles are driving around me where I sit. There's a policeman just in front of me in a tunic, with white cuffs directing traffic. Old buses are struggling with the tight corners. Then there are the pens of sheep and cattle, the men bartering on the seat next to me.

Again, I see the other kind, the otherworldly creatures. They stand apart from the crowds, watching as I watch. Sometimes they only appear in my peripheral vision as bright, human-like forms. There are two of these watchers standing with a woman in a blue coat to my right. They stand on either side of her like bodyguards. I swear they're carrying swords. This woman, she's the one who is following me, and now she's walking towards me.

'Hello, Inspector Angelis,' her voice is shaking. 'David

Angelis?' Her bodyguards turn and fade away as she speaks to me.

I swallow the last bite of a chicken salad sandwich. 'Yes,' I say. I'm wondering if she's seen me on the TV or she's going to complain about something. But I'm seriously wondering why she has the armed guard.

'You won't remember me, I'm sure. My name is Rachael Thorne. I'm a nurse. Is there somewhere we can talk privately? I have some information about you I need to tell you.'

'About me? How do you know me?'

'I met you in hospital. I was with you when you died.'

I follow her through the smoked-glass doors of the cathedral and walk past the stewards, greeting us as we enter. Rachael Thorne takes us to a pew seat, away from the centre aisle, next to a pillar. I feel strange in here, a sense of familiarity, expectation. I see shapes and shadows all around me, pressing in, watching. I mustn't focus on them. I look into her eyes and wait until they have gone.

'So, what is this about?' I ask her.

'I came a few days ago to see you, but I was too anxious to go through with it. As I have already told you, I was with you when you died.'

'I heard you, Ms Thorne, but can you elaborate?' As I say that, I remember what Driscoll told me, the rumours she heard.

'I know how that sounds—I've been a nurse for 20 years. Two years ago you were in a coma. You were in one of the side rooms in the intensive care unit. You had been unresponsive for several days, and I was talking to you about something. I can't remember about what exactly. You just slipped away. Your heart stopped, and they tried hard to bring you back. The doctor called it, and everyone agreed. It was then up to me and Jenny, my friend, to get you ready to go down to the morgue. We prepared you, and Jenny took you down with the porter while I did some paperwork. I got your things together and took them down to the morgue about an hour later. When I went down there, you were still on the trolley. You were well and truly gone, Mr Angelis.

'Then I saw you a few days ago on the TV. I would recognise you anywhere. You are very distinctive.'

'I'm sorry, Rachael. You're either mistaken, or you've had a mental health episode.'

'I am not mistaken.' She sighs and looks deflated. 'I may be religious, but I'm not a crackpot.'

'I'm sorry, I wasn't meaning—'

'Jenny said people have been asking questions about you in the last few days. And when I told her about you being on the TV, she was really spooked. They questioned her about how you died, going over and over it. Someone else out there knows you'd died, too.'

'Who was asking questions? Are you saying someone is trying to cover it up?'

'It was some official government office. She doesn't know. I know someone tried an experimental drug on you while you were in a coma, and I think they're wondering if that brought you back.'

'But Ms Thorne—'

'Rachael, please.'

'Rachael, what you're saying is impossible. I don't doubt what you saw, but there has to be another explanation.'

'I take it you're not a religious man, Inspector Angelis?'

'I used to be, a long time ago.'

'So, you are aware of these things. I saw something when you died,' Rachael says, looking up at the high ceilings.

I think it's about time I call this conversation to a close. I know she's well-meaning enough, but this could go round in circles.

'Rachael, I have to go—'

'You were a small point of light. You left the room and went over to the sculpture in the garden. You were there for a while, and then you floated away. I know that sounds crazy! But it's what I saw, and I've never seen it since.'

But that was a dream. I hold my breath to slow my heart.

'Rachael, some of what you are saying is making sense, okay. I won't deny it. I also have recurring dreams that are always just out of reach when I wake. I go somewhere else. I can't explain it.'

'I think you are somewhere in between worlds. Or you exist in both places?'

'That's far too deep for me, Rachael.' I can see she's serious, but she shrugs the idea off and smiles for the first time. She has a warm smile. 'What I will tell you is I have been given a gift.'

She twists towards me like I've poked her.

'A gift? Since what happened to you?'

'Yes. I can see things other people can't. I can see the truth behind what people are saying. I know when people are lying. I'm not really meant to talk about it. It's telling me you are totally sincere...'

'Go on,' she says.

'I see other places around me, like layers of history, existing alongside us. I see different kinds of people, creatures. Not dead people but other kinds of—'

'Angels?'

I laugh but realise she's serious.

'I'm not making sense, am I.' I wonder if she's as deluded as I am, but I get nothing like that from her. She's honest, scared, considered in her thinking.

'Mr Angelis, you are making sense. I had to tell you these things. I had a dream where an angel told me to find you.'

I shake my head.

'Rachael, please. I stopped believing years ago. I respect your views, but...'

'It must be for a reason. All I am saying is, reconsider. What you see is the spiritual realm. You are supernaturally discerning what people are thinking. You can see a dimension that others cannot, and the creatures that surround us that live in that realm.'

'I don't know about angels, Rachael. They don't have wings or play harps.'

Rachael looks at her watch and stands up.

'I have to go, too. I've said what I had to say. Thank you for listening to me. You can go on denying the truth if you wish, but that is not my problem.'

'Have I offended you?' I don't understand her reaction.

'No, I just think you need to do some searching for yourself. Maybe pray while you're in this lovely place?' She smiles at me and tilts her head. 'I would dearly love to see the things you see. God gives us gifts for a reason. You need to remember what that reason is and why he brought you back. Goodbye, Inspector.'

SIXTEEN

Martina pulls up in the forest car park on Selhurst Park Road, which reaches across the top of the Downs on its way to the Goodwood Racecourse. There is no one else here. She is under cover of tall conifers and out of sight from the road. She lowers her window and listens to the birdsong filling her ears. She has never heard how intricate it is before. Since her last fix, as she now calls Dettori's payment for services, her senses have become more acute, crystal clear. She earned herself an important extra dose that will hopefully save her if everything goes to plan. She's placed it inside a small plastic tub, and it's ready on the chair beside her.

His car turns into the car park and parks next to hers. She's met him once before, but now he looks different, dishevelled, and empty. He looks across at her, winds down his passenger window and nods.

'What have you got for me?' she asks him.

'You're going to be arrested,' he says. 'Could be later today or tomorrow. There's video footage of you throwing away your bag outside Grant's house. The bag's been recovered, and it's ready to be sent to Forensics. So, it's going to be more than Grant's word against yours.'

'Shit! I'm fucked then.'

He reaches down into the passenger footwell and holds something up in a police evidence bag.

'You are unless this gets lost.'

'I have what you want.'

'Show me.'

Martina lifts the tub, opens it, and there is a hypodermic syringe. 'It's one dose. Doctor Dettori says it should be all he will need to reverse the effects.'

'That's all it needs to do, Ms Hayes.'

Martina gets out of the car with the tub.

'DS Harris, this will be the last time we speak of this. Agreed?'

'Yes. You may still be arrested, but without the bag, there's no link to you and that bloodstained tea towel we found.'

Martina reaches into Harris's car, puts down the tub and snatches the evidence bag. She examines it for a few moments and returns to her car. Harris wipes the sweat from his hands onto his trousers. Finally, both cars leave the car park in opposite directions.

McCall and Cheung have arrived at the Jacobs's holiday home in Victoria Road, Dartmouth. Only one comfort break was required and a quick bite to eat. They called ahead before arrival and have been met by two police officers. The tall one with a taser has taken a fancy to McCall, but she's not interested in the slightest. She and Cheung put on their stab vests and check their handcuffs and batons.

'It's the white house up the steps, Sergeant,' says PC Stone, the tall one. 'There's no back entrance, just a pair of French doors facing us. The front door is around the side of the building. There's a tree in the front garden that partly blocks the view. By the time she sees us, we will be nearly upon her.'

'Thanks for that constable—very efficient,' says McCall. People are stopping to watch now. 'Let's get on with it. You've both seen the photograph of her?'

'Yes, Sergeant,' both officers say together.

The road is on a hill, leading out of Dartmouth, and the house is above them up some steep steps. McCall lets the uniformed officers take the lead, and they find the door key in the key-safe. The place looks dark inside.

'It doesn't look like she's going to be here,' says Cheung.

'We still need to check,' says McCall.

The first officer is in, taser drawn. 'Police with taser! Show yourself!' There's quiet. The other officer enters. McCall watches through the French doors to see the officers sweeping the place. McCall shakes her head.

'As you said, Sarge,' says Cheung, 'we still have to search the place.'

'It's all clear, Sergeant,' says PC Stone. 'Looks like no one's been here for a while. Sorry.'

'Thanks for your support,' says McCall.

'Any time.'

McCall watches them walk to their car. 'Did he just wink at me?'

'I think that was for me, Sarge,' laughs Cheung.

McCall tries to call Angelis, but she has no phone signal. She types a text, and it fails to send.

'Let's have a look around. I just hope this wasn't just a jolly day out, as nice as it was to spend it with you, Po.'

While Cheung searches upstairs, McCall sits in the lounge, looking through the junk mail she found by the door. It's a light, spacious room with polished floorboards, brown leather sofas and floor to ceiling bookcases in the alcoves, on either side of a wood burner.

McCall is allowing herself to enjoy this moment of quiet and is reflecting for a moment. She has decided to tread carefully with Angelis, taking one step at a time and seeing how things go. She just wishes she had more girlfriends to talk it over with. They are all job friends. That needs to change, she thinks.

'Come on, girl!' she says to herself. She should be looking for any sign of Vanessa having been here recently. She's concluding they're on a wild goose chase.

She turns her head with a start. She sees someone in the corner of her eye, standing by the bookshelf. There's no one there—just a trick of the light.

'Shit!' she says. 'I'm seeing things now.' One of the antique encyclopaedia volumes is protruding slightly. She must have missed it. McCall walks over to push the book back in, but notices something unusual with it. The edging is slightly damaged and bent. She pulls out the book and opens it. It's hollow, and inside is a memory stick and folded piece of paper. On the memory stick, in indelible ink, is written *Oberon* on one side. McCall opens the note:

Send to police if anything happens to me. K x.

'Hi, sir, it's me,' says McCall into her mobile. She and Cheung are travelling back now, and it's dark. They've stopped off for a McDonald's and a toilet break, with McCall taking over the driving now. Standing in the car park, she can just see Po sitting in the car eating her food. McCall is speaking into her phone against the sound of traffic.

'I'm off duty,' says Angelis, 'you don't have to call me sir.'

'Yes, of course. Sorry I couldn't call sooner. There was no

signal, and we just got caught up with everything. Vanessa wasn't there, and it looks like she's never been there.'

'So, I sent you out on a wild goose chase.'

'We used that exact phrase. I'll just call you David then?'

'That is my name. Never Dave and especially not Davey. There's only one person in the world who calls me Davey.'

'Intriguing. This is going to be so weird. Anyway, Edie gave us permission to look around the house in case there was any clue to Vanessa's whereabouts. There was nothing regarding Vanessa Grant, but we found something odd. We checked with Edie, and she said that neither she nor Ted knew anything about it. There was a memory stick and a note hidden in a cut-out of a book. It says send to police if anything happens to her, signed initial K. It must be Katherine.'

'Shit, she knew she was in danger. How long until you're home?'

'Two hours. Shall I meet you at yours?'

'Yes, sure, as long as it's not too late for you.'

'No worries. I'll see you soon.'

Cheung watches McCall as she practically skips back to the car. Cheung is staring at her.

'What?' says McCall. 'Haven't you looked at me enough today?'

'How was Angelis?' asks Cheung.

'Great.'

'Great?' Cheung's laugh sets McCall off, too.

Considering she's been on the road for eight hours today, Helen looks remarkably fresh and cheerful standing at my door. She has brought the note and the memory stick, and I have my computer ready.

I've made her peanut butter on toast and hot chocolate as requested, and when I come back into the lounge, I catch her looking at my family photos.

'Your parents look sweet,' she says. 'I love the old car! My grandpa had one of those, a blue one with wood on the back. And is that your sister?'

'Yes, they are sweet and far enough away, so I don't have to give an account of myself every single day. The car is dad's pride and joy. She's called Gracie. The girl is my baby sister, Gemma. Dad is from Trinidad and Tobago—mum is from Worthing. Don't ask how that happened.' Helen laughs.

'Is there a photo of your son?' She's looking around for it.

'One minute.' I get up and bring down the photo from the drawer in the bedroom.

She's looking at it and stroking his face with her finger. Her smile is making me weak at the knees.

'He's gorgeous. You can tell he's your boy. Did you know he was going to have Down's Syndrome before he was born?'

'No. It floored me at first, to be honest. But I wouldn't change him for the world. I just wish I could see him.'

Helen comes over to sit on the sofa with me. She's sitting close to me, and I can feel her warmth against me. I see her overnight bag at her feet, and I'm not sure if that makes me nervous or excited. It was something I never asked her to do. Perhaps she thinks going through this evidence is going to take us into the early hours. She notices me checking out her bag.

'I didn't want to leave it in the car,' she says. 'I've got my stab vest and warrant card in there.'

'Yes, of course.' But she knows what I'm thinking and smiles, sipping her hot chocolate.

Like some old ham, I've dimmed the lights a little and put some music on, a bit of gentle soul just to keep us going. My MacBook is on, and Helen has the memory stick ready. I copy the contents into a folder on my desktop, and Helen pops the stick into an evidence bag and seals it.

'Are you sure it's not too late for you?' I ask. 'We can do this at work tomorrow?'

'Yeah, right, like you won't sneak a peek before you go to bed.'

'Let's get on with it then.'

There are two folders inside. One is called *Docs*, containing emails, memos, and other documents. The other is called *Start Here*. I open that folder, and inside is one video file called *Angelis-Watch-This*.

The video starts with Kate talking to the camera. It's paused. She looks a little different from when I saw her last. Her hair is shorter, and her makeup is different. It's a shock seeing her there, and Helen can see my expression.

'Are you sure you're ready to do this?' McCall asks me. 'This case seems to have focused on you again. You seem to be caught up in the middle of it somehow.'

'Driscoll wants me to carry on with it, as does Walsh. But you're right, I'm not that comfortable with it,'

'We're here now. So, are you okay to carry on?'

'Yes, I'm okay. Hopefully, this will shed some much-needed light.'

I press play, and we're watching Katherine Jacobs talking confidently to camera, formal and businesslike at first. She talks about Hudson Biotech, the Operation Oberon programme, and the development of Y9-Alphapase. It's then I need to pause it.

'So, this just confirms what Driscoll told me,' I say. 'They've discovered a drug has side effects that effectively make people superhuman?'

'That's what Katherine's saying. It sounds so far-fetched, but then there's you!'

Doctor Katherine Jacobs to camera:

Dettori gave me a choice to do as he said or get fired. We somehow had permission to work from Brighton's major accident and emergency hospital to look for a suitable candidate for the trial. How Dettori got that consent is beyond me. Bizarrely, as opposed to the programme as he was, Colin volunteered to assist me. He would prepare the Y9 dose for me... Amanda and I separated because of this. She thought I should have just resigned. She told me I had betrayed my values...

Anyway, it wasn't long before we found a candidate that might benefit from the drug. He wasn't a stroke victim or a dementia patient, but he was still of some interest to Dettori. They brought in a police officer with multiple stab wounds and a fractured skull. He was in a terrible state at first, but they saved him. He was in a coma, and they weren't sure if he had suffered brain damage or not.

11th December 2019

'So, what is the drug you're giving him,' asks Rachael Thorne.

She has seen Doctor Katherine Jacobs several times on the

ward but has never actually spoken to her. Doctor Jacobs has kept herself to herself most of the time. She attends a few multi-disciplinary team meetings, but sits at the back, not wanting to stick out.

'It's a trial drug to help brain function,' says Doctor Jacobs. 'I can't tell you too much about it as it's hush-hush at the moment.' Jacobs nods at Colin Decker, her assistant, who is waiting with a tray and a phial of clear liquid.

Decker takes the phial, and Doctor Jacobs watches him as he cross-references the batch number against a number on a list. He prepares the drug ready to inject and hands it to Doctor Jacobs.

'Ready when you are,' he says.

'You're sure you want to do this?' asks Doctor Jacobs.

'You know my thoughts about it.' He pushes up his spectacles and looks away, scanning his notes.

'He doesn't sound too confident,' says Rachael as she steps out of the way.

'No, it's fine,' says Jacobs. 'It's just... He'll be fine.'

Jacobs delivers the dose in Angelis's left arm and stands back. Rachael records the first set of observations and takes a seat next to him.

'He should be monitored every half an hour for the first eight hours,' says Doctor Jacobs. 'We are not expecting there to be too many issues.'

'Too many?' asks Rachael. Jacobs tries to ignore the question and tidies everything away. 'What are you expecting to happen?'

'I'm expecting the patient to respond soon. Let me know when he does.'

'Okay. Hopefully, my stimulating conversation will help him.' Rachael smiles to be friendly, but she gets no response.

The doctor and Decker say nothing else and leave the room.

Rachael watches Angelis, and there is no response so far. She is alone with him now and takes his hand and squeezes it. She knows his family is so worried about him. They've been told to go home and rest. She is happy to stay by his side and be his family while they wait for any news. She will have her lunch on the ward today as not to be far from him. She found a juicy red apple in her bag, which her husband must have sneaked in there for her. She will look forward to that later.

She knows Angelis can't hear her, but she prays anyway. 'God, please help this man.'

Doctor Katherine Jacobs to camera:

> *I administered 10 millilitres of Y9-Alphapase into Angelis's bloodstream. After a few minutes, when the most notable adverse reactions occur, all was well—all his observations were normal. I checked in two hours later—no change. About 3 hours later, Colin came into my office. He looked anxious, and he said we need to get all our stuff together quickly. Angelis had died. After calling Dettori, I packed up everything quickly and left the office. I thought that was the end of it—I did everything I could. The trial was unsuccessful.*

'Died?' says Helen.

My palms are sweating now, and Helen notices the change in my breathing. She places her arm around me.

'We need to go on,' I say. Helen's arms are still holding me.

The following week, it all went crazy at Hudson. Colin Decker confronted Dettori about how the trial had deteriorated and how Dettori was just picking random subjects without getting informed consent. He felt vindicated after the trial on the police officer failed. He stupidly threatened to expose Dettori, even report it to the police. It created a great deal of animosity, and they suspended Colin pending a hearing.

The news came that they had found Colin dead on the road one night. They said he had been murdered. I thought this was too much of a coincidence. I confronted Dettori, who said it was all a fantasy. He said Colin had probably pissed someone else off. He was known for his volatile temperament.

Two nights after Colin's death, Amanda called me. She was distraught. She said Colin had spoken to her the night before he died. He told her something important about the trial involving the police officer. She wanted to talk to me about it. I was still angry with her and couldn't face her. Less than two months later... Amanda lay down in the fast lane of the A27 after taking a cocktail of drugs and alcohol. Valentine's day. I'll never forgive myself.

I resigned from Hudson, and in my leaving letter, I vowed to Dettori that I would ruin him and Hudson. As soon as I had the evidence, I would give it to the police. Dettori didn't take it seriously. They knew I had nothing.

In September last year, a woman approached me. Her name was Driscoll. She said she was from the police but some special department somewhere. She said she was investigating what happened to David Angelis in the hospital. I didn't know what to say at first. I explained to her I was acting on behalf of Hudson, and I had resigned. When I told her Hudson was responsible for Angelis's death, she was puzzled. She said to me that David Angelis was very much alive. I couldn't believe it. After all this time, I never knew. I was furious that they hadn't told me.

She said I could be in serious trouble, administering the drug with no lawful consent. To cut a long story short, I did a deal with her. I'm not proud of myself, but it was the only way out I could see. She wanted me to watch Angelis. They wanted me to move next door to him, befriend him, and study him. I finished moving in next door to Angelis in November. They told me he was showing some unusual behaviour since his recovery, and they wanted it monitored. They installed covert cameras in his home. I had to log in, record it via my mobile phone, and pass it on to Driscoll. I did what they wanted, but I hated it. I still do. He is such a nice guy. Quirky but nice. There are some bizarre things he does. Some things I can't explain. But I just do my side of the bargain... for now, anyway.

'Quirky,' says McCall. 'I'll agree with that. Are you still okay?'

'Yes, thanks,' I say. This is so strange, hearing Kate again. The Kate I thought I knew.

It was around that time Vanessa Grant, the head of security at Hudson, secretly approached me. She told me she had found evidence of Dettori's illegal activity, both with the drugs trial and his associations with Christopher Dalton. Vanessa had found evidence on Colin's old laptop that supported his claims against Hudson. And then, deciding to go through a box of Amanda's belongings they had put into storage, she found a memory stick with a backup of Colin's evidence. The memory stick you are watching this video on.

We were worried about bringing any accusation to Dettori at first. Vanessa believed that her life was now in danger because of what she knew. So Vanessa moved in with me after leaving her husband. She wanted to move somewhere safe, unknown to Dettori. Since she has been with me, Vanessa and I have become close. Very close.

We agreed that the safest thing is to build up the evidence and use it against Dettori. But we disagree on what we should do with the evidence. She wants to go to the police, but I have other plans. I just want to get away from everything, to move into the countryside somewhere.

If you are watching this, then it's likely I'm dead. It's partly my fault. I've been blackmailing Dettori—that was my plan. But I think the plan is going to work as they won't want their reputation ruined. I want out of all of this. I want to set up a nice home somewhere with Vanessa. I love Scotland. Far away with Vanessa and Max. I'll also be sad as I'm just getting to know David. He's a nice man. If I was really into men, then I imagine I would have been into him.

Also, my parents and my darling Lizzie... I'm so sorry, and I love you.

The video fades for a moment.

'This strongly implicates Dettori,' I say. 'We need to bring him in.'

'I agree,' says McCall. 'And Wheelhouse? So do you think Dettori, Martina and Wheelhouse could be working together?'

'Yes, most definitely. We have the tea towel connection to Martina Hayes, which is pretty good evidence. Dettori may have just been organising it all, and Wheelhouse is working for Dettori now. But we need some solid evidence to link them all working together with the murder.'

When Kate returns to the camera, it looks like a different day, and she's looking brighter and slightly further away from the camera. She's not so personal now, more professional:

According to David Angelis's psychiatric notes, he's suffering from some sort of PTSD, inducing hallucinations, audible and visual. It's clearly not Charles Bonnet. He's not showing the same psychopathic or narcissistic tendencies as Wheelhouse. Their conclusions are that David's acute sensory activity is causing his brain to generate imagery. These hallucinations bring to light the tiniest of details that he sees and hears. He picks up on micro-movements, the smallest of gestures, eye flicker, even down to how cloth hangs on someone's clothes. It's absolutely fascinating. He doesn't know about my study of him yet, but I will disclose it at the right time.

There is something else, though. Something I have absolutely no explanation for at all. Wheelhouse doesn't have this. It's not only sensory information that presents itself to David as hallucinations. There's something else, too. He's described it to the psychiatrist, and Professor Allen calls it a spiritual perception. I don't know how else to describe it. Professor Allen is baffled, too. I wonder if Allen's building a case study around it.

David is highly empathic. He can easily read people's emotions, motives, and intentions. It's staggering sometimes. But there is, and I cringe when I say this out loud, also evidence of telepathic abilities. Very sci-fi, I know, but the evidence is there. The scariest part is that it can work both ways. He can read other people's thoughts and influence other people's opinions and feelings, even to the point of making them see and feel things that aren't there.

Helen is looking at me like she's just realised something. I can see a sudden mistrust in her eyes. 'I know you've explained this to me before, but what can you do to me? Are you making me feel—'

'No, Helen! Stop it. I would never do that to you. I promise you. Even if I wanted to, you'd know I was doing it.'

'Yet, these new powers would be a godsend to someone who would get off on controlling others. How bloody ironic would that be!' She is no longer sitting close to me. Her legs have turned away, and there's a look of panic on her face.

'Listen to me, Helen! I want nothing more in the world but to hold you right now. To kiss you. Am I making you do it? No! What kind of friendship, relationship would that ever be? I'm not that man anymore. If you need to go now, then that's fine. I completely understand. I've only ever been honest with you about it—from the very beginning, I told you. Do you remember?'

'Your unorthodox methods, you told me.'

'Yes, those. I have this gift for a reason. I'm not completely sure what that reason is yet. Perhaps it is to help people, to mend things that are broken... God knows. But I do know I really care about you, Helen.'

She's looking at me again now, and she's softened again. 'Have your eyes always been that colour?'

'No. My eyes were brown, like yours, although not as nearly as pretty.'

'Flattery won't help you, sir.' Her smile has returned.

'The colour change is called Acquired Heterochromia. They think it was after the brain injury.'

'I can't believe you had brown eyes.'

'Well, I'm black, in case you hadn't noticed.'

She moves closer to me again.

'What did you say you wanted to do to me?'

16th December 2019

Amanda Wilson brings back a large white wine and another pint of Guinness for Colin. The pub is nearly empty, but it is a Monday night. There are a few lairy farm labourers in tonight at the bar. Colin keeps sending them withering looks as he's trying to hear Amanda speak. He's getting threatening glares back.

'Dettori is playing us all for mugs,' says Colin. 'I couldn't let him get away with it.'

'But what about Kate, Colin?' says Amanda. 'Why didn't you tell her what you did?'

'Don't be stupid. She would have run to Dettori and told him. I won't let this be on my conscience.'

A stocky man in a black t-shirt is walking up to the jukebox.

'But he died anyway,' says Amanda. 'Look, I get it, and I agree with you. These trials must stop. They are completely unethical.'

'I told Dettori that. Now, I'm out of a job. But I won't let him get away with it.'

Mariah Carey blares out.

'Sodding Christmas songs! Tosser!' Colin shouts at the black t-shirt man. He turns to approach Colin.

Amanda holds up her hand to him to apologise.

'Careful, Colin! There's three of them, and you've had too much to drink. I shouldn't have bought you the last one. And I've probably had too much myself.'

'Sorry, I just hate Christmas.' Colin finishes his pint. 'You're too good for Kate, Amanda. You know that. Have you ever been with a man?'

'Stop it, Colin! Anyway, Kate and I aren't together anymore. That's not what we're here to talk about. Frankly, I don't know what to do with what you've told me. I may go back to that policeman's family and tell them. Someone should know.'

'You can't, though, can you. It's official secrets and all that. And what would you say to them, anyway? Sorry, your son is dead. The drugs we gave him weren't legal, but it wasn't our fault he died.'

'I suppose you're right. It sounds stupid.'

'Too right it does. But not half as stupid as Mariah Carey.'

'What are you going to do, Colin? You're a clever man, even when you've had too much to drink. Where will you go?'

Colin pushes up his glasses and thinks for a while. Then smiles through alcohol blurred eyes.

'I will fight him. I'm not frightened of him. In fact, it's not him I'm going to talk to next. It's Dettori's boss. I will let Andrew Hudson himself know what Dettori's been doing.'

'Colin, you know what friends Dettori has now. You be careful.'

'I'm not frightened of anyone, Amanda. If anything happens to me, then it's all on my computer. Everything is there and also... on this...' Colin pulls out a memory stick from his jacket pocket. 'Actually, lovely Amanda. Would you give this to Kate for me? She may need it.'

He drops the memory stick onto the table, and Amanda picks it up.

'I'll try,' she says. 'But she's not happy with me at the moment.'

'Then send it anon... anon... secretly.'

'I will. I promise. Just take care, Colin. I'll be thinking of you.'

'You do that, Amanda. You bloody do that. I like the thought of you thinking of me. The same way, I often think of you at night.' He gives a lascivious laugh. 'If you spent one night with me, you would know what a real man felt like. I promise.'

'Come on, I'll take you home.'

She drags him up out of his chair, being watched by the men at the bar. Colin is fading fast. She picks up his wallet and phone and walks him towards the door.

The pub car park is dark, and Colin is about to drop headfirst into the gravel. Amanda puts his arm around him and drags him to her car. It's then she feels his fingers in between her legs and climbing up her skirt.

'Get off!' she says. She lets him go, and he falls.

'It was an accident!' He laughs as he gets up to his knees.

'You can walk home, you dick! The walk will sober you up. What is it with men?'

'Oh, come on, Amanda. It meant nothing.'

Then she sees two men in the shadows.

'You okay, sweetheart?' says a deep voice.

'I'm not your sweetheart, and I'm fine, thank you.'

'Okay, okay. Keep your knickers on. We'll take care of him for you. Where's he going?'

'Sorry. I just need to go home. Thank you. He lives in the next village.'

'Don't you worry—we're heading that way.'

Amanda gets in her car and locks the doors. She shouldn't be driving, but home is only fifteen minutes away. Amanda drives off, opening her window for the fresh air on her face, and heads along the Funtington Road towards home. Ten minutes later, when she comes to the first streetlights, she sees Colin's wallet and phone on her passenger seat.

'Oh, shit!' She steps on the brakes, and the car comes to a halt, with the anti-lock brakes pulsing. 'Calm down, Amanda,' she says to herself. She decides she'll drop Colin's things through his letterbox and run.

With a U-turn, she hopes no one saw, Amanda heads back

into the darkness of the Funtington Road. Along a straight mile stretch, she passes two men in dark clothing walking in the road.

'Idiots. They'll get themselves killed in the dark.'

She speeds up past them—Colin's place isn't far now. But it's too late when she sees a man lying across the carriageway. His glasses are the first thing Amanda sees, reflecting white flashes from headlights. She brakes hard, but the wheels are over his head and stomach. The car's front bounces with a clump and then the back, finishing Colin Decker for good.

She screams.

SEVENTEEN

8th March 2022

Helen and I enter the office separately to avoid embarrassment. She's already gone home and changed. I'm trying not to look too cheerful.

I see Cheung coming back with a coffee, and she has a tight-lipped smile as she passes me. 'Good morning, sir,' she says.

'Good morning, Po. Excellent work yesterday. I hope you weren't back too late. Helen has filled me in.'

'I'm glad she has, sir.' I catch the glint in her eye.

Harris is looking sharp again. He has notes for the briefing ready, but I must see Walsh first to tell him about the video. Helen looks up from her desk and watches me as I go in.

Walsh leans back in his chair and looks up at the ceiling while I'm talking to him about the video. To give him credit, he never makes a judgement until he has all the facts. The concern, in this case, is that I have become a central player in it.

'Sir, I'm asking that we restrict the video on the memory stick. It highlights certain aspects of my condition that others are not aware of, even though you are. I would hate this becoming unused material in this case—the defence and his wife will know about me, too. It will get out and scupper my career.'

'Thank you for being frank with me, David,' he says. Walsh pauses for a moment and is now watching a pen balancing on his finger. I don't know if that's a metaphorical judgement in the balance or not. 'The major element here is bringing Katherine Jacobs's killers to justice. So, Dean Dettori is in the frame now, too. God, as is Nathan Wheelhouse, Martina Hayes, even Vanessa Grant and Peter Grant. Lock them all up—they're all as guilty as sin. I despair! With the documents on that memory stick, you have the corroborating evidence of the emails, the laboratory notes, photographs. We need to go in and seize the original files from their servers. This is one major operation, David. Do you think we have the resources for it?'

'Not really. It's a Major Crimes job. It's a stretch with everything we're working on.'

'Bloody hell! What a tangled web we weave. Dalton and Dettori! I don't know what Hudson's head office criminal involvement was in this, either. Then, there's this recent information about you. I have to say, I have heard nothing like it in all my years. Your abilities are unique, I always thought that, but they go far deeper and further than I ever imagined, than you let on, anyway.'

'I'm sorry, sir.'

'That's okay, David! Laura Driscoll says she has this in hand. And how could you have told me without me sending you back to the funny farm? Oh, I shouldn't call it that, should I.'

'Sir, this video's disclosure has put me in a difficult position. I'm not sure how much of it you want to put out there.'

'It's a fair point you're making, David. I will need to talk to Driscoll and the Chief. Hopefully, they'll be able to give me the advice on that one.'

'Thank you, sir.'

'Driscoll's a funny one, isn't she?' says Walsh quietly, as if she could be listening. 'So many secrets going on there. Studying you under the microscope like that. Don't lose your humanity in all this, David. Whatever you can do, whatever strange powers you possess, you are still a human being underneath it all. The senior officers are right behind you.

'Do your Operation Greenwood briefing. Don't mention the video to anyone—consider it restricted. Obviously, McCall knows, but leave it at that. She's in Driscoll's *circle of trust* now, too.' He smiles and shakes his head. 'Major Crimes will take on the illegal drug trial side of things because of the complexity and serious nature of Hudson's research. Your focus should now be on finding and arresting Vanessa Grant, Dettori, and Hayes, too. All three of them. Let's have a party.'

'Op Greenwood briefing is now in progress,' says Harris, 'so can we have less of the chatter, please.' The office is suddenly quiet, apart from the pockets of calls going on regarding other cases.

'Thank you, James,' I say. 'Thank you, everyone. So, we now know Vanessa Grant has not visited the Jacobs's holiday home in Dartmouth. Recent evidence found from that location by Po and DS McCall casts doubt on Vanessa's motive for murdering Doctor Jacobs.'

'Even with the fingerprints and trace DNA on the knife, sir?' says Sam Gregory.

'Yes, that is a problem,' I say, 'but the motive is missing now. I know there are fingerprints, but we'd expect there to be more of her DNA on the handle if she were cutting and stabbing. Vanessa Grant may have been helping Doctor Jacobs to blackmail Dettori over the drug trials. We've restricted details of those drug trials before anyone asks.'

I suddenly see a large, black bird with a curved beak landing on James's shoulder. It's come out of nowhere, and I don't have a clue what it means. He sees me frowning at him.

'Sir?' Harris says.

'No, it's fine,' I say as I gather my thoughts again. 'Operation Greenwood has suddenly got a lot more complex.' Laura Driscoll enters the office and stands at the back. I nod to her.

'So, what are our priorities now, boss?' asks Daley.

'Major Crimes is taking over the primary investigation of the drugs trials, working together with assistance from the Medical Research Council. We need to bring in Martina Hayes and Dean Dettori today. Sam has suggested that we take Hayes while she's at work. Thanks for your leg-work, Sam. I'd like an armed response unit on standby, please. Her bag should be with forensics by now, and there should be enough of Doctor Jacobs's DNA in there from the tea towel to convict her.'

'Muhammad,' says Harris, still with the agitated bird pecking at his shoulder, 'you sent the tea towel to Forensics—any news yet?'

'Um,' Essam looks dazed, 'I haven't checked. Sorry, I didn't realise—'

'Get on with it then,' says Harris abruptly. The bird is flapping his wings.

Essam is bright red.

'Let me know when Dettori and Hayes are in,' I say.

Helen appears at my door. She has a frown on her face as she's examining a list of property log printouts.

'Excuse me, sir,' she says, almost as if last night never happened.

'DS McCall, how can I help you?' I say with a smile.

'There's a problem.'

We are in one of the side offices above the Custody Suite, well out of the way from everyone else. I'm sitting at the desk, logged onto the property system. McCall and Essam enter the office and shut the door.

'So, exactly what has happened?' I say to McCall.

'Muhammad contacted forensics after the briefing,' says McCall, 'and they have not received Martina's bag we seized from the skip near Peter Grant's house.'

Essam is looking very pale, and there is a line of sweat along his top lip. I look at the property database, and I see Essam booked the bag in and marked it as evidence to go to Forensics. It should have been in the property store, ready to be collected.

'DC Essam,' I say, 'did you put the bag, exhibit reference JL/03, bag number P301102, into the property store, or did something happen to it on the way?'

'Sir,' says Essam. He clears his throat. 'I delivered the bag myself.'

'Did anyone see you?'

'No, I was on my own.'

'What's happened to this vital piece of evidence?'

'I don't know, sir. I put it in there, with the appropriate label.'

'DS McCall, has the property store manager turned the place upside down looking for it?'

'Yes, sir,' she says.

'So, we have these alternatives: the bag was lost, transferring it to the van going to Forensics, someone removed the bag from the property store after DC Essam booked it in, or last, DC Essam is lying.'

'I'm not lying, sir,' says Essam. I study him for a while. He's a hard-working but anxious lad. I see nothing about him that tells me he's lying.

'Muhammad, I believe you.'

He gives a loud sigh.

'So,' says McCall, 'it was either lost or removed. I've checked with Forensics, and they have received the five other items that were also marked for delivery to them.'

'Thank you, DS McCall,' I say. 'Are we sure it wasn't taken away for destruction?'

'Absolutely, sir.'

'In that case, someone has removed the evidence. You're dismissed, Muhammad.'

'Thank you, sir,' Essam says as he stands. 'I'm sorry.'

'What are you sorry about? You've done nothing wrong. If you have any suspicions, then let me know.'

Essam leaves McCall and me in the office together, and I look at her. She looks amazing—glowing.

'Well, DS McCall. We are officially in the shit. If that evidence has disappeared, then we have nothing on Hayes other than circumstantial evidence.'

'Do you think someone deliberately removed it to clear Hayes?'

'Possibly, but it could be just a big cock-up. I would rather it was a cock-up than the other.'

'That's for sure.'

'You look incredible, by the way.'

'Thank you, sir,' she says, grinning at me. 'I do my best.'

'Email everyone in Chichester to see if anyone has booked out the wrong item. We need to be as upfront as we can. I'll tackle Walsh. I still want Hayes arrested. She may yet give us a confession.'

'Yes, sir, you never know.'

Paul takes James's head in his hands and forces him to look at him.

'I would never, ever have asked you to do this, James. I thought you knew me. Never in a million years.'

James backs away and leans against the kitchen counter.

'I did this for you, Paul! I did this for us! I can't live a day without you. I can't watch you fall apart slowly over months and years, drifting away from me. The very idea you won't even recognise me kills me!' James holds up the syringe in his hand. 'This will give us hope. This will give us a future!'

'But at what price, James!' Paul beats his fist against the countertop. He points a finger at him. 'At the price of you letting someone get away with murder? At the price of you going to prison for God knows how many years? Doing what you did has broken my trust in you, James. You were a man of virtue, honesty. I don't want to be the reason you throw that all away!'

'Paul! Just take it, please! I beg you! I'll tell them what I did. I'll face the consequences. But please, just take this. I don't want to lose you!'

'No! I will not!'

Paul swipes James's hand and grabs the syringe. He pushes the plunger and ejects a stream of clear fluid onto the floor.

James slips down onto the floor, sobbing. Paul crouches in front of him and holds him tightly.

'Martina is in the cells, sir,' says Daley outside my door. 'We're just waiting for her solicitor to arrive. I hear she came quietly, almost like she was expecting us.'

'Thanks, Dan,' I say. 'What's happening with Dettori?'

'No one knows where he is. Sam and Po have gone to his golf club. He's probably heard about Martina's arrest by now.'

'Shit! We need Dettori. Is DS Harris in the office?'

'I haven't seen him since before lunch. I thought he'd gone to get Hayes.'

'No, he didn't. No worries. If you see him, let him know I'm looking for him.'

I check the duty sheet and type in his details—he's booked off duty. I'm feeling uneasy. I look up his mobile number and call him.

'James?' I say as he answers. 'Is everything okay?'

'Sir,' he says. His voice sounds strained and shaky. 'No, everything isn't okay... I've let you down.'

'Okay, talk to me, James.' I hear a train announcement telling people to stand back. He's standing on a platform somewhere. I signal to Daley and tell him to get McCall.

'I took that bag, sir. I gave it back to Martina Hayes in exchange for the drug.'

'For Paul?'

'Yes. For Paul. I just can't be without him, you see. I don't want to see him decline, to forget who I am.'

'So, you gave him the drug in the hope it would prevent Paul's Alzheimer's?'

'I offered it to him, but he's a much better man than I am. He refused it. He's so much better than me.'

'James, I'll be honest with you. This is going to be difficult for you, but I can help—'

'No, it's okay. You're a good boss. Very fair. But it's too late. There's a note in my house. We're doing this together.'

There's another voice I can hear. It must be Paul. 'Yes, DI Angelis. It's okay. This is the only way. We want to do this together.'

'James! Where are you? What are you doing?'

I can hear the rumbling on the tracks of a train coming, full speed... and then nothing.

I'm sitting with Walsh, Driscoll, and Helen. We're all speechless—it's just such a senseless loss. I've had a message from BTP near Horsham. The remains of James and Paul have been located. I keep thinking about that poor train driver; there was nothing they could have done.

'I think it's best we send the team home,' I say. 'Including you, Helen. I don't want there to be any speculation or anything.'

'Yes, I think you're right,' says Walsh. 'What about you?'

'I'm okay. I'm staying to interview Hayes.'

'With all that raw emotion, David, I'm not sure that's wise. We can get someone from Major Crimes in.'

'I'm okay, sir, honestly. I'm the best one to find out the truth here. We can cut through the crap right now.'

'I agree with Superintendent Walsh,' says Driscoll. She sits on the desk in front of me. 'This is all highly charged. You have lost one of your own, and Hayes is responsible.'

'Sir,' says Helen to Walsh. 'I know this isn't a vote, but I think DI Angelis is ideally equipped to get to the bottom of this. We don't have the bag now, and Hayes has probably long disposed of it. We need someone who can cut through to the truth.'

There's a pause because everyone knows Helen is right.

'I will go in with you,' says Driscoll. 'The first sign of anything unprofessional, then I will take you out of there.'

'Thank you, ma'am,' I say. 'Helen, I will see you later, okay? Tell the others to go home for the afternoon.'

As Driscoll and I watch the team leaving, she turns and steps in close to me.

'David,' she says, quietly. 'I don't care what you do in there with Hayes. Just get that bitch with whatever it takes.'

'Okay. I need to go back to the house, ma'am. I'll meet you in the interview room in about an hour.'

I pull back the boarding just enough for me to slip inside. The place is in semi-darkness. I'm hit by the overpowering smell of bleach.

It's surreal to be back here again. There are things where Kate left them, books, a pen by the phone, a notepad with a scrawl on it where she's tested if it's working. There's a hair grip on the stairs. She could still be in here.

My stomach is churning, and my heart races. I must stay focused and detach my feelings. I need to see. Is it still too soon? Will it still be a mess of shadows and faces?

I close my eyes and slow my breathing.

'I want to see.'

When I open my eyes, I see layer upon layer of time surrounding me. It's a cacophony of images, moving about me, walking through me. I see Kate and Vanessa. I see the previous tenants. I see builders and plasterers. I focus and peel away one layer at a time, moving forward, coming closer and closer. The more recent they are, the more I struggle to see. They become blurred with movement and colour. The further back I look, the dimmer the images become, washing away into history.

I see something. I tune my senses to see Kate being pushed across the room. The table goes flying as she falls.

She's fighting back, kicking. There are two of them standing over her, just blurred shapes. One of them grabs Kate and lifts her off the ground. I follow them to the kitchen, and she's pinned to the table. They're men. Dark clothes. The focus is going. They're tying her, and she's kicking, screaming. And then they are still, and I see exactly who they are. There's a knife...

I fight to get out into the fresh air. I can barely breathe. The world is turning around me, layer upon layer, sweeping past my eyes. I'm falling away, drowning as each layer smothers me. A hand touches me, steadies me.

'Come on, David,' a voice says. 'It's okay. It's okay.'

She holds me tightly until I return—until I can see and hear again. But just before she comes into view, she's gone, slipping away into the breeze, into the light of a breaking cloud.

Martina looks as cool as a cucumber when we step into the interview room, and she knows it. Next to her is Arthur Spooner, her solicitor. He's expensive and very thorough. He's old school, and I always thought he should have been a barrister. Martina doesn't even look up at us but continues to examine her nails. I know nothing about fashion, but I can tell that dress she's wearing is expensive, showing off her figure. I wonder who that is for? Her boss?

Driscoll is as cool as Martina, positively icy. She has this fixed half-smile on her face as she opens a folder containing photographs. I'm looking at Martina now, and I'm getting the darkness, the violence and anger. It's exuding from every pore of her skin. I see another face, repeatedly projected onto her own. A man with a beard, moving inside her. In phase with her every move. So, already, I know she's working with someone.

I press the button on the computer screen and wait for the warning tone to stop.

'I am Detective Inspector A2470 Angelis, and this is a video interview being conducted in the Chichester Custody Centre. It is Tuesday, 8th March 2022, and the time is 1432 hours. Also present is...'

'Detective Chief Superintendent D2001 Driscoll.' Driscoll nods to the solicitor, who raises one of his bushy eyebrows.

'Also present is your solicitor...'

'Arthur Spooner of Spooner and West.'

'Please state your full name...'

'Martina Ellen Hayes.' Martina looks up at the camera on the wall.

'While you are here, you have the right to free and independent legal advice, and you have chosen Mr Spooner here to represent you. You do not have to say anything, but it may harm your defence if you do not mention when questioned something which you later rely on in court. Anything you do say may be used in evidence. Do you understand the caution, Ms Hayes? Can you explain what it means back to me?'

'Inspector,' says Spooner, 'my client is an intelligent woman and has had the caution explained to her. Can we move on, please?'

'As you wish.' I smile and take a small sip of water. I won't be rushed. 'Ms Hayes, you were arrested this morning on suspicion of conspiracy to murder and perverting the course of justice. This is in connection with the murder of Doctor Katherine Jacobs. Did you know Doctor Jacobs?'

'Inspector,' Spooner again in a theatrical tone. 'My client has prepared a written statement we would like to give you, and she will not be answering any questions you put to her.'

Spooner passes me a typed piece of paper. I scan it and give it the Driscoll.

'Very nice, Ms Hayes. You know I will ask you questions, anyway.'

'You haven't even read it properly, Inspector!' Spooner leans forward. 'Come on, lad!'

'Mr Spooner, my name is Detective Inspector Angelis. Not lad or boy. I hope I have made that clear?'

Spooner grumps as he sits back in his chair.

'Martina,' I continue. 'What were you doing from 9 p.m. on Sunday, 27th February 2022?'

'No comment,' says Martina.

'It's in the statement,' says Spooner. His sigh is worthy of the Royal Shakespeare Company.

I look at Martina and wait. I allow myself to focus once more. I can see the hundreds of suspects sitting in that chair, people moving around me. Men, women, and children, blending into each other. But I focus on Martina.

Spooner huffs. 'What are you doing, Inspector? She gave you her answer?'

'Mr Spooner,' says Driscoll. 'Please stop interrupting, or we will have to find Ms Hayes other representation.'

I see that darkness again. It's twisting inside of her, whispering to me, cursing me. I see her memory. She's sitting in a car with two others. They're waiting in the shadows, watching Peter Grant at Kate's front door. There's Vanessa. Then I reach in, and I make her break the silence.

'You were outside Katherine's house,' I say. 'I know you were. You were with two others.'

She flinches like I've struck her. She's desperately trying to control her tongue, but I'm forcing it out of her. She's blinking rapidly, groaning. It's hurting her, keeping silent, holding back the truth. The vein in her neck is throbbing. Her face is swelling.

'I was with Nate and Dettori,' she says. I see her relief as she lets the tension go like she's been holding her breath for too long.

'Thank you,' I say.

'Martina,' says Spooner. 'Stick to the statement!'

'Ah, the statement!' I say. 'Let me read that part... It says you were at home alone. So, you wish to retract this prepared statement?'

Her head is hurting as she resists. So much anger, darkness. That other face is yelling at her.

'Yes!' she says. She is sweating. She's trying to stop talking, but she can't.

I rip up the statement, and Driscoll is nearly at a full grin. She's enjoying this.

'Martina, what were you doing with Dettori and Nate?'

'We were waiting for Peter Grant to leave Katherine Jacobs's house.' Martina is struggling to sit still. She is moving around as if something is biting her.

'And just to confirm? Who is Nate?' I say.

'Martina!' bellows Spooner. 'Do you wish me to carry on representing you?'

'Yes!' she pleads. 'I can't stop...'

'Mr Spooner!' says Driscoll. 'Calm yourself, please. You are intimidating your client.'

'Nate is Nathan Wheelhouse. He's my brother. My twin brother.'

'Hayes is your married name?' asks Driscoll.

'Yes. But I'm divorced.'

'Why were you waiting for Peter Grant to leave Doctor Jacobs's house?' I say.

The darkness inside her is trying to fight back. She clenches her fists, digging her nails into her palms until they bleed.

'Inspector,' says Spooner, pointing his finger at me. 'My

client is clearly unwell. We should suspend this interview immediately.'

'Are you feeling unwell, Martina?' I ask.

'No, I'm absolutely fine.' She nods her head vigorously.

'She's fine, Mr Spooner. Martina, where were you while you were waiting for Peter Grant to leave?'

'In a car, just out of sight.'

'Is this you in the car that night? I'm showing Martina Hayes a still from a nearby garden security camera. There's a black car with three occupants. Exhibit JH/04.'

'Yes.'

'By the way, Martina, the exhibit reference JH/04, means it is James Harris's fourth exhibit. That's DS Harris. I think you knew him. I'll talk about him later.'

Tears are rolling down Martina's face.

'I understand,' she says. 'You want to talk about the bag.'

'Ah, that's right, Martina,' I say. Driscoll grips her pen and nearly breaks it. 'But first, what time did Peter Grant leave Katherine Jacobs's house?'

'I don't know. I wasn't there.' She's trying to fight back again, but it's getting harder and harder for her.

'Martina?' I'm holding her tighter. 'Answer the question, please.'

'We saw Peter Grant leaving just before 9.30 p.m. I was there, Inspector. I was there. I was definitely there.'

'Thanks for clearing that up. What happened then, Martina?'

'I went to see Vanessa—Dettori wanted me to. I told her Dettori wanted to talk, to make a deal with her. I walked her to the car... Nate and I grabbed her, and he hit her. We tied and gagged her and put her in the boot of the car...'

Martina is turning pale.

'Have some water, Martina,' I say.

'I need Dettori. I need my fix.'

'We would like to know where he is, too.'

'What are you taking?' asks Driscoll.

'Y9. Dettori gives it to me.'

'We can get the nurse for you, Martina?' I say.

'No, I'll be fine. Carry on.'

Arthur Spooner has given up defending his client. He has been doodling on his notepad.

Martina takes a sip of water. Her hands are shaking.

'It feels good to tell the truth, doesn't it?' I say. Driscoll is nodding in agreement. 'What happened after you put Vanessa in the boot of the car?'

'Nate and Dettori went in to see Katherine. I stayed in the car. Vanessa was unconscious, so I just waited. Twenty minutes later, they came back. Ran back to the car. Dettori was wiping himself with a tea towel. They were smothered in blood. Nate had a computer under his arm.'

Martina's face is glistening with sweat. Driscoll frowns and is about to speak.

'Dettori handed Nate a knife. He put the knife in Vanessa's hand to get her fingerprints. Then he ran down the road to drop it in one of the rubbish bins.'

'Martina, who murdered Katherine Jacobs?'

'It was both of them, Dettori... and Nathan.'

Martina is really shaking more now.

'David, that's enough now,' says Driscoll.

'James Harris,' I say. 'Did you hear what happened to him? He and his partner killed themselves today, Ms Hayes. I just wanted you to know. I wonder how that makes you feel?'

I take a deep breath. I must stay calm.

'I... I'm sorry.'

'Martina.' I bring her back to look at me in the eyes. 'I suggest that you planted that tea towel in Peter Grant's house to make the police think he was guilty of killing Katherine. How does that sound, Martina? Is that true?'

'Yes, it is,' she says. 'I put it in Peter's laundry basket after we had... after I beat him.' A trickle of blood runs down her nose.

'Did Dettori tell you to do that, or was it Nathan?'

'Both. They suggested it. If I didn't do it, then I wouldn't get the Y9.'

'David. We'll stop this now,' says Driscoll.

I turn my head and close my eyes, and Driscoll sees it. The light in my eyes, just for a moment. As I let Martina go, she screams.

'What the fuck did you do to me! You bastard!'

Spooner jumps from his chair, but Martina already has the table over and smashed against the wall. She tries to grab me, but she can't find me. I'm behind her, in front of her. She's confused. Driscoll has hit the alarm strip, and it's all over as Martina collapses on the floor.

EIGHTEEN

He's wrapping her up in chicken wire, pressed in tight against her flesh until her skin looks like a pink quilt. Then comes the sacking. It's as long as she is tall, pulled up above her head and tied. The gag is tighter still with its wired reinforcement. He's carrying her again, and he whispers to her as he walks across the garage floor.

'Not long now, ugly bitch. You'll be dead soon. Hopefully, you won't have to hang around for long.' Then he's whistling again, some untuneful noise warbling from his lips as he walks.

She can just see through the weave of the sacking. He probably doesn't realise. The back door of a van opens, and he throws her in. The pain is no longer hers. She's long lost a sense of what is real and what is not. She's in the dark once more. How long has this ordeal been? He had so many questions, but she won, she won.

A phone rings somewhere, and he's talking.

Driscoll is in Walsh's office. Walsh isn't there—he's visiting James's family. The Investigations office is eerily quiet. There's a couple of uniformed officers copying CCTV footage in the corner, and that's all. She closes the blinds, shuts the door, and makes the call.

'Hi, it's me. Yes, I've just witnessed him in action, so to speak. It was terrifying. In my opinion, he is a real danger left to his own devices. If he went rogue, then it would be difficult to stop him... No, it's not likely at the moment, but he's volatile... I don't think we could restrain him... There's a lot more to him than we think we know... You know full well what I will recommend... The minister will have to wait a few hours. I'm clearing up a few things here first. We must wrap up Dettori and Wheelhouse first, and then we can decide. Turns out Martina Hayes is his sister. Yes, he is probably screwing her... Well, that's the sort of animal he is.' She hears someone moving around outside. 'I've got to go. Someone's outside.'

She opens the office door, and her intuition is correct. It's Angelis.

'David, that was a... dramatic interview.'

'It was what you wanted, wasn't it?' says Angelis, slipping off his jacket.

'To sort this out quickly, yes.'

'The thing is, ma'am, you forget what I'm capable of.'

'I don't think so. You achieved what we needed perfectly. The video won't show any hint of intimidation or coercion techniques.'

'That's not what I meant.' Angelis is looking directly at her. She can feel pressure in her temples. She's not sure if he's causing it or not.

'Sorry, I don't understand you.'

'You forget I can tell when people are lying to me. You remember me, don't you.'

Driscoll swallows. She's feeling the first hint of apprehension now.

'I think you ought to go home, Inspector. You've had a difficult day.'

'Alison, your sister. She and I went out together half a lifetime ago. You would have known me, but I never met you. You always avoided me. Why was that?'

'You're Davey!' Driscoll tries to look surprised.

'You know who I am, ma'am. You've known for a long time. You thought Alison was too good for me back then, that kid from the estate. After the attack, you took a special interest in me when you found out who I was. I know full well you consider me a threat. For the record, I don't feel safe around you either.'

'Alison often spoke about you. She was infatuated. She was so clever, as well as kind. We thought you were pulling her away from her studies.'

'I expect it was you who stopped us.'

Driscoll runs her hands through her hair. 'Look! This isn't helping. It's all in the past.'

'Years later, there I was again. Helpless in hospital. Was that it? Morbid curiosity? Alison must have been diagnosed with cancer by then. Did you tell her you'd come across me again?'

'Yes, I did. She prayed for your recovery, even when she was ill herself. As did our grandmother, until she died in February last year.'

'Joyce Mayhew. I've sat on the bench in the copse. I've even seen her there praying.'

'You are full of surprises, David! I bought that bench in her honour. The old one had rotted away. She used to pray for you there and for Alison, of course. That's all she ever did. It was her answer to bloody everything. Alison's, too. Now look where we are.'

'I'm sorry you lost your sister.' Angelis sits beside her. 'But I am not a threat to you or to anyone. I'm not a fucking terrorist!'

'No one can stop you, can they, David. You could even change the course of democracy if you used a little imagination. If you fell into the wrong hands...'

Angelis shakes his head and sighs. 'What do you want me to do, ma'am? Throw myself in front of a train?'

'David! That's hardly appropriate.'

'Well, short of getting rid of me, what can you do?'

'Come and work for us.'

'Work for you?'

'Yes. I was going to ask you. You've read me completely wrong. You've let your emotions get in the way. So, at least we know where you're vulnerable.' She takes a deep breath, as do I. 'There's a whole level of national security that urgently needs your skills. If people realised how close to the wire it gets with domestic terrorism, there would be a meltdown. We need someone with your skills.'

Driscoll knows Angelis is trying to read her, but she won't let him. Her face and neck are tingling, and she can feel pressure in her sinuses and ears.

'It would save you a problem.'

'Yes, it would. Of course, it would. I'm sorry I never mentioned that I was Alison's sister. Was that Terry I met at her memorial, a friend of yours?'

'Yes, and Alison's.'

'Tell him he's an oaf.'

'He knows. But he's a charming oaf and a good friend.' Angelis allows himself to smile. 'And I'm sorry I got it wrong.'

'Get some space, David. Have a think. In the meantime, we need to find some resources to find Vanessa.'

'I have the money for you,' says Dettori. 'Did she tell you anything?'

Wheelhouse puts the phone closer to his ear.

'No. I hurt her real bad and nothing. I'm going to dispose of her. She's just wasting our time.'

'They've arrested, Martina.'

'What the fuck!'

'Calm yourself. She got that bag back, and she's destroyed it. They can't link her to anything. The police are coming after me next—that's what you two need to worry about. I need you to get me out of here. I want to get back to Venice.'

'That's going to cost you an awful lot of money, Dean. How about your poor wife? She will be devastated.'

'I don't care about her. Just get me out of here. Whatever the cost.'

'Okay, 250 thousand on top of what you owe me to get you to the airport safely, plus the wife thrown in.'

'You are sick, Nathan!'

'I was fine before you gave me your magic potion, Dean. I was a good boy. Whatever I am is down to you.'

'I'll give you 400 thousand. Half the money upfront and leave my wife alone.'

'What about the Y9? I'm going to need a lifetime supply.'

'Yes, I know. I'll give you the key to a lockup nearby. It's all in there. Enough for you and your sister. You should slowly wean yourselves off it, Nathan. It could kill you if you don't. You can't stop suddenly.'

'Give me three months' supply now and the key. Then it's a deal.'

'Yes, yes. Whatever! Just get me on that flight. I've booked it for tomorrow, midday, from London Gatwick.'

'We'll go by train. My van and your car will ping on the police ANPR.'

'Train! Everyone will see us!'

'We'll be hiding in plain sight. Stop panicking. Listen. Leave your phone on. Get one of your skivvies to deliver it to one of your depots in Liverpool, anywhere far away. Wipe everything from your phone and wrap it up in the parcel. If anyone wants to trace your phone, then they'll get sent on a wild goose chase.'

'Right, will do.'

'Be at Chichester railway station tomorrow by 9 a.m. latest. Make sure you have everything I want, or you'll go nowhere.' Nathan ends the call and leans back to talk to Vanessa. 'I'll still have his wife.'

He dials another number, but there's no answer—the phone is switched off. So, it's true. They have her.

I'm walking in the city. There's so much in my head, and I don't know where to start. I head towards South Street, and an image of the old city gate and wall comes into view for a moment and disappears as I walk through them. The street is busy with late morning shoppers before the forecasted heavy rain comes our way.

My head is cast down, and my mind plays a mix of worries on an endless, repeating loop: James, Driscoll, Helen, Vanessa, Kate. I never got to question Martina about James. I get why he took the evidence. But what sort of life would he have had, knowing what he had done? If only he spoke to me. If only I could have seen it coming. Then I'm thinking, can Helen and I make it work? Am I going to become that controlling monster again? And is this job too much for me? Am I good enough and strong enough to carry on? It all just goes round and round in my head.

For some reason, I'm back in the cathedral, sitting away

from the central aisle. I didn't think I was a religious man, but I've seen such darkness today. I need to step into the light again. I look around, and I'm struck by the silence. This is one of those thin places. I'm wondering if the people praying over the centuries have punctured a million holes between heaven and Earth. Is that how it works?

A choir begins its practice, and their voices reverberate all around, creating a heavenly sound that vibrates through my chest and stomach. I'm alone and exhausted. I feel blind, naked, and utterly wretched.

I don't know if I have found the cause of my differentness or not. Kate wanted to believe it was that Y9-something-or-other drug. She thought it did something to my brain and brought me back to life. But then a memory comes back to me: Amanda. She visited me in the hospital—that note. Whatever happened to that note? I never read it. It must be in my old junk box in the wardrobe.

'God,' I whisper, 'what about me? Why am I so different? I can't sort my shit out at all. What do I do now?'

I raise my head, and I see the creatures are here again. I sense their intelligence and feelings. I see two or three of them standing around me at first. I'm not sure what they want with me. But they keep coming, hundreds and hundreds surrounding me, too many to count. I feel my flesh prickling like they're bringing a storm to me, covering me on every side. The cathedral is fading now. The sound of the choir gets louder. It's then I realise there was no choir at all—it's the creatures, singing together, with intricate harmonies, ground shaking basses. One of them crouches beside me, and I recognise them from somewhere.

'Hey, David,' they say. 'Yes, we have met before.'
'Who are you?' I say. 'I see so many of you.'
'Watchers, messengers, angels, friends.'

'I'm here trying to sort the crap out in my head. What's happening?'

The creature laughs, and others join in.

'While you try to sort your crap out, David, I have a message for you.'

I see Vanessa appear among them. She's pale, broken, and terrified. 'Help me!' she says to me.

'Where are you? We're trying to find you. Tell me where you are.'

'The robin,' says the creature. 'Follow the bird.' With that, the music stops, the creatures and Vanessa suddenly turn to vapour and disappear.

There's a fear growing in my gut, and my heart is racing. The robin. I remember the yew forest, crouching, my hand on the moss, the bird. Then the shape hanging in the tree. It's her!

Someone sits quietly next to me.

'I couldn't just leave you on your own,' says Helen. She grips my hand, and I kiss hers. I hold her tightly and want to cry.

'I know where she is!'

She doesn't remember hearing the engine start; a drop into a pothole must have woken her, jarring her even more. Those broken ribs digging in. Now he's stopped and switched off. Her own smell is making her wretch, but it doesn't matter. It will be over soon.

He has lifted her somewhere high above the ground, and now she is hanging by her feet. Her lungs are burning, her head is banging. She cannot cry or move. She is simply waiting to die, and she prays for her husband, her mother and father, and to be taken soon.

Helen is on her phone, pacing outside the cathedral until Gregory answers. We walk together up the steps and stop by Saint Richard's statue. Helen gets a car to meet us, and Saint Richard is blessing us as she gets a search dog organised. I'm still focusing on what I saw, and everything floods in on me: the Watchers, Vanessa calling for help. I see the place by the beautiful shoreline, the fruit, the Woman. I stagger and hold on to the base of the statue. Helen is facing away from me, and the world folds up around me...

'David, you lovely man,' says the Woman. 'Where have you been? I've missed you.'

We are sitting outside a small wooden hut overlooking the turquoise sea. She is laying back on a long deckchair, alongside my own.

'I don't know,' I say. 'I really don't know what I've been doing.'

The Woman laughs and sips a drink from a tall glass. 'I told you we were friends. Do you remember?'

'I think I do.'

'Friends talk to each other.'

The Woman stands up, and she beckons me to follow her. We walk up to the shoreline and let warm water lap over our toes. She takes a deep breath and turns to me.

'So, you're about to use your gift for something good, I see.'

'Am I? I just don't want Vanessa to die.'

'She won't die. She's a friend of mine, too. We go way back.'

'Why is everything so bloody cryptic? It would be a lot easier if it wasn't.'

'Why go for a walk in the woods when you can look at a map or a photograph?'

'I walk in the woods to experience it.'

'Yes, to experience it, to learn from it, to let it change you from the inside. That's why it's *so bloody cryptic.*'

'I see. Look, I'm not religious, okay. But I have a good idea who you are. Are you expecting me to go to church or read my Bible? I just don't know if I can do that.'

'Oh, David! Chill!' The woman laughs. 'Don't go all religious on me. The Church is cool. It's full of people who know they are as broken as you are. You're family. You can't be more family than you already are. Your Bible is cool, too. It's got a great ending, but don't get hung up and lost over it. Get yourself lost in me.' And when she laughs again, the heavens spin wildly, and the sea raises up, and there comes a tremendous roar as the waves crash over us. I'm swept onto the sand, and the sea falls away.

I see a hand stretching down to lift me up. This is a man now. His skin is darker than mine, glistening in the light of the stars.

'David, my lovely friend,' he says as he pulls me off the sand. He's tall and strong, with eyes like fire, and thick braided hair down to his waist. 'There are going to be some changes coming. Don't be afraid of them. I'll look after you. Send my love to that beautiful boy of ours. Josh is one of my shining stars.'

'David!' says Helen. 'Are you okay?'

I'm still holding onto the statue.

'I'm here,' I say. I'm still dazed.

'But you weren't. You faded out... You scared me.'

'I'm okay. What's happening?'

'There's a car being dropped off for us here. A search team is being organised, and a dog unit is blatting it from Worthing. Let's go.'

I'm in the lead car, with Helen driving. When we arrive in the car park at Kingley Vale, we let the dog unit go in front, with the other three officers behind. The sky is overcast now, and the wind has picked up. We don't want the rain.

'That was the 25th of February, 11 days ago,' says Helen. 'You had a premonition of this 11 days ago?'

'I know, I know,' I say. 'It sounds crazy. You can't tell anyone, okay?'

'Of course. I'm under orders. If it wasn't you, I would have just laughed it off.'

'I'm not sure what the creatures are. I can see them anytime, anywhere. Often in special places like hilltops, deserted beaches, religious places, where people pray.'

'I didn't take you as religious.'

'I'm not. Well, I didn't think I was.'

She squeezes my arm. 'It's okay. It doesn't matter if I understand or not. I believe you.'

The last car pulls in and parks up.

'We're all here. Let's get going.'

There's a team of us, and we follow the path from the car park for about twenty minutes. There's a drone flying overhead, trying to search through the gaps in the trees. Passing through a gate, we walk into the Kingley Vale nature reserve. There's that hush again, the silence of the trees, so ancient and trustworthy. The dog is sniffing the ground for a scent.

'Nothing yet,' says her handler. We stop.

'To the right, here,' I say. 'There's a really old tree there and a narrow path just off of that.'

The clouds are heavy with rain now, and there are a few spots. The black German shepherd happily charges onwards—she's enjoying this game. Her tail is high and wagging furiously. She pauses, we hold our breath, and then off she goes at speed.

'She's got something!' says the handler as he runs behind her.

I'm ahead of Helen as we pass the old tree with the gaping mouth and beard and cut our way across onto the bramble covered path. We all stop in the clearing. This is it, where the robin led me the first time, but there is nothing here.

'Is this the place?' asks Helen.

'Yes,' I say. 'I'm certain.'

I crouch down and run my hands over the moss. It is raining now, and there's a faint rumble of thunder in the distance. It's then I look up. Above us is a length of sacking hanging from a tree branch, like a chrysalis ready to hatch.

Helen looks up. 'Oh my God!'

'Let's get her down,' I say. I'm climbing the tree quickly. The others are still trying to find a way up. I reach the rope.

'I'm coming up, sir!' another officer calls up.

The rope is in my hands, and the officer is with me. The knot on the branch looks tight. We pull at it, and nothing happens. I've taken the body's weight while another officer takes a knife and cuts the rope above the knot. We take the body together and use the rope and lower it. The body feels stiff, and my heart sinks at the feeling of rigor mortis. We are too late.

We lower her to the ground. Everyone is silent apart from the whimpering of the dog. We cut away the sacking, and we see the chicken wire wrapped around a naked woman. The leg twitches.

'She's still with us!' says Helen.

We cut away the mesh, and I see purple hexagons scored into the flesh. There's a murmur.

'We've got you, Vanessa,' I say. 'Help is on its way.'

We lay a blanket of police jackets on top of her, carefully wet her cracked lips with water until she can take a few sips, and we wait for the paramedics to arrive.

It's still pouring outside. In the dark, I can hear my gutters overflowing, splattering onto the patio below. Helen is asleep next to me. She's on her side, wrapped tightly in a white bedsheet. I'm following the beautiful curves of her body, like the soft lines of a marble statue in this semi-darkness.

The image of Vanessa suspended in that tree keeps coming back to me. I'm grateful that we found her. I'm thankful for the mystical woman on the shore and her Watchers. She's not the God I had imagined as a child.

I turn over, and there's my wardrobe. There was something I had to do—what was it?

I'm in the spare room now, trying to adjust my eyes to the raw, unshaded light. On my desk, I've placed a shoebox full of stuff and rubbish that I meant to go through. It's been in the back of my wardrobe for the last 18 months. I carefully empty it, piece by piece. There are old batteries, keys to locks I threw months ago, ends of pencils and screws. Why don't I just chuck this stuff? Underneath are pieces of folded paper, old receipts, and my mum's flapjack recipe.

'Did you know there's a naked man in your spare room?' It's Helen. She's still wrapped in a bedsheet and wearing her glasses. I think she looks cute in them.

'Sorry! I didn't mean to wake you. I just remembered something?'

'It couldn't wait until morning?' She's yawning.

'No.'

Then I see it. I recognise the hospital logo on the top.

The note that Amanda gave me. It's folded tightly, several times over. I carefully peel it open.

Helen can barely open her eyes. 'What is it?'

'A note someone gave me in hospital. It could be important.' I read the note. 'Shit! It is.'

NINETEEN

9th March 2022

Sam Gregory is watching the sun lifting above houses from the window of Harting Ward. She's with a PC she knew when she joined up. It's been nice to catch up, but now the conversation has run dry. He went into firearms, and she became a detective. He's married and has a baby girl called Rosie. She's still single, with a cat called Mo. He's scanning through Facebook, watching stupid videos, which leaves Sam watching the sun.

Vanessa Grant is still unresponsive. It was a very close thing; much longer and she would probably have asphyxiated. She's still on a hydrating drip. The marks from the wire are all over her body, but the doctor says they will quickly fade.

A nurse approaches. He's wary of the man with the big gun watching Facebook.

'Mrs Grant's husband is here to see her. Is it okay if he pops his head round?' The nurse's name is Roger, and he's been supplying tea, toast, and hobnobs to the officers.

'It should be okay,' says Gregory. 'If she wakes, then he may have to leave.'

The nurse comes back with Peter Grant. He walks in carefully, as if he's scared to wake her. His shoulders are hunched, face pale and unshaven.

'Just look at her,' he says.

'Mr Grant,' says Gregory. 'There's still no change, I'm afraid. She's in the best place now. Her broken ribs will mend, and the bruising will go down, eventually. It's the psychological damage that's harder to guess.'

'She's a tough cookie. As much as we had our differences, I would never have wished this on her.'

Gregory looks at the firearms officer next to her. 'She's safe here.'

'Have you arrested Dettori?' says Peter.

'Not yet. We'll find him soon.'

'Thank you for what you've done for her.'

'It was DI Angelis who found her, Mr Grant. She wouldn't still be with us if it wasn't for him.'

Vanessa stirs and moves her head towards Gregory.

'Get the nurse, please, Peter,' says Gregory.

Vanessa opens her eyes and reaches out her hand to Gregory.

'Vanessa, my name is Sam. I'm a police officer. You are in hospital, and you're safe.'

'Wheelhouse,' she says to Gregory. The morphine is slurring her speech. 'It was Wheelhouse.'

'Did Nathan Wheelhouse do this to you?'

'Yes.' She is struggling, but she grips Gregory's hand. She drifts for a moment, but her eyes are urgent. She won't let go of Gregory. 'He's taking Dettori... Gatwick... midday flight to... Venice. He's meeting him at... Chichester Station... at 9 a.m.'

Gregory checks her watch: 8.05 a.m.

We're in the office after taking Sam Gregory's call. Walsh and Driscoll are here, and the rest of the team all want a piece of Dettori. Some of us have kitted up. Bob Lister is standing next to me. He's put the city's CCTV on the main screen, covering the entrance to the station.

'He's just so unpredictable,' Lister says to me. 'I've seen people like Wheelhouse before. No respect for life if it suits him. I reckon he'll dump Dettori and make a run for it.'

'He doesn't know we're watching him,' I say.

'It won't take him long to work it out. Have you ever met him?'

'No.'

'I bet he knows you and McCall.' He turns to me so only I can hear him. 'I know you're gifted. I've seen it myself. But don't take him for granted, sir. He's extremely dangerous.'

I have a question on my face, but Driscoll interrupts.

'How long until armed response will be here?' says Driscoll.

'They've given an ETA of twenty minutes, ma'am, silent approach,' says Cheung. 'BTP can't get there for another 30 minutes, but they'll hold the train for us at Chichester station.'

'Who's down there now?' says Walsh.

'Two early shift response units and DS McCall,' says Cheung. She's holding her police radio, relaying the updates.

'Keep them out of sight,' says Walsh. 'Get onto BTP. I want the train they're going to catch emptied at the previous stop, which is where?'

'For that train, it's Southbourne, sir,' says Daley.

'I want everyone off the train at Southbourne,' says Walsh, 'but keep it running to Chichester. Dan, get over there, now. Take a ride with a response car and go on blues.'

'Yes, sir,' says Daley.

'I want to limit the number of people getting on that train in Chichester—none, if possible. But don't spook them. If we can trap Wheelhouse on the train, then it reduces the risk to the public.'

'The station is 5 minutes away on foot,' I say. 'We want the north side.'

Cheung is calling the response team on the radio. 'It's the north side you want. Let me know as soon as you see them.'

'Giles,' says Driscoll, 'As you're covering things here, I'll head to the station with Angelis.'

I check my watch it's 8.48 a.m. I have a covert stab vest under my coat. Driscoll and I head out, running to start but walking as we approach the station gates. We stay in the shadows, walk alongside the cycle racks, and pass the bank machine. Dettori and Wheelhouse aren't here yet. We get into the station office and join the others, watching the station CCTV.

Several cars are pulling in and leaving the station car park, but there is still no sign of them.

'They're cutting it fine,' says Driscoll. She's chewing her nails now.

I'm standing next to Helen. The foyer suddenly fills with college students in tracksuits.

'Shit!' says McCall. 'That's the last thing we want.'

It's too late. Wheelhouse and Dettori are entering the foyer. Wheelhouse has a bulging shoulder bag, and Dettori is wheeling a small suitcase. They blend in with the crowd.

The radio is busy, and everyone tenses.

'Just let them get their tickets,' says Walsh over the radio. 'Stay calm. Once they're through the barriers, we need to limit those coming through.'

I'm watching Wheelhouse. He's tall, muscular, and he walks as if no one can touch him. The college girls are looking at him, and he loves it. He's a narcissist. Wheelhouse is looking around now, and I can see something in his movements. He senses the tension. He knows something is wrong—Lister was right.

'Ma'am,' I say. 'He knows we're here.'

'No, how?'

'I believe the drug gives him acute perception,' I say. 'He knows we're here, believe me, but he hasn't told Dettori. Why?'

'Armed Response is here, ma'am,' says McCall.

'It's too dangerous,' says Driscoll. 'Just let him get on the train.'

'The train is clear of passengers,' Daley updates over the radio from Southbourne station, the previous stop.

'Good work, Dan,' says Walsh.

Dettori heads for the barriers, and Wheelhouse is behind him. They walk casually through, using their tickets. Wheelhouse looks around him and back to the cameras.

'Get them to close the ticket barriers,' says Walsh. 'Tell everyone they're faulty.'

A man in the office clicks a button, and red crosses appear on the ticket barriers. There's a queue of students, and they are moaning amongst themselves.

Dettori pulls up the suitcase to his side and checks his watch. A notice appears on the display; there's a four-minute delay. He sees Nathan is busy looking around him. He's doing that thing he does with his eyes, flitting from one thing to another, taking everything in.

'What's wrong?' says Dettori.

'Not sure,' says Wheelhouse.

'That's not reassuring! Remember the deal. I transfer the money when I'm on the plane. I'll give you the lockup location and the passkey when I go through the departure gate. Not before. You've got enough of the Y9-Alphapase in that bag to last you twelve weeks only.'

'Yeah, yeah. Stop worrying, my Italian friend.'

'What about Martina? How are you going to help her? She's already overdue her next dose.'

'Screw Martina! She's fucked us all up. She can pay the consequences.'

'Nathan!' Dettori pulls at Wheelhouse's collar. 'Don't you know what will happen to her if you don't help her?'

'I think you've made that clear already. And now I've just doubled my supply.'

'You really are scum,' Dettori steps away, and Wheelhouse laughs. The display now says three minutes.

'When were you going to tell me about Angelis?' says Wheelhouse. 'You gave him a dose, too.'

'Where did you hear that?'

'Martina told me. What did it do to him? Has he been altered, too? Why didn't you tell me it just needs the one dose? Instead of getting me and Martina hooked on this stuff. You just wanted to control us, didn't you!'

'It was part of the experiment, you idiot. That's all.'

Wheelhouse turns and sees that the ticket barriers are closed. There are only a few others on the platform. The train is two minutes away.

'But we only needed the one dose, Dettori! I don't want the rest of it. I'm going to come off it. Not cold-turkey. I'm going to take this supply and reduce it slowly. I won't be your slave anymore.'

'Fine, try it if you want, but it's probably too late. You won't get the rest of the money until I'm on the plane.'

'Do I need that money, I'm asking myself? Do I actually need the whole 400 thousand?'

Dettori's heart pounds in his chest. What is Wheelhouse doing?

'If you drop me in it, Wheelhouse, you drop yourself in it.'

Driscoll watches Wheelhouse's expression as he looks up at the camera.

'You're right, David,' she says. 'What is he going to do?'

Then I see it. It's as clear as day. I grab a radio.

'Sir, he's going to kill him! He's going to kill Dettori!'

'Go, go, go!' says Walsh.

I'm out of the door, and two uniforms follow me. There's the sound of boots running into the foyer, a police dog is barking, and kids screaming. I'm over the barrier first and onto the platform. Dettori sees me, and his face is white. Wheelhouse is smiling at me—he knows me. He grabs Dettori.

'Get off me, you fool!' says Dettori. 'You need me. You can't ever stop taking it now. Your body needs it to survive. It's too late for you!'

Wheelhouse lifts Dettori by his neck. Dettori flails his arms and kicks his legs in terror. I freeze just before I get to him, but Wheelhouse throws Dettori from the platform onto the tracks. There's a bright blue flash and a loud crack as Dettori lands and burns on the live rail. The train brakes hard and screeches to a halt over Dettori's smoking body. The horror gives Wheelhouse time.

'Armed police, get down on the floor!' comes from behind me. I duck right down, but Wheelhouse has gone. There's no safe shot. He's climbed onto the overhanging roof and is running along it. The officers are aghast, shouting into their radios.

I'm running and back over the gate. I can hear others running behind me, but I'm nearly as fast as Wheelhouse. I've left the station, and I'm outside in the bright daylight. I scan the area, running into the taxi rank. There he is. I see a dark shape heading towards the multi-storey.

'He's heading into the multi-storey car park,' I say over the radio. Officers are calling up and on their way.

I climb a metal staircase, and I'm on the top floor of the multi-storey. Where is he?

'DI Angelis,' comes a call from Driscoll, 'leave him to Firearms.'

I hear footsteps.

'Too late, ma'am, he's found me.'

This was a ruse to get me alone with him. I've walked straight into it.

'David Angelis! He shouts. 'So good to meet you at last.' Nathan Wheelhouse is walking towards me slowly.

'Nathan, this is it. I'm arresting you on suspicion of the murder of Katherine Jacobs, Dean Dettori, and Julie Dalton, and the kidnap and attempted murder of Vanessa Grant.'

'What do you mean, attempted murder? Don't tell me you found her! I must be slipping.'

'Yes, Nathan. We know you tortured her and hung her up to die.'

'Really, Inspector. Do you think I'm going to let you arrest me?'

I can hear police vehicles racing into the multi-storey.

'Give it up. Martina has told us everything we need to know. She's going to be charged tomorrow.'

'Will she now, then that's her screwed. I don't need her, anyway. So, it's just you and me, Angelis. But I won't let there be two of us. Just me, no one else. We've been genetically altered. Did you know that? That drug buggers with your DNA permanently. There's no way back now. There's so much I can do. I'm practically a god! They can't touch me, Angelis! I will be the first and the last. There will be no others beside me, thus says Lord Nathan Wheelhouse!'

'You do not have to say anything, but it may harm your defence—'

'Blah, fucking blah!'

Wheelhouse begins his run at me, and then I see the blade.

9th March 2022, 2.37 a.m. Angelis and Helen.

'What is it?' says Helen.

'A note someone gave me in hospital. It could be important.' I read the note. 'Shit! It is.'

'What does it say?'

'I don't understand... But how am I what I am?'

Helen strokes my arm. 'Read it to me, David.'

I show her the note:

> Mr Angelis. Don't believe them, whatever they tell you. Colin Decker told me what he did in the hospital. He swapped the drug over that Doctor Jacobs gave you. It can only be God who brought you back to us, Mr Angelis. Because Kate gave you a placebo. Colin swapped the drug for a placebo. It was just saline. Amanda.

Now...

. . .

Wheelhouse begins his run at me, and then I see the blade. I raise my hand, and Nathan's legs buckle, making him crash to the floor. His eyes are wide with horror.

'The thing is, Nathan,' I say, 'you and I are not the same. Not in the slightest.'

There's the sound of boots running, and Nathan grips the knife.

'What do you mean? How?'

'Katherine Jacobs didn't know what Colin Decker had done. Not until two years later.'

'What the fuck are you talking about?'

'Colin had swapped over the drug intended for me for a placebo. I wasn't given the Y9-Alphapase at all. Amanda Wilson visited me in hospital, and she left me a note. She explained what happened.'

'But how are you the way you are?' Wheelhouse says, rising to his feet again.

'It's a mystery to me. I died, Nathan, and someone brought me back for a purpose. That's all I know.'

'Armed police! Put down the knife!' There are guns trained on him.

I'm stepping back towards them with my hands in the air. The officers move closer, and red dots appear on Wheelhouse's chest.

'Drop the knife now, or you will be tasered!'

Nathan just looks at me and screams. There's a shot.

'Taser, taser, taser!' The taser barbs penetrate his top but have no effect. Nathan rips them out.

'Armed police! Drop the knife now!'

'We're going to take those drugs away from you, Nathan, and get you the medical help you need.

'It won't work, Inspector!' He's sobbing now. 'It just won't work. I never wanted to be like this. I can't help it. It just happened. I lost everyone. My sister killed my dad, my mum killed herself. I had nothing! I found my own way in life. I was a survivor until I met fucking Dalton and Dettori. They found my sister and used her against me. They lied to me and now look at me. What's the fucking point?'

'Come on, Nathan. Drop the knife. Let us help you.'

But Wheelhouse is fast. The edge of the blade is raised before any of us realise. He holds it horizontally across his throat and does the job in one slice. A few seconds later, he drops to the ground in a growing pool of blood. There was nothing anyone could have done. Not even me.

I'm watching as the light gathers from within him, stretches and breaks free from his body. It circles his remains and rises. But then it stops, and I see another kind approaching from the shadows. There's no light in them at all, just cruel shifting shapes. Nathan Wheelhouse's light wavers in the air and then slowly falls back to join them in the shadows until it finally extinguishes.

TWENTY

'I've never known such a high body count,' says Driscoll to Walsh. 'I'll be continuing enquiries from HQ. I didn't realise Chichester was such a dangerous place.'

'What's happening with Hudson,' I ask.

'We're working with the Department of Health,' she says, 'and they will have to answer for the breaches of the Human Medicines Regulations. That's a heck of an investigation, which I'm sure someone in Major Crimes will look forward to getting their teeth into.'

'Thanks, ma'am, but why didn't you move on Dettori sooner? You found Katherine Jacobs and somehow got her to work for you. She must have given you enough to stop Dettori?'

Driscoll looks at me coldly. I've hit a nerve somehow, but it's a perfectly logical question. She looks up at the ceiling, controlling her breathing, trying to find the words. 'Katherine didn't give us enough at first, but as the case moved on, as the link to you became more apparent, we decided to... wait and see what happened.'

I still can't read her, but I see the layers of secrets closing around her like a flower closing for the night. I suspect she's learned how to block me—or she thinks she has.

'It's just that if you had acted sooner, Katherine Jacobs would still be alive. Was the covert information gathered about me really worth that?'

Driscoll flushes, and her lips tighten. 'Hindsight, David, is a wonderful thing, isn't it?'

It's time for me to leave—I've made my point. Walsh nods as I leave his office, and Helen is watching me. She follows me into mine and shuts the door.

'How can I help you, Sergeant,' I say.

'Well, sir,' she says. 'I was considering making some lewd and sexual remarks to a senior officer, but I thought better of it.'

'Perhaps you could try that this evening, Sergeant. Say about 7.30 p.m.?'

'How about 6.30 for dinner at mine?'

'Agreed.'

'Are you okay? You look tired.'

I rub my eyes. 'I'm just glad that's over.'

'I have to tell you something.' Helen pulls me in closer to her. 'When I went to see Lizzie, she told me that her sister gave you a Haribo.'

'A Haribo?' I laugh.

'I think she meant placebo. Katherine Jacobs knew all along. She must have read Colin's notes.'

'It must be what she was trying to tell me at the pub the night she was killed...' I have Helen's attention, so now is as good a time as any. 'Helen, we need to talk.' I can sense the immediate worry rising in her.

She looks down at her shoes. 'Bad news?'

'God, no! You know I want to be with you. I want you and me to work, okay?'

'So do I.'

'What do you think about me taking up Driscoll's offer? I'd continue to work here, but I'd be on call if I was needed—an extra resource for them.'

Helen is frowning. She's not sure. 'Only you can make that decision. As long as you're not leaving us for good. You've only just arrived.'

'No. I wouldn't want that.' I'm looking into her eyes. 'I have everything I want right here.'

Helen blushes and smiles as she backs out of the office. 'You do. See you when you're done.'

I'm about to leave the office—it's been a day like no other. I'm just grateful we have a great media team to take on the press.

I've written my statements and updated all the case files I can do for now. I look out my office window and see Helen patiently sitting at her desk, drinking coffee, and waiting for me.

Someone looking smart in a dark suit stops by her and asks her something. She points towards my office, and he walks towards me. Then I recognise who it is, and I realise I have not once ever thought to speak to him, to ask him how he survived that night, over two years ago. Tom Hobbs is standing at my door in two minds if he should knock. I open the door to him.

When he looks at me, he notices my eyes. He lets out a small gasp and then a smile.

'Inspector Angelis, I hope you don't mind…' he says.

'Tom,' I say, and then I'm stuck for words.

Tom saved my life that night. I'm told he kept me alive until the paramedics came. He stemmed the bleeding. He's not so fresh-faced anymore but has a hint of something stronger, steel earned through experience. Meeting Tom completes something I never knew needed completing. I didn't realise it was still hanging over him or me. Tom needs to know he wasn't to blame, and I hold no blame against him. Healing and mending what is broken.

'I just wanted to see how you were, sir. I heard you'd returned to duty.'

'I'm so sorry, Tom. I never said thank you.'

'I wish I could have done more. I should have been—'

'No, stop,' I hold up my hand to him. 'I didn't risk-assess it properly. It was my fault. You saved my life, and I'm grateful.'

'Really? I thought I had let you down.' I'm seeing a weight falling off his shoulders.

'No, Tom. Not at all.'

'I still dream about it, sir. It broke me. I've been off sick with PTSD for a while.'

Helen has made her way over to us with her coat on and her bag over her shoulder. She's reading my face, and she can see my shame. I never considered how that night had affected him. Not once.

'Helen, this is Tom,' I say. 'He was with me when I was attacked in Brighton. Tom kept me alive until the paramedics came. He kept my attacker from causing me further harm. If it wasn't for him, I wouldn't be here.'

Helen looks surprised and smiles as she shakes Tom's hand. Tom's relief is palpable. His cheeks flush.

'I'm Helen McCall.' She checks his lanyard. 'You're a DC? Where are you based?'

'Haywards Heath. I'm looking for a transfer. I'm taking my sergeant's promotion board.'

'Sergeant!' I say. 'Last time I saw you, you were a probationer.'

'Yes, sir. I'm on a fast-track scheme. I was hoping to transfer here. But I totally understand...'

'Excellent!' I'm shaking his hand. 'You'd be really welcome

here. Let me know how you get on, and I'll happily have you on my team.'

'Thank you, sir!' He looks over his shoulder. 'I have to go now, my lift...' An officer is waiting near the entrance.

'Good to see you, Tom. I'm so glad you came by.'

We watch him leave, and Helen hooks her arm underneath mine.

'That was amazing,' I say. 'But I can't believe I'm so selfish sometimes.'

Helen punches me in the arm. 'We've all got stuff to learn, and you've been on a roller-coaster for the last two years. Don't be too hard on yourself.'

'He probably thinks I'm wearing coloured contact lenses.'

'Why?' Helen laughs. 'Oh, they're not brown anymore... Come on, freak, I'm hungry.'

'You're always hungry.'

22nd May 2022

Mr and Mrs McCall open the front door to Helen as she walks down the path. Behind Helen, a shy young woman waits with her hands behind her back, and beside her is a tall, skinny man covered in tattoos.

'Hi Mum, Dad,' says Helen and gives them both a hug.

'So,' says Mrs McCall, 'this lovely young lady must be Lizzie.'

'Hello,' says Lizzie. She pulls out a large bunch of carnations for Helen's mum from behind her back.

'Oh! How lovely!' Mrs McCall squeals with delight and Lizzie laughs.

'And this fine young man,' says Helen, 'is Jake, one of Lizzie's support workers.'

'Pleasure to meet you,' he says.

Just then, there's the sound of claws hurriedly scuttling over a wooden floor. A cocker spaniel leaps out of the front door, straight onto Lizzie. The dog's tail beats rapidly from side to side, and Lizzie is being licked all over.

'Max!' says Lizzie. Her face is alight.

'Come on in, all of you,' says Mrs McCall. 'Come through.'

Everyone follows Helen into the garden. Then she sees David and Josh Angelis coming out of the potting shed, wiping compost off their hands. It seems her dad has already given them something to do.

'Hi! I'm Josh,' he calls to everyone. 'This is Dad. You can call him David.'

Helen walks over to Josh and has to stop herself from hugging him straightaway.

'Hello, Josh. I'm Helen.'

'You are Dad's girlfriend.' Josh sniggers and gives her wide grin.

'Girlfriend!' says Lizzie. 'Don't cry, Jake. There's plenty of fish in the sea.'

'Oh, okay, Lizzie,' says Jake. Pretending to rub his eyes.

'Hello, handsome.' Helen kisses Angelis on the cheek. 'Your son is lovely.'

'I know,' says Angelis. 'He gets it from me.'

'Aren't your parents here yet?'

'They're on their way. Dad won't be rushed driving Gracie.'

'Are you nervous about them meeting me?'

'No, but...'

Helen rubs his arm. 'It will be great. I'm so looking forward to it. What time is your meeting with Driscoll later?'

'4.30, but I'll be home around 6.'

'Don't expect me to cook for you. I'm not your woman indoors.'

'I wouldn't dream of it. I think a takeaway, don't you?'

Carol enters the room quietly, and she sees the woman is asleep again. She hasn't touched her lunch or her drink. Carol takes a moment, in the quiet, to look out of the window onto the lawns below. She holds onto the bars and wishes she could climb out there into the sunshine. Carol's desperate for a cigarette, but that will have to wait until she's finished here.

She changes the water in the flowers and stands up some of the woman's cards she has knocked down.

'Why do I bother?' says Carol.

Turning to the woman, Carol strokes what's left of the woman's short, white hair and gently rubs her cheek to wake her. 'Come on, my darling. You haven't touched your lunch. It's roast chicken. You like roast chicken. I've mashed it all up for you.'

The woman stirs and squints hard to see who is talking to her. 'Don't want it! Fucking shit dinner! I want sausage and beans. Where's Mum? Dad's dead, Nate. He hurt me—stuck his dick in me. So I killed him, Nate. He deserved it. Get Mum!'

'Mum's not here, my darling. You are in hospital, do you remember?'

'I'm going dancing. Get my dress, the red one with the split.'

'It's not here today.' Carol checks the woman's sallow, wrinkled skin and her nails. 'I can do your nails for you'd if you'd like me to. How about that?'

'Fuck off!' The woman rocks in her bed and pushes Carol away with her scraggy arms.

'Come on now, Martina. No need to be like that, or you won't go out dancing today.'

'Argh. Get Nate! Stupid woman! Have you got a passkey? I can let you in.'

'Let me change your pad for you. You'll feel a lot better.'

Martina sinks her chin into her chest and lets Carol clean her. Then she drifts away and dreams of dancing with Nathan once again.

EPILOGUE

I've taken a walk into the forest once more. The little cocker spaniel dashes around my feet, darting into the bushes. I stop for a moment. Ancient yews surround me, and it's silent here. I watch the journeys of ten thousand souls winding their way through the forest, as I do now. The Watchers are here, waiting in hushed reverence for The One who walks with me. Her breath blows through the boughs and branches, and her sweet fragrance fills the warm summer air. Her Spirit alights on a bramble cane as she waits for me to follow her beyond this place, where the passing hours ebb away, and all time belongs to her.

'Not now,' I say to her. 'There's more I need to do. There's that son of ours for one thing. I won't be long. Hold that place for me.'

'I stand by my promise, lovely man,' she says to me and kisses my forehead. 'I'll see you real soon, David Angelis—real soon.'

BOOK 2 - HIDE HER AWAY

Alice is alone and terrified. He's hidden her away, and no one can find her. Can her strength of will, forged in an abusive marriage, bring her through this terrifying ordeal?

DI David Angelis, hit hard by personal tragedy and self-doubt, must solve the puzzle of Alice's disappearance and the trail of murder that ensues.

Hide Her Away, a gripping supernatural crime thriller and the next instalment in the Detective Inspector Angelis series, follows the first novel, *Chasing Shadows*.

HIDE HER AWAY - CHAPTER 1

Kingston Upon Thames, Thursday, 13th October 2022.

He's by the front door, putting on his coat with his briefcase balanced between his brogues. Alice is fresh out of the shower in her dressing gown, waiting for him to leave, watching him fumble with the zip on his coat, that deliberate procrastination he does so well to drain any last drop of patience she has. Her loathing of him is masked by a good-natured smile as she folds her arms tightly over her chest to hide her shaking hands. She shifts her weight between her legs to stop her knees from trembling. He must not know, and he must never suspect.

'What are your plans for today?' John asks.

'Why?'

'My sister has asked us for dinner at hers. You don't have to look especially nice—just your normal will do.'

Alice tries not to react. 'No real plans,' she says as brightly as she can. 'I was thinking of popping over to Charlotte's. She's not been well.'

He delves for the car keys in his coat. He's found them but

pretends he hasn't. She's waiting for it, that supercilious smile, that fake interest, riding his will roughshod over hers.

'Sounds like you've made plans to me,' John says. 'Charlotte's probably had loads of her friends over to see her this week, and you don't want to tire her out.'

'She invited me.'

'Did she? When?'

'Yesterday.'

'You didn't tell me.'

'Sorry, I forgot.'

'Did you, really?' John studies her with those cold, blue eyes, fixing his petty accusation on her. He produces his car keys from his pocket. 'She probably didn't mean it, anyway—just being polite.'

'Okay.' Just agree, let him go.

'Anyway, I'll see you at the usual time. I don't expect to be late. There's not a lot going on at the moment.' Does he know? How can he know? 'Love you. Call me if you need me.'

She won't say it. She's not been in love with him for over six years. 'Will do.'

John raises one of his bushy eyebrows, and she's sure he's noticed something's wrong. He takes her keys off the hook, puts them in his coat pocket and opens the front door. There's a cold draught entering the house, and she shivers.

'Melody would like to see more of you, Alice. I've always said she could be a sister to you too, and you could learn a lot from her. She's always had an even temperament. We got that from our father.'

'It's cold, John. Don't make yourself late for work.'

He sighs and nods his head, then checks his pockets for something again. 'I'm sure I've forgotten something.'

Alice is going to scream at him, but he turns and closes the front door behind him. She stands frozen to the spot, and her nails are digging crescents into her palms. She won't let him stop her now.

She waits until she hears the engine start, then Alice rushes to the front room, standing back from the window so she can't be seen. John's warming the car, clearing the windows from the misty October dew. God, why won't he just go! The engine revs and then goes quiet. The car door opens. He's coming back!

Alice races up the stairs to the bathroom. He removed the lock years ago. Her stomach twists, and she puts her back against the door.

'I left my phone!' he calls up the stairs. 'You could've told me.'

She doesn't answer. Is he coming up the stairs?

He calls up again. 'I just thought, did you make my sandwiches? I can't find them.' She's fighting to catch her breath. 'Alice? I said, did you make my sandwiches?' Fuck it! She didn't.

She flushes the toilet and waits a few moments, forcing her weight against the door again.

Alice calls out—her voice is shaky. 'Buy something for yourself at work.'

'I'll just have to make my own. You've made me late for work, by the way.' Why doesn't he just get on with it? Charlotte will be here soon! 'What are you doing up there?'

'I thought you said you're late.' She's answered him back. He's definitely going to suspect something now.

There's silence, and Alice thinks he's abandoned the thought of making his own lunch. She never forgets to make it for him. Why today of all days? There's a click from the hallway, and then she hears the car starting again, and tyres roll on the gravel. There's the change of gears and the acceleration into the distance. Has he gone? She opens the bathroom door and heads downstairs. The house is empty.

Alice has a plan, and she's behind on time. She goes into the kitchen and pulls out the kickboard from below the built-in oven. Her hands are shaking with the adrenaline, and she can't see straight. Alice has this constant fear the package won't be there. It kept her awake half the night. So many times, he's ruined everything at the last minute, and she dares not imagine what he would do if he found it. He doesn't beat her as much now. No, now it's more subtle. He took away her phone and stopped her from seeing any of her friends until all she had left was Charlotte. Now he controls absolutely everything, and she can't even breathe unless he says so.

She reaches under the unit, and thank God, the package is there. She unzips the small black case and opens it. There's the reply from the solicitor, the Deed Poll letter, Charlotte's old mobile phone and the new SIM card, her passport, birth certificate and the cash. She's had to steal food so as not to spend the money he's given her for housekeeping. She has over 800 pounds here, every penny she's had to fight for. The number of times they've argued about missing receipts, and she's even forged a few. He thinks that's beyond her capabilities.

Alice has taken a large shoulder bag from the top of her wardrobe, and she stuffs the contents of the package into it. She checks the time on the watch he bought her—Charlotte will be here in fifteen minutes.

The nausea is getting worse, and she breathes her way through it. Alice couldn't eat breakfast, and John saw that. He sees everything.

'Oh, come on, Alice!' she says to herself.

She must get dressed. She has her favourite jeans and boots ready, her warm cashmere turtle-neck, and the Chanel perfume she bought herself when he used to let her work. She puts on a little lipstick and then her green Barbour, untucking her long, blonde hair. She stops and looks at herself in the mirror. This is the Alice she used to know, the one who had the dreams of friends, of a career in writing, the one who got a first-class honours degree.

'Hello again,' she says to her reflection.

Alice tugs off her wedding and engagement rings with no ceremony, and she goes to the kitchen, where she's found the pliers and hammer in the kitchen drawer. With hot, raging tears, she squeezes the gold bands in the jaws of the pliers, twisting and cutting the soft metal into meaningless fragments.

'You fucking monster! Fuck you!'

She puts the mangled pieces of gold and loose diamonds onto the kitchen island, along with the pliers, then removes the watch and places it next to them. The hammer goes down hard three times on the watch, crushing the token gift of atonement for the beatings she suffered. Out comes the letter she spent a day writing. She doesn't fold it but places it securely underneath the hammer.

Alice hears a car horn, so she grabs her shoulder bag, and the rucksack stuffed with her favourite clothes, wash things, tampons, underwear, makeup, a photo of her late mother, and that first scan picture, hidden inside her moleskin journal. The journal that kept her sane all these years with him. It's the best friend she has.

She rechecks her face and hair—it's good enough—opens the front door, and stands on the step. Charlotte has pulled up on the opposite side of the road, avoiding the doorbell video camera. She winds down her window, but then the house phone rings.

'Shit!' Alice stares wide-eyed at it. She can't leave it. What if it's John? He's checking on her. He's taken the house keys, for fuck's sake. What else does he want?

'Don't answer it, Alice,' Charlotte calls out.

Alice answers the phone.

'I can see there's no one at the door, Alice,' says John in his faux calm voice. 'Where are you going? What's wrong with you today? You didn't eat your breakfast, and you're tense. Your time of the month isn't for two weeks. I know, would you like me to get you a present? I'll get you something nice to wear for later.'

'John, listen.' Alice gags—she tastes the burning bile in her mouth. She takes a deep breath.

'Are you ill, Alice?'

'I want you to know something. Listen carefully.'

'Okay? It sounds like my little wife has something important to say.'

'I hate you. I've despised you for years. You're vile. So, so vile. You've tormented me, raped me, controlled me, beaten me. You've been hurting me since the day we were married. And I've had enough of your disgusting, perverted affairs—those girls were barely out of school! I'm leaving you today, and you're never going to see me again. You'll never find me, so don't bother. You're a piece of shit!'

'Alice! Calm yourself! Stay right there—I'm coming home.'

'No, I'm not fucking staying here! What are you going to do? Beat me? Lock me in again? If you follow me, then I'll go to the police, and I'll tell your bosses.'

'You're being hysterical! We can talk about it when we get home from Melody's tonight. Okay?'

'What, do you really think I want to see that twisted, evil sister of yours? So, what are you going to tell her, John? What lies will you come up with this time? That I've run off with someone? That I'm sick again?'

'You *are* sick! You have no money. Where do you think you'll go? Don't be so silly. You're obviously in one of your moods again. Don't move—I'm on my way.' He hangs up the call.

Alice hurls the phone against the wall, and it smashes open —the batteries clatter over the polished floorboards. She runs out of the front door to Charlotte, whose arms are wide open to her.

Alice finds it hard to catch a breath. 'I told him. Now he's coming.'

Charlotte puts Alice's rucksack in the Volvo, and they get in, heading off into the traffic.

'Well done, girl,' says Charlotte. 'You're so brave! Have you got everything you need?'

'Yes. Everything. I just need to buy the ticket.'

'Call me when you're safe. You've remembered to bring my old iPhone? Charged it, and the SIM card activated?'

'All done. I haven't used one for years.'

'You'll work it out. I was upgrading my contract, anyway, and that one works just like John's iPad.'

'Thank you so much, Charlotte.'

'So, I'm taking you to Surbiton station, sweetheart. Is that right?'

Alice nods, still breathless. 'Yes. He'll expect me to stay with my cousin in Brighton, and he's the only relative John knows about.'

'But you're not.'

'No, I'm heading to an old school friend in Dorset.' Alice is lying, and she hasn't even told Charlotte about the letter from the solicitor. The fewer people that know, the better, and Alice knows how John can twist this around to look like her fault. He'll try to bring everyone onto his side.

'Well, it will give you a chance to start again. Get a job, and then divorce John.'

'I will, and once I've settled in, I promise we can meet up again. I don't know I would ever have been able—'

'Stop it, Alice. You'll set me off.' Charlotte's phone rings, a withheld number. 'Hello?'

'So, where are you taking her?' It's John's voice over the speaker.

'She's going, Johnny. There's nothing you can do now.'

'Where are you heading, Alice? Going to stay with that cousin of yours?' John is spitting his words into the phone. 'I will find you! You know I will.'

Alice is trembling, unable to breathe. Charlotte ends the call.

'Come on, Alice! We're only ten minutes away from the station. I guess me and Tim aren't on John's Christmas card list now either.'

'He can rot in hell for all I care. I hope it's sooner rather than later.'

They arrive at the station, and Alice takes her bag and rucksack from the back of the car and hugs Charlotte one last time.

'I'll call you once things have settled,' says Alice. 'Don't let him intimidate you. Thank you for driving me.'

'It's Tim's car, not mine. Don't worry about John—I'm not scared of him. Tim will give him a good slap if he tries anything.'

Alice sees Charlotte is eager for her to go. Perhaps she's finding this harder than Alice thought.

'Goodbye, Charlotte. Thanks for everything.'

Alice wipes away her tears and turns towards the entrance to Surbiton railway station and never looks back.

Printed in Great Britain
by Amazon